...ok, one of the great ... , page-turning romance novels. L... ut to have a fantastic romantic read that we kno... won't be able to put down!

Why don't you make your Little Black Dress experience even better by logging on to

www.littleblackdressbooks.com

where you can:

 ♥ Enter our **monthly competitions** to win **gorgeous** prizes
 ♥ Get **hot-off-the-press** news about our latest titles
 ♥ Read **exclusive** preview chapters both from your **favourite** authors and from brilliant new writing talent
 ♥ Buy **up-and-coming** books online
 ♥ Sign up for an essential slice of romance via our **fortnightly email** newsletter

We love nothing more than to curl up and indulge in an addictive romance, and so we're delighted to welcome you into the Little Black Dress club!

With love from,

The ...

Five interesting things about Nell Dixon:

1. I once crashed a Sinclair C5 into a tree. (Sinclair C5s were weird little concept cars that looked like go carts.)

2. I'm scared of heights and got stuck on a rope bridge on an assault course and had to be rescued by a very nice army man.

3. I used to be a midwife and have delivered over a hundred babies.

4. I sing to the music in supermarkets, loudly and tunelessly. Strangely, my family prefer me to shop alone.

5. I have dyscalculia which means I can't remember numbers and often read them back to front.

By Nell Dixon

Marrying Max
Blue Remembered Heels
Animal Instincts

Crystal Clear

Nell Dixon

little
black
dress

First published in 2010
by LITTLE BLACK DRESS
An imprint of HEADLINE PUBLISHING GROUP

A LITTLE BLACK DRESS paperback

1

Cataloguing in Publication Data is available from the British Library

ISBN 978 0 7553 5435 1

Typeset in Transit511BT by Avon DataSet Ltd,
Bidford-on-Avon, Warwickshire

Printed and bound in Great Britain by
Clays Ltd, St Ives plc

Headline's policy is to use papers that are natural, renewable and
recyclable products and made from wood grown in sustainable forests.
The logging and manufacturing processes are expected to conform to the
environmental regulations of the country of origin.

HEADLINE PUBLISHING GROUP
An Hachette UK Company
338 Euston Road
London NW1 3BH

www.littleblackdressbooks.com
www.headline.co.uk
www.hachette.co.uk

For my long-suffering family, especially Robyn, Corinne and Alannah who endured numerous research trips and acted as photographic assistants and note-takers for this book.

Acknowledgements

My grateful acknowledgements and thanks to Kate Tomas, crystal therapist and expert, and also to renowned medium Lorraine-Lilly Ash. Any errors or mistakes are entirely mine. My thanks also to the good people of Brixham who willingly answered all my questions about buses, safe deposit boxes and one hundred and one other things and who have allowed me to fictionalise their lovely town.

'It's your mother.'

Three simple words that chilled me to the core as I accepted the phone from Joyce, the school receptionist. Point one, my mother never, ever called me at work, and point two, she'd never say she was my mother. She was always Marla – even as a child I had never been allowed to call her Mum.

'Hello, this is Zee.' That was something else that was annoying – my name. My given name is Azure Dawn Millichip, but everyone calls me Zee. Who in their right mind would call their child Azure Dawn? Marla, that's who – and no, I'm not sure she's ever been in her right mind.

'Darling, your mobile was switched off.'

'I was teaching in class. I always check my mobile for messages at lunchtime.' Marla has always struggled with the concept of time. As a child I'd frequently been either too early or too late for everything until I was old enough to request my own watch. Then I'd taken over the task of getting us to wherever we were supposed to be at the right time.

'Oh, isn't it lunchtime now? I hate bothering you, sweetie, I know you have a very *important* job, but I really need you to pop home this weekend. If you catch the traffic at the right time you could be here for supper.'

I ignored the implied criticism in her tone, since something was definitely very wrong. Marla never asked me to visit. She knew I would come down to stay anyway in a couple of weeks' time during the school holidays. 'What's the matter?'

'I'm sure Simon would run you here if you asked him. It might be good for both of you, a weekend at the seaside,' she chirped on, ignoring my question. Now I knew for certain that something was wrong. Marla disliked my fiancé, Simon, even more than she disapproved of my choice of career.

'Mum – I mean, Marla, what's going on?' I dropped my voice when Joyce gave me a curious look. 'It's the last day of term and I've tons of things to get done.'

'Zee?' A male voice came on the line. Rich and sexy with a low, throaty growl to his tone.

The speaker sounded familiar. 'Who's this?'

'It's Drew.'

A weird prickly feeling ran down my spine. 'Drew?'

It couldn't be. Not *my* Drew – not that he was mine – or ever really had been mine, now I came to think of it.

'Yeah, um . . . listen, Zee, Marla really needs you to come home.' His voice was deep and serious, and I heard my mother protesting in the background. 'I made her call you. She wanted to wait it out but I thought you should be here.'

Okay, this was beyond weird; I hadn't seen or spoken to Drew since he'd broken my heart in my final year of teacher training. He'd gone away to travel the world and I'd gone back to university. The last thing I'd heard was that he'd gone to live in Australia. Now it seemed he was home and ringing me about my mother – it didn't make sense.

'Please can you just tell me what's wrong?' It had to be something serious for Drew to feel he had to get her to call me.

Marla came back on the line. 'I told Drew I didn't want to worry you.'

'Marla?' A tension headache started to niggle over my left eye.

'I went to the hospital today.'

Oh dear God, Marla never went to the doctor, let alone a hospital. She didn't believe in conventional medicine. 'What? A hospital?'

'I have to have surgery. I'm being admitted on Sunday.' Her voice wobbled. 'I need you here, darling. There's the shop and the allotment and the cat. Drew's been an absolute angel but . . .'

I sank down on the spare chair with the wonky back that stood in the corner of the office. My knees had liquefied and there was a whooshing noise in my ears. 'What kind of surgery?'

'Really, Azure, this isn't the way I wanted to tell you about this. I'll explain everything tonight.'

There was no point arguing. I could tell by her tone that I wouldn't get anything else out of her right now.

'Okay, I'll ring Simon and see if he's happy to drive me over.'

Simon wouldn't be happy; I knew that already. He and Marla didn't see eye-to-eye on anything.

'Darling, Drew will come and get you if Simon is busy.' Again there was a faint inflection on the word 'busy', implying that she knew full well Simon would hate to drive me to her house in Devon.

'Don't be silly, Marla. Simon and I will be down as soon as he can get away from the office.' Anxiety made my voice waspish.

'Then I'll see you tonight.' She rang off.

'Is everything all right?' Joyce took the phone back from me and slotted it neatly back in its cradle.

'No, it's not, unfortunately. My mother has to have surgery.' The words slid out of my mouth and that was when it hit me. Marla needed urgent surgery. 'I have to call Simon.'

Joyce pursed her lips and passed the phone back to me. 'Ring him from here, dear. You look like you've had a bit of a shock.'

Under normal circumstances I would have gone back to the staffroom to ring him on my mobile but I didn't think my legs would support me on the short walk along the corridor. I dialled his number and waited for him to answer. A bee buzzed lazily against the window-pane outside while Joyce tapped away on her keyboard and pretended she wasn't going to listen to my conversation.

'Simon Farrington.'

I pictured him sitting at his desk, crisp white shirtsleeves rolled back as he frowned at his laptop and waited to find out who was calling him.

'It's me, Zee. Marla called me a minute ago. I need to go home tonight to stay for a few days.'

There was a pause. 'Can't it wait till tomorrow? The traffic will be hell.' He sounded distant and I knew he was simultaneously reading his email.

'She's not well. She's going into hospital, she needs an operation.' My throat felt all thick and choky.

I heard Simon sigh. 'I don't know what time I'll be able to get away from the office.'

'I have to go tonight, Simon.' Mentally, I counted to three. Marla always said Simon was selfish. If I'd rung to say we'd an invitation out to supper tonight he wouldn't be making excuses about finishing late, but a visit to my mother was a rather different proposal.

'Okay, I'll get home as soon as I can.' I could hear another phone ringing in the background as he spoke.

'Thanks, love you.' The sunlight flashed off the diamond in my engagement ring as I passed the phone back to Joyce again. I knew the journey to my mother's home in Brixham would be filled with sulky silence.

'Are you all right to finish off this afternoon?' She peered at me over the top of her glasses.

'It's fine. My mother is a bit of a drama queen, I'm sure everything will be okay. I'll probably get to her house and find it's nothing.' I forced a smile to reassure Joyce. It was a fib, of course; my mother might be eccentric but she was rarely perturbed by anything. I wasn't sure if my lie was intended to soothe Joyce's concerns or my own.

There was a tap on the office door and a small worried face peeped in.

'Please, Miss, Daniel Sugden keeps going into the girls' toilets and I can't find Mrs Mount.'

'I'll be right there, Lucy.' I forced myself up from the office chair and followed the girl out into the corridor. Outside in the playground the children were laughing as they played. Only faint screams coming from the toilets confirmed that Daniel was indeed teasing the girls.

I dispatched Daniel back to the football field and resumed playtime supervision. The conversation with Marla still niggled in my head along with long-repressed memories of that last summer with Drew. I'd thought I'd forgotten, forgiven and filed all thoughts of Drew away in my mind. Yet if I closed my eyes, I could see him as he had looked the day we'd said goodbye. I could remember the smell of his skin and the taste of his lips on mine. As if I didn't have enough to worry about with Marla's operation, it sounded as if I would have to face the ghost of my romantic past when I returned home.

Lucy reappeared at my side. 'Shall I ring the bell, Miss?'

I nodded and she scampered away, eager to please. The large brass handbell clanged and the children began to line up, jostling for position in readiness for the end-of-term party. I stuffed my memories back in their box and focused on being efficient Miss Millichip for the remainder of the school day.

*

The flat I shared with Simon was a short bus ride across the city. By the time I slid my key in the lock it was after five. I stepped over the post that lay on the hall floor and went to dump my bags on the granite breakfast bar in the kitchen. The room felt hot from being closed up all day and there was no sign of Simon.

I collected the post and placed it in its appointed spot for Simon to read when he got home, then unpacked my bags from school. Several boxes of chocolates, two mugs bearing the legend 'World's Best Teacher' and a bedraggled bunch of flowers later, I'd cleared everything away. The sounds of the city filtered through the double glazing and the air was stuffy and oppressive. From my third-floor vantage point the traffic trickled below like streamers of multicoloured ribbons on the tail of a kite.

I poured myself a glass of juice from the fridge and carried it through to the bedroom. Thirty minutes later I'd changed out of my work clothes into a cooler cotton summer dress and packed our bags ready for Devon. I stacked the matched Louis Vuitton cases on the dark red satin throw that covered the bottom half of the bed and looked around the room.

Simon and I had been together for two years. He'd proposed at Christmas, hiding my ring inside a fake Christmas bauble that he'd hung on the tree. I'd moved into his flat on Valentine's Day, so the choice of décor was predominantly Simon's. He didn't like what he called 'clutter', so pictures, soft furnishings like cushions, and ornaments were virtually non-existent. Everything was orderly, modern and streamlined, arranged to 'show home' perfection. It was the kind of apartment I'd dreamed about when I was younger.

I perched on the edge of the bed and finished my juice. Marla's home was anything but orderly and streamlined. Knick-knacks and doodahs filled every surface. Crystals were placed in strategic positions around the house to ensure good health, prosperity, happiness and luck. Feng shui principles were considered wherever possible while wind chimes and sparkly glass objects dangled from every window.

The hi-tech alarm clock on the bedside cabinet caught my eye. Simon was late. I walked back through to the open-plan living area and stashed my dirty glass inside the dishwasher. Restless now, with my immediate tasks completed, I paced up and down the polished wooden laminate floor of the lounge and waited for Simon.

I tried to hope that Marla was overdramatising the whole situation and that I'd arrive to discover she was booked in for nothing more sinister than bunion removal. Somehow, though, I didn't think that would be the case. She never went to the doctor, preferring to use her homeopathic remedies or crystal therapy to treat whatever was wrong.

Plus, there was Drew. I hadn't even known he was back in England, let alone that he was in touch with Marla. My flesh goose-bumped on my arms and heat tugged at my stomach when I pictured his green eyes. I was going to see Drew again.

I wondered if he'd changed, if he'd married or had a girlfriend. I tried to repress those thoughts, yet the logical, sensible, school-teacher part of my brain told me that all of those things were perfectly possible. After all, I was engaged to be married and living with someone, so why wouldn't Drew have similar commitments?

Except the Drew I'd known didn't do commitment – that was why we'd broken up. He'd wanted to travel around the world, see new sights, try new things. I'd wanted stability, order, roots . . . all the things I'd never had while I'd been growing up. So Drew had left with a back pack and his guitar. I'd gone back to college and lesson plans. There had been the odd postcard from various parts of the globe, to be pored over and treasured. Then nothing.

Simon's key rattled in the front door and I snapped back to the present.

'The traffic is hell. I suppose you still want to go to your mother's?' He dropped his leather briefcase on the kitchen floor and picked up his mail from the worktop.

'Everything's packed.' I waited for him to finish reading and look at me.

'Okay, give me ten minutes to change.' His voice was resigned.

'Thanks.'

He dropped his post down and came over to give me a hug, holding me close to him for a second before placing a kiss on top of my head. I savoured his solid safeness and the smell of his expensive cologne. Simon was everything Drew wasn't. Simon was security.

The traffic was every bit as bad as Simon had predicted. By the time we reached the outskirts of Bristol and the start of the motorway section we were down to a crawl. Perversely, being proved right appeared to lift Simon's spirits and he delved enthusiastically into the bag of wine gums on the dashboard as the middle lane of the motorway came to a full stop once again.

'So Marla didn't say what her operation was for?' he asked.

'No, she said she didn't want to tell me over the phone. I don't think she would have called at all if Drew hadn't made her do it.' I stared out at an uninspiring view that comprised the side of a coach and a car-transporter lorry.

'Who's Drew?' Simon frowned.

I'd never told Simon about him. There had never been any need to, and besides, I was sure Simon had old flames that I knew nothing about. He even had some that still worked in his building that I *did* know about.

'Just a guy I used to know. I thought he was still in

Australia.' The inside of the car smelled of wine gums and guilt.

'And he's a friend of Marla's?' Simon slurped on his sweet.

'I suppose. You know my mother.'

We lapsed back into silence. Everyone in Brixham knew my mother. Marla regularly gave talks on the local radio about alternative living and crystal therapy. She'd even been on television a couple of times when she'd pulled some crazy stunt. In addition to the crystals, she was known locally as Marla the mystic and gave mediumship readings. As a self-conscious teenager I'd hated it. I wanted her to be like my friends' mothers. They all drove four-by-fours, had dogs and shopped at Sainsbury's in their designer clothes. Marla rode a bike, grew her own vegetables and dressed like a gypsy.

The traffic picked up speed and we were soon climbing up Telegraph Hill. This was the point in the journey where I began to don my mental armour, ready to cope with my mother and all her eccentricities. I imagined that this time I would need extra protection, since I was going to see Drew. I wondered if he would look the same or if his shaggy hair, bleached by the sun, would have been cut short.

I glanced across at Simon with his corporate close crop and trendy semi-shaved look that hurt my lips when I kissed him. In his designer sunglasses and T-shirt he looked every inch the successful young businessman. It was no surprise that the office girls in his building all fancied him like mad. Somehow, though, he never appeared so desirable when we were in Brixham. Maybe I should have taken the train and left Simon behind in the city. Immediately I felt guilty at being so disloyal and offered him another wine gum – one of the red ones, his favourites.

Finally we were outside my mother's house, a narrow white-painted Edwardian terrace high on the hillside with vertigo-inducing views of the harbour. Simon squeezed his BMW into a precious tight parking space and hoisted our bags from the boot. The sky above the horizon was streaked with bands of pink and silver from the setting sun; overhead the seagulls wheeled and called to each other. I stood for a moment and allowed the beauty of the place to seep into me before squaring my shoulders ready to face my mother.

As I put my key in the lock I heard the faint sounds of my mother's meditation music. I'd insisted on keeping a key in case of emergencies when I'd left home. Marla was prone to locking herself out. Simon followed me into the hall with our bags as the evening breeze rippled the wind chime that dangled over our heads. I stepped around the huge chunk of lucky hematite crystal that lay on the quarry tiles of the hall floor like a trip hazard and walked towards the back of the house in search of Marla. I knew where she was likely to be, I simply followed the music and the sickly sweet smell of incense to the small courtyard at the back of the house.

As I'd expected, Marla sat cross-legged on a pile of cushions surrounded by candles, blissfully oblivious of our presence. Simon coughed and she opened her eyes.

'Azure, darling!' She leapt to her feet in a swirl of Indian-print fabric to hug me and plant kisses on my cheeks. 'Simon.' She dropped me to pounce on my fiancé, knowing he hated her open displays of affection.

'Marla.' He stood stiff and awkward in her embrace, nodding his head in greeting as he clung to our luggage like a drowning man to a life raft.

'Take the bags upstairs and I'll get you both a drink. You must be parched after driving in this heat.'

Simon didn't need telling twice and disappeared off inside the house, leaving me with Marla. I switched off her music.

'What's going on? What's this operation for?' I knew I needed to tackle her straight away. If I didn't she would dance around the issue for ages.

True to form, she didn't answer me, but walked back inside the house and into the kitchen.

'Marla?' I had to know what was wrong. When she'd first sprung up from her yoga position in the courtyard she'd looked her usual healthy self. Now, as she collected a jug of iced water from the fridge, I saw her hand trembling.

'Sit down, Azure.' She indicated one of the small stools she kept under the postage-stamp-sized breakfast bar.

I did as she asked, sliding into the narrow space between the bar counter and the rough stone wall. She poured a glass of water from the jug and took a sip.

'I have cancer.'

A loud buzzing noise sounded in my ears and my

breath stuck in my throat. Unable to speak, I gaped at her and tried to comprehend what she'd said. It wasn't possible, there had to be a mistake.

'I found a lump in my left breast. I waited a few days and did some crystal therapy but nothing changed, so I went to a doctor.'

Old people and smokers got cancer. Not Marla, she was the poster child for a healthy, organic diet. She lived on seeds, nuts, vegetables and wheatgrass. She was only forty-seven. She couldn't have cancer.

'What did they say? Have you had tests? How long has this been going on? I've called you every week and you've never said a word about this before.'

'It's all happened quite quickly. They have this new system – well, I don't know if it's new, but they call it a fast track. I had a mammogram and a biopsy, then the consultant went through the options with me. They want me in this Sunday.' She moved her shoulders in a resigned sort of shrug.

I stared at her as the meaning of her words finally began to sink in. She appeared the same as always. Slender and delicate with her wild, dark hair loose about her shoulders. Clad in her familiar fitted T-shirt and flowing gypsy skirt with a gold bangle round her ankle. She looked well and healthy. It didn't make sense.

'What are they going to do?'

She took another sip of her water. 'It's a lumpectomy. If they find it's more when they do the operation then they'll . . . remove the whole breast.' This was the point where her voice quivered.

'Oh my God.' I jumped up from my stool to hug her, causing the water in her glass to splash out on to the counter.

'It should all be fine. Depending on how it goes they'll decide my follow-up treatment quite quickly. Probably radiotherapy, they said.'

Tears poured down my face and wetted the shoulder of her T-shirt.

'Azure, my sweetheart, I knew you would be like this. Positive thinking, darling, that's what's required,' Marla chided.

I fumbled in my pocket for a tissue and dabbed at my eyes. I could hear Simon walking around on the squeaky floorboards upstairs, no doubt busy unpacking our bags and hanging our clothes neatly inside the wardrobe.

'How long will you be in hospital?'

'Only a few days. I'm told it's not a big procedure if everything goes to plan.' I suspected she was down-playing the seriousness of the situation to avoid upsetting me.

'I can't believe it. Why didn't you ring me sooner?'

'There wasn't anything you could do, and besides, everything has happened so quickly.' She picked up the water jug again and poured me a glass. 'Your grand-mother would no doubt have suggested brandy for shock,' she commented wryly as she passed me the glass.

I took a dutiful sip of water. Brandy sounded like a good idea to me, iced water wasn't quite the same.

'Drew suggested I ring you as soon as I got back from

the hospital. I'm going to need your help for a while to look after the shop.'

'Of course. Simon has to go back on Sunday but I'll stay for as long as you need me.' My mind went into a whirl with all the things I needed to plan for my stay. The upstairs floorboards squeaked again, reminding me of Simon's presence. I longed to ask about Drew and where he fitted into all this, but decided to wait.

'Anyway, we can sort everything out tomorrow. You and Simon must be starving,' Marla announced, and opened the fridge door to peer hopefully at the contents.

Simon appeared in the kitchen at the mention of his name.

'How about some fish and chips? My treat.' She closed the door and I guessed there wasn't anything in there that Simon would eat. She looked around the kitchen for her purse.

'It's okay, we'll walk down and get it. Would you like something?'

I needed to talk to Simon. I wasn't sure how well he would take the news of my staying in Brixham. From what Marla had said, I would need to be here for the whole of the six-week holiday.

'Nothing for me, darling. I ate not long before you arrived.'

Simon and I left the house and walked down the hill towards the chip shop. The evening air had grown cooler and goose bumps appeared on my bare arms. Simon looked as shocked as I had been when I told him Marla's news. It still hadn't really sunk in, and I knew the least little thing would start me crying again if I thought about it too much.

'How long do you think you'll need to stay here for?' Simon asked after we'd collected our chips and were trudging back up towards the house.

'I don't know. At least for the next six weeks or so. I'll know more after she's had her operation.' We paused by a low stone wall and looked back towards the harbour as we caught our breath. Pretty coloured lights gleamed in the dusk like jewels in a necklace and the boats in the harbour bobbed gently up and down in their moorings.

'I don't know how often I'll be able to get down here.' Simon frowned.

He wasn't very good with illness. If I had a cold he would avoid me completely, even sleeping in the spare room in case I contaminated him. Add in the fact that he disliked Marla almost as much as she disliked him, and I knew he wouldn't be rushing to come here, not even to see me. It was probably just as well. Marla would be under enough stress without the added strain of pretending to be nice to my fiancé for my sake.

'I'll have to be here to look after Marla, and then there's the shop. It has to stay open, it's the busiest time of the year for her.' Marla had a shop on the main street called the Crystal Palace; she sold all kinds of gem crystals and holistic therapies, charms and doodahs. Some of her stock was for the tourist trade but she had other, more expensive things for the serious collector.

I poked a hole in my paper bag and extracted a lovely

fat vinegar-soaked chip. I nibbled thoughtfully on the end and ignored Simon's disapproving expression.

'Until she's had her surgery and I see how the land lies, I won't know the extent of the help she'll need.'

We carried on walking. I knew Simon wouldn't eat his food till we were back inside the house and he had a knife and fork, but I carried on picking and eating as I walked, relishing the tang of the salt and the warmth of the hot potato. It would have been nice to take our food down by the sea and sit on one of the benches overlooking the water, but Simon disliked al fresco dining.

Not like Drew.

The traitorous thought sprang up from nowhere and I remembered an evening sitting on a beach. The sand had still been warm from the sun and we'd fed each other chips and drunk cider, cold from the bottle, while we watched the sun set. We'd listened to the dull roar of the waves and laughed at silly jokes.

Simon led the way into Marla's kitchen. 'I'll find some plates.'

Somehow, once we were seated and our supper was taken out of the paper bags, the pleasure had gone and the food didn't taste the same.

3

M arla had already left to open the shop when I
went downstairs to breakfast with Simon the next
morning. I'd arranged to meet her there so I could
reacquaint myself with everything.

'You won't have to be there all day, will you?' Simon
clumped around the kitchen opening and closing the
cabinet doors on a futile quest for cornflakes.

'No, I don't think so. Marla has people who help out
at weekends. It's so I can get used to the till and stuff.' I
found Marla's big plastic tub of homemade muesli and
put it on the breakfast bar in front of him.

He pulled a face and sipped his orange juice. 'We
could go out for the afternoon, have some supper at a
restaurant?'

'Sounds nice. Marla might like to join us for a
meal. She probably won't eat any of the hospital food
when she's admitted tomorrow.' I ignored the sour quirk
of his lips at the mention of my mother joining us for
supper.

'I thought I might go into Torquay for a few hours.'
He picked an apple from Marla's hand-carved fruit bowl

and polished it on a tea towel. 'Shall I text you when I'm done, and we can meet for lunch?'

'Good idea.' I finished my drink and collected my bag, ready to leave. Simon would enjoy browsing around Torquay's designer menswear shops and sitting in one of the outdoor cafés by the marina where he could admire the yachts.

The morning air was already warm with the promise of a hot, sunny day. Marla's shop, the Crystal Palace, was situated in the centre of the town. I sauntered down the hill, enjoying the feel of the sun on my skin and the sound of the gulls, but not looking forward to working in the shop. During my childhood we'd moved dozens of times until finally, when I was fourteen, we'd settled here, in Brixham.

Marla had opened the Crystal Palace and I'd spent weekdays after school had finished, weekends and holidays serving in the shop. The customers usually fell into two categories: they were either tourists, looking for sparkly knick-knacks as souvenirs, or they were bona fide crystal junkies. The genuine aficionados were the worst. They knew the meaning of every crystal and wanted advice on wands and elixirs for various illnesses.

My pace slowed of its own accord as I reached the main street. The shops were full of local people hurrying to get their shopping done before the park-and-ride bus started to deposit the holidaymakers. The bakery, greengrocer and newsagent all seemed to be doing a roaring trade. Further along by the harbour, numerous gift shops were displaying stands of shrimping nets, postcards and saucy bumper stickers.

The Crystal Palace had a double front with windows either side of the door. Over the shop, in common with the rest of the street, was a small flat, which Marla sublet to a rather dour middle-aged single woman called Esme. It gave her some extra income and provided security for some of her rarer crystals by having someone on the premises.

I could see silver wind chimes and ghastly resin fairy figurines through the window, glittering in the morning sunlight. Lurid dragons and feathered dreamcatchers were positioned at the perfect height to catch the attention of children looking to part with their holiday spending money. Instinctively, I took a deep breath. Nothing had changed since my last visit. I don't know why I thought it would have. The Crystal Palace had always looked the same, right down to the giant stone fossil centrepiece on its podium in the middle of the shop floor.

The wind chimes tinkled as I pushed the door open. The scent of roses and lavender from the baskets of pot-pourri at the side of the cash register was thick on the air. A pretty, dark-eyed girl, aged about sixteen and with long brown hair, drifted towards me.

'I'm Zee, Marla's daughter.' I held out my hand.

The girl gave a hesitant smile and took my fingertips in a brief handshake. 'I am Katya.' Her English had a heavy accent and I wondered where she was from.

'Azure!' Marla swept in from the door at the rear of the shop which led to the stockroom and the upstairs flat.

'I see you've met Katya. She's a real treasure.'

I smiled politely at the young assistant. 'That's great. I'll need all the help I can get.'

The wind chimes overhead sang out as the shop door opened behind me.

'Hi, Zee, I see you made it back.'

Even before Drew spoke, I'd known it was him. A sixth sense told me he was near me. Hell, five minutes in my mother's shop and I was already behaving like her.

'Drew.' Annoyingly, his name squeaked out of my mouth as I turned round to face him.

My heart skipped a beat. He hadn't changed, though his shoulders were broader and the tanned muscles of his arms indicated a life spent working outdoors. He was still unmistakably Drew, from the faded tan T-shirt stretched taut across his chest to the well-worn snug-fitting denim jeans. The crinkles at the corners of his eyes were deeper, as were the smile lines round his mouth. My mouth dried at the note of challenge in the dark green depths of his gaze.

'You look good, Zee.'

I fought the urge to toss my hair back in a flirty flick. I'd taken a little extra care with my clothes this morning, choosing fitted navy capri trousers and a pretty blue strappy top. I didn't want to examine my motives for this, nor for doing my make-up so carefully. 'Thanks. You still have your hair.'

Where had that come from? Probably some subconscious wish that he might have gone bald in the last nine years so that I wouldn't find him attractive any more.

He raked his hand through his dark gold mop of hair, a slightly puzzled frown on his face.

'Yep, it was still there this morning when I showered.' A glint of mischief appeared in his eyes.

My pulse picked up just as I heard a soft and disapproving 'tsk' noise from Katya; probably she had a major crush on Drew. That could mean that he spent a lot of time around here, maybe too much for me to feel comfortable.

'Well, you know, people's appearances change. It's been a long time.' I tried to ignore the heat creeping into my cheeks.

Marla brushed past me, the swirling cotton of her long skirt cool against my calf. 'Katya, please can you help me unpack this stock?' She waved a graceful hand in the direction of a stack of boxes in the far corner. Katya followed, her frequent backward glances towards Drew betraying her interest rather too obviously.

'I didn't know you were back in Brixham.'

He gave a careless shrug. 'No reason why you should.'

He was right. There was no reason at all why I should have known he'd returned to Brixham, but somehow I still felt I should have done. 'Are you home for good?'

Another shrug, making his T-shirt – which advertised a big rock band – ripple with the movement of the chest muscles beneath the fabric. 'Not sure.'

I lowered my voice and glanced over to where my

mother and Katya were arranging snowglobes on a shelf. 'Thanks for making Marla call me.'

Drew shifted his feet and looked uncomfortable. 'Yeah, well, I thought you should know.'

Okay, so Marla and I weren't especially close. I love her, she's my mother, but we're very different people. It doesn't mean I don't care or that I neglect her. I call her at least once a week. I visit every school holiday and, before Simon, I used to pop down for weekends. Drew had no business judging me, since his relationships with his own family had always been pretty strained.

'Are you living near here?' He can't have been that far away as Katya appeared to know him quite well and he'd clearly been spending time with Marla.

'Um, yeah, quite close.' He cleared his throat. He looked uncomfortable and I wondered what was bothering him.

'Marla said you were engaged. Congratulations.' He glanced at my left hand.

The large princess-cut diamond twinkled on its gold band as I shifted my fingers and felt strangely ill at ease.

'Thanks. How about you? Are you engaged or married or anything?' I tried to keep the enquiry casual. I knew Katya and Marla were both listening in on our conversation, even though they were pretending they weren't.

The corner of his mouth lifted upwards in a wry twist. 'No, you know me, I like to travel light.' He looked directly into my eyes as he spoke and I knew he was remembering parts of our past.

'Rolling stones collect no moss.' I forced the phrase out. My initial irrational elation that he wasn't married with a family was instantly deflated by the knowledge that Drew hadn't changed at all. Nine years later it sounded as if he was still unable or unwilling to commit to anyone or anything.

Marla got up from where she'd been kneeling on the floor and walked back over to join us, her bracelets jingling as she moved. 'I'm going to show Azure the stock and refresh her knowledge of the till. Why don't you come back in an hour or so – you could go for coffee together and catch up?' She smiled up at Drew.

'I said I'd meet Simon for lunch.' I wasn't sure about spending time alone with Drew.

'Sure, it's early still. Plenty of time.' He smiled. He knew I felt uncomfortable.

'Great, see you in a while. Take the back stairs, it'll save you walking round,' Marla said.

'Thanks.' He strode across the shop and disappeared through the door that led to the stockroom and the stairs of the flat.

'Where is he going?' I hissed the question in Marla's ear.

'I've rented him the upstairs flat. Esme has emigrated to live with her sister in Canada. I needed a trustworthy tenant and Drew needed a place to live. Fate is a wonderful thing.' She beamed at me, her clear blue eyes, so like my own, appearing innocent of any hidden intent.

'Wonderful.'

Drew was living upstairs. My stomach gave a funny little flip at the thought.

Marla had always had a soft spot for Drew, and I'd sometimes wondered if that was why she didn't like Simon. Drew and Marla had a lot in common. Like my mother he loved to travel and experiment with new things and new places. Marla's adventures had been severely curtailed when she'd had me, but I knew she still dreamed about all the places she wanted to go and the things she longed to do.

I'd experienced enough travelling in my childhood when Marla had moved us from place to place. One day we would be living in a camper van and eating noodles from plastic bowls, the next we would be squatting in some palatial old house which the owner had left empty. Every time I made friends or settled into a school we would be off again.

Customers began to trickle into the shop and Marla took me to the till for instructions. It surprised me how quickly it all came back once I'd rung up a few sales. Katya was very good at answering enquiries, although I couldn't shake off the feeling that she didn't like me much. It wasn't anything in particular that she said or did, it was just a vibe I got whenever we spoke.

Time passed quickly as I found my way around the stock and familiarised myself with Marla's routines. Before I had a chance to think of a good excuse to avoid going for coffee with Drew, he was back.

'Ready for a break?' He leaned his forearms on the

side of the counter as I carefully wrapped a delicate amethyst crystal in tissue paper.

'I think I should stay here and—'

'Of course she is. You two go and catch up with each other.' Marla deftly removed the crystal from my grasp and sealed the tissue wrapping with a shop label.

Katya glowered at me as I bowed to the inevitable and followed Drew out of the shop. The streets were crowded now, bustling with holidaymakers and locals alike who browsed in windows and caught up with friends. I folded my arms defensively across my chest as Drew led me down the street towards the harbour.

I knew where we were heading. Five minutes' walk would lead us round the sea wall where children would be catching crabs with nets. Right across the road was a small café. It was the place we used to meet in, the place we'd sat inside on wet days and watched the rain come down while we drank tea and ate scrambled egg on toast.

I had to trot to keep up with Drew's long-legged stride, and the bustle of people walking past made conversation difficult. We arrived at the café just as an elderly couple were vacating one of the outside tables. I took a seat while Drew went inside to get drinks. He hadn't asked me what I wanted.

He emerged a few minutes later carrying two tall white mugs.

I stared at the contents of my cup. Hot chocolate with extra cream and pink marshmallows. I hadn't drunk that combination since I'd been twenty years old – since I'd been with Drew.

'Is this okay? You do still like chocolate?' He leaned back in his shiny aluminium café chair and took a sip of his drink. I knew he had coffee, black, with one sugar. Inexplicably my heartbeat had kicked up a notch simply from his being near me. This was wrong, all wrong.

'It's okay, though I usually have tea these days.' I watched as the creamy float on the top of my drink started to fizzle around the edges, sinking a chunk of pink marshmallow into the chocolate.

We sat in awkward silence for a moment while I ate the marshmallows with the long-handled spoon that accompanied my mug.

'This is weird. Until yesterday I thought you were still in Australia and that my mother was well and happy. Now I'm here with you, and Marla has cancer.' Tears filled my eyes as the enormity of everything that had happened in the space of twenty-four hours hit me.

Drew put down his mug and leaned forward in his seat to catch hold of my hands. 'It's okay, Zee. Marla will be fine. The surgeon says they caught it really early.' He passed a napkin to me, so I could dry the tears that had tumbled on to my face.

'But I'm frightened. Marla is all I've got.' The words came out as a whisper even as I drew comfort from the warmth of his hand holding mine.

'And Simon. You have a fiancé now, too,' Drew reminded me. He withdrew his hand from mine, a blank expression on his face.

My engagement ring winked at me in the morning sunlight, a guilty reminder that on some subconscious level I'd been enjoying Drew's touch just a shade too much.

'Yes, Simon too, of course,' I agreed, feeling rather shocked that I had apparently forgotten all about my fiancé.

'Marla tells me you're a teacher at a primary school.' Drew leaned back in his seat again.

'Yes, year five. It's a challenge; most of the kids come from difficult backgrounds.' I took a sip of my hot chocolate, relieved our conversation had taken a more neutral turn. 'What about you? What are you doing now?'

'This and that.' He stretched his legs out in the sunshine and wriggled his bare toes under the leather strap of his sandals as if the subject of work bored him.

'How did you come to meet Marla again?' I still hadn't figured out why Drew had been the one to call me about her operation. Marla had a lot of female friends and I would have expected one of them to be the bearer of bad news. Fran, perhaps, or Wendy; Drew was an unlikely candidate to offer support to anyone or to play the middleman.

He played with his mug as it stood on the table, sliding his finger up the curve of the handle. 'I got back to England a few months ago. I spent some time in

London and then came back down here. I'd gone to see my family one day and bumped into Marla in town. She seemed upset, not herself. We went for coffee and she told me she had to go for tests.'

'You knew when she was having the tests done? But nobody called me.' My hand shook as I put my almost-empty mug down on the table.

'Hey, it was only a test. It could have been nothing. She didn't want her girlfriends to know because she knew they would ring you. She didn't want to worry you when it could have been something minor,' Drew continued.

I sucked in a breath. 'Who went with her for the biopsy? She didn't go by herself, did she?'

He shook his head. 'I took her and waited with her. I made her call you as soon as we got back to the house.'

I stared at him. I was grateful Marla hadn't been on her own, but I was her daughter. 'I should have been with her.'

'Zee, there was nothing you could have done. I wanted her to ring you beforehand but you know Marla, she's a law unto herself.'

He was right, I shouldn't be feeling angry with him. If anything, I probably felt bad because I knew I should make more effort to visit Marla, to call her and to involve her in my life.

'Thanks for being there for her.' I finished my drink.

'It's okay. Marla's all right, you know.' His green eyes looked into mine.

I knew. My mother had always been perceived as cool by my friends. It should have been good, but when I was growing up I hadn't wanted a cool mother – one who kept trying to be my friend – I'd wanted a mum, a traditional mum with rules and routines. Marla spent most of my teen years trying to get close to me yet, perversely, had only pushed me further away.

'I should get back. Simon wants me to meet him for lunch.' I glanced at my watch and slipped the strap of my handbag on to my shoulder. 'You could join us if you want.'

Drew rose from his seat in an easy languid movement. 'Sorry, Zee, I think I'll pass. Two's company and all that.'

We walked back around the edge of the harbour. The men who sold tickets for the boat trips along the bay appeared to be doing a good trade.

I wasn't sure why I'd asked him to join us for lunch, except it had seemed impolite not to. Simon certainly wouldn't have been very happy if I arrived back at the cottage with Drew in tow, especially after I'd told him Drew was an old friend. 'Okay. I guess I'll see you around,' I said.

'Yeah, I expect you will.'

Drew accompanied me to the front of the Crystal Palace and we stopped in front of one of the windows. People parted to walk round us like waves round the breakwater.

'Well, thanks for looking after Marla.' I should have worn my heels. I'd forgotten how tall Drew was compared to me. When I wore my pumps my nose came level with the top of his chest.

'No prob. If you need anything, just give me a call, Marla has my number.'

My pulse raced at his proximity and for a brief second I thought he was going to kiss me on the cheek. He appeared to hesitate, his green eyes thoughtful as he looked at me.

'I'll be in touch.' He took a step backwards and walked away to be swallowed up by the crowd.

I stared after him. My mobile buzzed in my handbag and I fumbled to get it.

Bk at M's. R U coming 4 lunch?

It was probably just as well that Drew had gone. Seeing him again and spending time with him was already having a distinctly unsettling effect on me. I replied to Simon's text and popped back into the shop to check that Marla would be okay if I went off to lunch.

The shop floor was busy with people browsing among the shelves. Katya gave me a frosty look as I joined Marla at the till where she was busy packing a gaudy resin pixie into a box.

'Did you have a nice chat with Drew?' Marla asked as she rang the sale into the register.

'Yes, it was fine.'

She handed over change and a receipt to the child who'd bought the pixie. 'That's good. I wasn't sure how you'd feel, seeing him again.' She blinked innocently.

'Nine years is a long time, Marla.' I wasn't sure how much my mother knew about what had happened when

Drew and I split up. I'd gone back to university the next day and hadn't come home for quite a while afterwards, pleading pressure of exams and coursework.

'Time is elastic, Azure. Nine minutes can feel like nine years with the wrong person – and vice versa.' She drifted along the counter to straighten up a display stand of handmade greetings cards.

I realised my jaw was clenched. My mother was prone to making statements like that and they always got me riled.

'Is it okay if I meet Simon for lunch now?' I didn't think there was much more I could do in the shop anyway. When Marla went into hospital tomorrow, however, I would have to manage on my own, with Katya for company.

'Oh, of course, darling.' She waved her hand, making her bangles jingle. 'I'll see you both later.'

I slipped out of the shop past the surly Katya and set off on the walk up the hill to the cottage. As I turned off the main street I caught a glimpse of a familiar male figure – Drew. My heart gave a skip before I realised he wasn't alone. A petite blonde woman in a short pastel-pink cotton strappy sundress was at his side.

I marched up the hill in the midday heat. I don't know why I felt disgruntled about seeing Drew with someone. It shouldn't be a surprise, he was an attractive man. An attractive *single* man, who could date anyone he liked. Why should I care?

Simon was in the back courtyard when I reached the cottage. He'd made himself comfortable in the sunshine and was busy working on his tan, lounging in a thread-bare deckchair. He sat up when he heard the click of Marla's beaded curtain as I stepped through it.

'Everything all right?' He shaded his eyes with his hand, in order to squint at me.

'Yes, fine. Where do you want to have lunch?' I busied myself with looking at Marla's flower tubs, tugging a few dead leaves from the geraniums that spilled out in colourful profusion over the stone ledges.

Simon stood and picked up his shirt from where he'd draped it over the back of the chair. 'I thought we could go to that place up the road.'

I presumed he meant the small café-cum-bistro that was a few minutes' walk away. 'Okay.'

As he buttoned his shirt I couldn't help contrasting Simon's neat, well-groomed appearance with Drew's casual scruffiness. Today he was wearing crisp cotton chinos in biscuit tan teamed with a short-sleeved shirt the colour of the summer sky which was murder for me to iron. He placed a hand possessively at my waist. 'Shall we go?'

I allowed him to steer me along the hallway and out of the house. We strolled along the street towards the café and he told me about his morning.

'Are you feeling okay, Zee? You seem quiet.' His forehead creased in concern as he peered at me.

'I'm okay. Just worried about Marla, I guess.'

'Ah, yes, well . . . I'm sure she'll be in good hands,' he said as we reached the café. He pushed the door and held it open for me.

The café was busy both inside and out, on the small terrace at the rear. We managed to get a small table indoors in the corner of the room. I wished everyone wouldn't keep telling me that Marla would be okay. I knew they meant well, but this was cancer. Why was I the only one who seemed to have grasped the seriousness of it all? I could understand Marla being in a state of denial – she had every right to do whatever she needed to get through her illness – but was nobody else considering the possibility that . . . ? No, I couldn't even think it.

I looked up to see Simon studying the menu. I, in turn, studied Simon. He glanced up and caught my eye. 'Have you decided what you'd like?'

'Salad.' I felt I needed to balance out some of those calories from the hot chocolate with something light, especially if we were going to eat out this evening, too.

He smiled approvingly at me and went off to give our order at the counter. I settled back in my seat and looked around the café. A flash of tan-coloured T-shirt caught my eye. Damn. The whole of Brixham, including Drew, had chosen the same café in which to eat their lunch. I tried to see if the blonde woman from earlier was with him but I only had a partial view through the open doorway and couldn't tell.

Simon resumed his seat and placed a glass of sparkling mineral water in front of me. There was a movement over his shoulder and I caught a glimpse of a pink sundress. Drew wasn't alone.

'Food should be about ten minutes.' Simon took a pull from his glass of lager. 'I'm starving.'

I smiled a polite but silent reply while Simon continued to tell me about why he needed to head back to London tomorrow morning and what he needed to do at work on Monday. All the while my gaze kept straying over his shoulder to catch glimpses of Drew and his girlfriend out on the terrace.

'So, if it's okay with you, I thought I might leave before lunch tomorrow. You'll be busy at the shop so I may as well miss the traffic.' He reached across to take my hand, nudging my engagement ring so the diamond was lined up straight on my finger.

'Yes, very sensible.' I only had a vague idea what he'd been talking about but I knew he would have found an excuse to leave early, no matter what. Being around any kind of illness made him uncomfortable, and it didn't help that he and Marla were distantly polite while in each other's company. I frequently felt as if I were refereeing some unseen tennis match when the three of us were together.

'Zee, is there something on my shoulder?' Simon stopped talking and peered at his sleeve before smoothing down his hair.

'No, sorry. I thought I saw someone I knew out on the terrace.' Heat flooded my face.

'Oh?' Simon swung round in his seat to take a look as Drew and his girlfriend walked in.

Drew's eyes met mine and my face burned hotter.

'Small world.'

He nodded.

'Simon, this is an old friend of mine, Drew. Drew, this is Simon, my fiancé.' I managed to force out the introductions in a fairly normal tone. Drew stretched out his arm to shake hands with Simon. The pretty blonde girl simply looked bored.

I knew they were sizing each other up from the way they did the whole hearty manly handshake thing. Drew made no move to introduce the girl at his side and I wondered how long he'd been seeing her. She appeared to be in her early twenties with a smooth bouncy ponytail and cute little wedge-heeled shoes. I disliked her on sight.

'Good to meet you. Enjoy your meal.'

The waitress arrived with our two plates as Drew spoke. Simon nodded his head in acknowledgement and Drew and his girlfriend left the café.

'I, erm, saw Drew earlier at the shop.' I spread a napkin over my lap.

Simon picked up the salt. 'Hmm?'

'He's lodging in the flat above it.' I waited for Simon's reaction. He was always a bit possessive where I was concerned. Not in a bad way, but he liked to know who my friends were and where we were going, stuff like that. It had always made me feel cherished and cared for before I'd moved in with him, but just lately I'd begun to find it smothering.

'I thought an old woman lived in that flat?' Simon frowned and tapped the salt cellar on the table.

'Esme's moved to Canada.'

He squinted at the holes in the salt dispenser to see if they were clear. 'Well, be careful, Zee. I know he's an old friend of yours but he looks a bit off to me.'

He got up and exchanged the cruets with the ones from the table next to us. I didn't say anything. Instead, I sat and ate my salad.

5

After lunch Simon headed back to the house to catch up on his tan in the courtyard while I pootled aimlessly around town. I returned to the shop shortly before closing time so I could learn how the alarm system worked.

'Hello, darling, did you have a nice afternoon?' Marla smiled at me from behind the counter as I entered.

Katya ignored me and switched on the vacuum cleaner, rendering my response inaudible above the noise. Marla continued to count the money from the till, bagging it up ready to deposit in the night safe at the bank. I tried not to grind my teeth with impatience while I waited for her to finish. Spending time at the shop with Katya hanging around wasn't my idea of a good time and Marla seemed to be taking for ever to finish up.

Katya finally switched off the Dyson and dragged it back into the store cupboard.

'Thank you for all your help today.' Marla dropped the last of the day's takings inside the cloth bag and smiled at Katya. 'I know that you, Wendy and Fran will be a great help to Azure.'

Wendy normally helped out at the shop during busy times. I'd forgotten Fran would be working in the shop most days. She'd been at the Crystal Palace ever since I'd left for college. Like Marla, she was really into alternative therapies and practised tarot readings as well as crystal therapy. She was pleasant enough but a bit wet – and she always smelled like stale cabbage.

'I am sure we will all work very well together.' Katya's expression didn't match her sentiment, but Marla didn't seem to notice.

I forced myself to smile at her by way of a response.

'Good. Well, time to lock up.' Marla put the float for the next day in the safe and then programmed the alarm using the keypad on the wall inside the store cupboard. I followed Katya outside while Marla secured the front door.

Katya made a huge performance of hugging my mother and wishing her all the best for her surgery, even to the point of pressing some tiny painted icon into her hand for her to take into the hospital.

'For good luck,' she said, dashing her hand across her eyes as she spoke.

Marla sighed as Katya, all blotchy and tear-streaked, finally disappeared round the corner to catch her bus. 'She's such a sweet girl.'

I didn't bother to reply; it all felt a bit fake to me, as if it was a show put on for my benefit. Instead, I strolled along beside my mother as we headed to the bank. The crowds in the streets had thinned and now there were just a few family groups wandering along, doing some window-shopping or looking for somewhere to eat. The town had settled into that sort of semi-lull that exists between the end of the day and the start of the evening nightlife.

'It's a beautiful evening.' Marla waved at someone she knew across the street.

'Yes.' It *was* lovely. The air was still warm and the sunlight soft, reflecting a mellow glow on the buildings.

'What are your plans for tonight?'

'Simon thought it would be nice if we all went out together for something to eat.' Okay, so it was a bit of a fib. Simon would probably prefer it if Marla stayed home while he and I went out.

Marla arched her brow. 'Really? I suppose it would be better than staying in. My bags are all packed for tomorrow and I plan to do a crystal healing session in readiness before I leave for the hospital.'

We paused at the night safe. She pulled open the metal drawer in the wall and deposited the bag of takings safely inside.

She reshouldered her natural hemp bag and we continued to stroll towards the harbour.

'You *will* be all right running the shop, won't you, Azure? I know it's the busiest time of the year and retail is not your "thing".' She did the speech-mark gesture in the air with her fingers as she spoke.

'Marla, I'm quite capable of managing for a few weeks while you recuperate. What matters is that you get well.' We stopped again, this time by a wooden bench next to the harbour where we sat down. We'd drifted towards the sea by a kind of unspoken consent. It would be difficult to talk tonight with Simon there and I wanted to make sure she was okay about everything.

'I'm sure I'll be fine. The consultant has assured me that he doesn't expect to find any nasty surprises when he operates. I have my crystals and Fran is making up some elixirs.' She leaned back against the seat and surveyed the sea.

I tried not to roll my eyes. 'You will finish the conventional treatment, though?' I hoped she didn't plan to simply have the surgery and then neglect any follow-up treatment. I knew Marla; she would rather rely on the hocus-pocus of her crystals and homeopathic remedies than on the more conventional radiotherapy.

'I promise I'll do whatever is necessary to make myself well again.' She crossed her slender legs, making her ankle bracelet tinkle.

'Well, okay then.' Her promise reassured me a little.

'I'm convinced this whole thing is a result of my life becoming misaligned. I've been working on rebalancing my chakras and getting the ch'i flowing properly again.'

'Misaligned? In what way?' I wondered if she'd had this conversation with her consultant. I always thought breast cancer was down to genetics, smoking, diet, bad luck . . . any number of ill-fated combos, but not misalignment of your chakras.

'There are things in my life I haven't achieved, Azure. I think those subconscious negative feelings of failure have been causing my physical symptoms.' Her face took on a dreamy expression as she watched the gulls swoop over the water.

It was exactly this kind of talk that drove Simon up the wall. His parents, Jonty and Evelyn, were middle-class surburban citizens. Nice and solid. Evelyn belonged to the WI and at Easter she knitted yellow egg cosies in the shape of chicks. Jonty belonged to the local golf club and read the *Daily Mail*. Poor Simon wasn't used to this kind of thinking. I'd grown up with a constant stream of New Age therapies, some good, some positively bonkers, so I wasn't as fazed as I might have been by Marla's theory.

'What kinds of things do you want to achieve?' I had bad vibes about this question. There wasn't much my mother hadn't done in her life.

'I never did see the sun rise over the Serengeti. And it's the place that inspired me to give you your name.' She heaved a sigh.

I'd heard the story of my name a million times. Apparently, when I was born, I opened my eyes and they were bright blue, the colour of the sky at daybreak over the Serengeti – or at least the colour my mother imagined it to be – hence Azure Dawn. I was actually born in a squat at a house in Milton Keynes where my mother happened to be living at the time.

'And you think that not having seen the Serengeti has made you ill?'

Marla pursed her lips the way she always did when she thought I was being obtuse. 'It's the imbalance, darling. The frustrations of unfulfilment. That's why I worry so much about you.'

Uh-oh, how did we get on to me?

She patted my arm reassuringly as I gazed blankly at her and wondered what might be coming next.

'Ever since you were a child you've seen things in black and white. There were never any shades of grey with you. An old head on a child's shoulders.' Her big blue eyes filled with tears.

Since my childhood had hardly been conventional it was no surprise that I'd had to grow up so quickly. When I was three we lived in a yurt in the middle of a potato field in Kent. Marla has photos of me in a Peruvian-style knitted cap, standing in a sea of mud outside a tepee-like structure. A succession of squats, a camper van and several rented inner-city terraces had rapidly followed until Granny Millichip died when I was in my teens. The inheritance provided enough money for us to settle in Brixham.

'Marla, I'm perfectly happy with my life. We were discussing *you*, remember?'

A seagull strutted across the pavement in front of us, his beady little eyes searching hopefully for a sign that we might have food secreted about our persons.

She grasped my hand in hers. The sudden movement startled the gull and he took to the air, calling his displeasure.

'Don't you see? That's the problem, you simply don't understand. I've failed you, Azure, and this illness is a physical sign.'

If I didn't know for a fact that my mother had stopped smoking the wacky baccy a few years ago, I would have sworn she was on pot. 'That's ridiculous. One in four people get—' I struggled for an alternative, not wanting to say the C-word out loud.

'Cancer,' Marla prompted.

'Yes.'

She squeezed my fingers and frowned at my engagement ring as the gold band bit into her skin. 'All things in life have a purpose. This is my wake-up call, Azure, I know it is. I feel it here.' She thumped her chest with her free hand.

'Once you've had the surgery and you're getting better, then you can do whatever you feel you need to do.' I felt uncomfortable sitting on a seafront bench discussing private matters while people strolled past.

'I know, and I need to make plans.' Her gaze bored into me. 'You'll support me on this, won't you, darling? It's terribly important.'

Her grip on my hand was cutting off the circulation in my fingers. 'Of course I'll support you. That's why I'm here.'

She released her hold and I had a horrible feeling that I'd just agreed to something I hadn't bargained for.

My mobile pinged in my bag. I knew who the text message would be from before I even checked the screen.

Where R U?

'Simon,' I said in answer to my mother's unspoken question. I sent him a quick reply to say we were on our way back.

'Darling, are you sure Simon is the right man for

you?' Marla asked as I replaced the phone in my handbag.

'We've had this conversation before.' I stood and brushed imaginary dust from the back of my capri trousers.

Marla remained seated on the bench, a calm expression on her face. 'I know, but it's been a while since I asked the question and you're living together now. I wondered if things might have changed since then.'

'I'm fine. We're fine, we're very happy together.'

'If you say so, darling.' She rose from the bench with an elegant swish of her skirt. 'We'd better go home, then, before he sends out a search party for you.'

If she wasn't my mother, and seriously ill, I might have shoved her into the sea. The thing that annoyed me most about the whole conversation was that there was now a tiny niggle, buried deep in my subconscious, that maybe my life wasn't as great as I made out.

We set off back along the street and up the hill towards the cottage. It was ridiculous, of course. Simon was the perfect man for me. He was smart, intelligent, had a good steady job and wanted the same things out of life that I did. We had a nice home, good friends and enjoyed ourselves. If I were honest, though, I'd have to say that most of our friends were actually Simon's friends. He didn't really hit it off with any of my colleagues from school, and by 'enjoying ourselves', I mostly meant us going to dinner with his friends.

Marla opened the front door and wandered off to the

kitchen. She hadn't spoken since we'd left the bench so I knew she could tell I was cross with her. I heard water running upstairs and guessed Simon was in the shower.

Meditation music began to drift along the hallway as I looped the strap of my handbag over the post at the foot of the stairs before making my way up to the bedroom.

Simon's shorts and T-shirt were folded neatly on the chair behind the door and his change of clothes was laid out on the bed. I lay down on my side of the bed, being careful not to disturb his stuff, and closed my eyes.

Damn Marla and her questions. I was happy with Simon.

I was.

Simon left the next morning, after we'd taken Marla to the hospital. I stayed with her while she was booked in by the nurse, then Simon dropped me off in time to open the shop. I hated leaving her there, in the ward, with a pale blue NHS theatre gown at the foot of her bed and her pillow of healing herbs resting inside her locker.

I hurried down the street, trying to remember the code for the alarm as I hunted in my bag for the keys. Katya was already waiting on the doorstep.

'You are late.' She folded her arms.

'I know. The traffic was bad coming back from the hospital.' I undid the top lock and pushed the key into the bottom keyhole, bracing myself for the alarm warning as I opened the door.

'Marla is okay, yes? She did not wish that you stay with her?' Katya was hard on my heels as I dashed inside and wrenched open the store cupboard door so I could switch off the alarm.

'The hospital doesn't like relatives to stay. They needed to get her all booked in and to prepare her for this afternoon.' I punched numbers on the keypad and prayed I'd got the right combination.

'What time is she having the operation?' Katya persisted.

I hit the last button and held my breath. Silence. I sighed with relief. 'About four o'clock – she's the last one today. Apparently, they have a backlog on the waiting list so the surgeon is doing extra sessions to ensure they hit their targets. That's why it's a funny time.' I decided to give Katya all the extra information in an attempt to stem the interrogation.

'It is not right that she is alone.' Katya shook her head and stalked off towards the store room.

I resisted the urge to kill my assistant with a heavy chunk of iron pyrite and concentrated instead on collecting the float from the safe and filling the till. With luck the shop would be busy and I wouldn't have time to fret about Marla. I'd felt awful enough, leaving her at the hospital, without Katya pressing all my guilt buttons. The nurse who admitted her had seemed nice and I had the ward phone number on a piece of paper in my purse so I could call and check on her progress.

Marla wouldn't have wanted me with her anyway; she was much more concerned about how I'd manage the shop and if I'd feed Jethro, her fat black cat.

The meal out last night hadn't been a success. The conversation had limped along; once we'd discussed the weather, the shop, her allotment and what had changed in Brixham since my last visit, silence had reigned supreme.

Simon had sulked because Marla had accompanied us, although he could hardly have expected me to abandon my mother the evening before she was due to undergo major surgery. It annoyed me because when he behaved in ways that she had predicted it only reinforced her bad opinion of him.

I'd said goodbye to him before hurrying to open the shop. I was a bit disappointed that he hadn't wanted to stay until the evening so that we could spend some extra time together before he went home. Still, I planned to go to the hospital once the shop was shut and Simon was anxious to get an early start to avoid the traffic. It would have been nice to have had him around, though.

Katya switched on the New Age music tapes and topped up the pot-pourri with essential oils. A few people drifted in and out of the shop and I wondered how my mother was coping with the hospital environment. She'd taken in the icon that Katya had given her, a chunk of rose quartz crystal she used as a meditation aid, and the mini pillow stuffed with healing herbs. I hoped she'd be okay.

Katya bustled over to the till with a customer and I moved across the shop out of her way while she dealt with the sale. There was something unnerving about the way she kept looking at me, or perhaps I was being paranoid. Today she wore a navy-blue and white patterned sundress, exposing olive-skin arms and legs. Her long dark hair was slicked back into a ponytail at the nape of her neck and her brown eyes were ringed with black liner. Two large silver hoops of twisted metal dangled from her earlobes and a tiny blue stud adorned the side of her nose.

I wondered where she was from and how she had come to meet Marla. She was young, but she definitely had a thing for Drew. That had been obvious yesterday from the way she'd reacted when he'd entered the shop. I couldn't figure out why she was so hostile towards me; it was unlikely that she'd know about our previous relationship – unless, of course – Marla had opened her big mouth.

The wind chimes tinkled as the shop door opened again. Drew strolled in.

'Hi, Zee, how's Marla?' He paused next to the giant ammonite fossil in the centre of the store, his hands pushed casually into the pockets of his faded snug-fit Levi's. His khaki-green shirt clung to his broad muscular chest and my tongue glued itself to the roof of my mouth, leaving me temporarily wordless.

'We took her in this morning. I've been told to call the ward at five and, all being well, I plan to go and see her tonight.' My voice came out all breathy and I could see Katya giving me the evil eye from behind him.

'Okay, let me know how she gets on. I hope everything goes well for her.' He seemed to fill the small space next to the display stand.

'Will do. Thanks for dropping by.' I knew my cheeks were heating up. This was stupid. He shouldn't have this kind of effect on me, not after all these years.

'Hey, KitKat, how's it going?' He turned round and crossed the shop to lean on the counter and talk to Katya.

I tried to act cool by tidying the trays of stones on the shelf while simultaneously attempting to eavesdrop on their conversation. It didn't work. I ended up having to help a small child choose a shark's tooth for her fossil collection while Katya simpered and fluttered her eyelashes at Drew.

By the time I got to the till to ring up my small customer's purchase, Katya and Drew's conversation had ceased. I rang the money into the register and passed over the bag that contained the tooth to the little girl.

'I'll catch up with you guys later.' Drew straightened up.

'Bye,' Katya called as he strolled towards the door.

I contented myself with raising my hand in a farewell gesture as he left the shop and walked past the window towards the harbour.

'Have you known Drew long?' I did my best to sound casual as Katya and I served another couple of customers.

'I meet him when I move here with my older brother Pieter. Drew is very kind to me. Marla is also very kind to me.' Her tone implied that I should take a leaf out of their book.

'Have you lived here long?' I didn't recall being uncharitable towards her. She, on the other hand, had been hostile since we'd met, but I was at a complete loss to know why.

'Not long. Why? You think I am here illegally?' Her dark eyes narrowed.

I'd begun to feel quite uncomfortable and, to be honest, I wondered if she was the full ticket. It wouldn't be the first time my mother had taken pity on some whack-job. I couldn't forget the incident of the homeless vagrant, when she'd let some tramp sleep on our couch. Marla had come home to find him passed out and dressed in her underwear after he'd drunk all the wine from the rack in the kitchen.

'I just wondered where you're from and why you've come to live here?' Brixham was hardly a bustling metropolis. Nearby Torquay had plenty of language students and a lot of the hotel workers and waiting staff were immigrants, but Brixham tended to be a little quieter.

Katya gave a dismissive sniff. 'You ask many things. Here is good place to live.'

She flounced off to serve a customer without really answering any of my questions. I wondered if Marla had bothered to ask Katya anything about her background before employing her. I made a mental note to check with Drew. He seemed to be on good terms with the teenager so he might know more about her.

The rest of the day felt a bit surreal. Katya avoided talking to me as much as possible. A few of Marla's friends stopped by to ask about her but since I wasn't certain how much she'd told them about her illness I kept things vague. Fran came in, presumably to ensure I hadn't ruined the business during my few short hours in charge. I checked my phone intermittently for any missed messages from the hospital.

I decided to close up half an hour early. Trade had become quiet towards the end of the day and I wanted to get home and call the hospital. I would have called from the shop but my nerves were stretched out like piano wire and Katya was getting on the very last one. Once the day's takings were safely stowed away in the bank's night safe I walked slowly back up the hill to the cottage.

Simon had sent me a text to say he was back at the flat and would call me later. There were also two missed messages from my mother-in-law-to-be, Evelyn. I let myself into the cottage and headed for the kitchen to use the phone. I took the piece of paper with the ward details on it from my purse and dialled the number. Long, agonising seconds passed before someone picked up and I stammered out my request for information on Marla.

'She returned from theatre a few minutes ago. We're making her comfortable now but she'll be drowsy for a little while. We suggest she only has a couple of visitors this evening as you may find she's quite tired.'

I guessed they must be busy so I didn't ask any of the questions I was dying to ask. Not that they would have the answers or be likely to tell me over the phone, even if they knew. I would have to ask the nurse in charge, or the surgeon, to find out how the surgery had gone, what they'd found and what Marla's prognosis was.

My hands were clammy with sweat and my legs were shaking as I hung up. I couldn't quite keep back the rush of tears that escaped to run down my cheeks and drip on to my pastel-pink T-shirt. Jethro the cat observed me from his sunny spot on the windowsill, his green eyes contemptuous in the face of my frailty. I wasn't even sure why I was crying.

I wandered over to the fridge and poured myself a glass of juice. The courtyard was filled with late-afternoon sunshine and the scent of Marla's favourite pink roses. I took a seat on the lounger that Simon had left out. A few sips of my drink restored my equilibrium. The sun seeped into my skin and I closed my eyes, breathing in the peace and quiet of the courtyard. Bees hummed lazily amongst the roses and the lavender and the anxious panic that had filled me while I'd been talking to the hospital started to drift away.

The peace didn't last long. My mobile, which I'd left on the counter in the kitchen, started buzzing. I forced myself back inside to answer, praying it wasn't the hospital with bad news.

'Azure, dear, Simon told us about your mother.' The cut-glass, Home Counties accent of my mother-in-law-to-be filled my ear.

'Hello, Evelyn.' I'd only met Evelyn and Jonty on two occasions. Once when they'd been on a day trip to visit Simon shortly after we'd started dating seriously and another time when I'd spent an excruciating weekend at their home shortly after we'd announced our engagement.

'I said to Jonty that I must ring and find out how Azure is coping.'

'That's very kind of you.' I noticed she hadn't asked about Marla, she'd only asked about me.

'Do you know how long you'll have to stay there, dear?'

I adjusted the phone so Evelyn's voice didn't grate on my eardrums quite so much. 'I'm not sure. My mother is only just out of surgery.'

'Oh, of course. I'm sure she'll be fine. Simon's gone back to the flat, hasn't he? I'm sure you won't leave him on his own too long.'

'Well, even if my mother makes a good recovery, she will need me for a while to look after her business.' Irritation riled in my stomach. I knew Evelyn was Simon's mother and he was an only child, but he'd been living on his own for a long time before I moved in. I was quite certain he could fend for himself for a few weeks.

'Oh yes, well . . . Tell your mother I asked after her, won't you, dear? And if it gets a bit much and you need a break, then you and Simon are always welcome at our home.'

'Thank you, Evelyn, that's very kind.' I finished the call while I was still able to control my temper.

Evelyn and Jonty had never met Marla. I knew they'd spoken on the phone a couple of times as Evelyn had taken it upon herself to contact my mother when Simon and I got engaged. She'd thought it was the 'proper' thing to do. They'd soon discovered that they had nothing in common and I suspect that Simon had filled his mother in on his own views of Marla and her alternative lifestyle.

I stood at the counter and finished my juice. My earlier feelings of peace had vanished and I had this eerie sense of foreboding that all the certainties I'd worked so hard to build into my life were about to be upended. Jethro jumped down from his spot on the windowsill and stretched.

'You are so lucky,' I told him as he sat and delicately began to clean a front paw with his tongue. 'I wish my life was as uncomplicated as yours.'

After a quick shower I changed into pale-blue linen trousers and a short-sleeved white shirt ready to head back out again. Fran had informed me that the number twelve from Brixham to Torquay was quite regular and ran right by the hospital. I grabbed an apple from the fruit bowl and made my way back down the hill towards the bus stop.

The evening air felt warm and the streets were still flooded with soft golden sunlight. Red geraniums and blue lobelia spilled from ancient wooden window-boxes and barrel-shaped tubs. Everything appeared bright and vivid against the white-painted walls of the cottages as I strolled along, munching on my apple.

The bus was already waiting at the stop, the only passengers a young couple occupying the back seats and a family group in place behind the driver. I paid my money and slid into a seat near one of the open windows in the hope of catching a breeze once we started to move.

'Two minutes till we go.' The driver turned the page on his newspaper, biding his time as he waited for stragglers.

I settled back in my seat and fanned myself with my hand in a vain attempt to move the stagnant air inside the bus.

A sharp knock on the window startled me and I turned my head to see Drew standing on the pavement with a bewildered expression on his face.

'What are you doing?' he demanded.

I could feel the other occupants on the bus all focusing their attention on me. My heart skipped a beat at the look of concern in his eyes.

'What does it look like I'm doing? I'm on my way to see Marla.' Embarrassment made me sound waspish.

A couple more people clambered on the bus.

'Where's Simon?' The creases on his forehead deepened as he looked along the bus.

'He had to go home.' Irritation burned through me as I realised how Drew would take this news.

The driver turned the key and the rumbling vibrations of the elderly diesel engine filled the air.

'So you're going to the hospital on your own?' Drew raised his voice above the noise.

'Yes.'

'Wait for me at the bus stop in Torquay. I'll meet you there!' Drew yelled as the bus pulled away from the kerb.

What the hell was that about? What bus stop? How was he going to meet me? The other passengers were all studiously pretending they hadn't noticed the kerfuffle. I forced myself to concentrate on the task ahead, forcing all thoughts of Drew and his cryptic conversation from my mind.

The bus chugged up the hill out of Brixham and into the stream of traffic heading along the bay. A welcome breeze filtered in through the open window to cool my heated cheeks. We crawled along at the genteel speed of an elderly snail, hemmed in on all sides by cars and vans. We made a couple of stops as passengers got on and off. Nervous tension hummed through my body and kicked up a notch with every halt as we drew closer to Torquay.

Eventually the bus rumbled to a halt at the stop in Fleet Street, the main thoroughfare. Fran had omitted to mention that on Sundays you couldn't get a direct bus to the hospital. I gathered up my bag and my courage and stepped out on to the pavement looking for my next connection. The street was still busy with shoppers and I caught snatches of German, French and Spanish as I hurried along the bus lane.

I spotted the stop for the bus to the hospital and made my way towards it through a crowd of teenage language students all dressed up for a night out in the amusement arcades. Behind me I heard the dull roar of what sounded like a motorbike. Clearly this was impossible, since it was widely signposted that only buses and pedestrians were allowed along Fleet Street. I turned my head to see the throng of people part to allow a large black motorbike through.

It halted right next to me and the rider pushed up the visor on his helmet. 'You should have told me you were on your own.' Drew, his voice muffled, proffered a spare helmet that was stashed on the bike.

'This is a bus lane. You'll get into trouble.' Behind him

I could already see one of the noisy vehicles inching its way round the corner. This was crazy, what on earth was he thinking? This was the side of Drew that had always worried me – the reckless, daredevil edge that slipped out from time to time when the circumstances were right.

'Then put on the helmet and let's get out of here.' He closed his visor, effectively ending the conversation.

Not having much choice, I pulled on the helmet and slid on to the back of the bike behind him. Heat from his body sizzled into mine as I leaned against him and the bike accelerated away ahead of the bus. The years fell away as we climbed the hill towards the hospital, the summer air rushing past my bare arms and Drew's firm, muscular back pressed against me. The engine of the powerful bike pulsated between my thighs and suddenly I was back in the past.

When Drew and I had been together he'd owned an ancient Triumph and we had toured the narrow green lanes of the coast, stopping at tiny secluded bays only accessible by determined walkers. We'd made love in fields of high ripe corn and in sheltered woody glades, lost in our own little world.

He pulled to a stop in the visitors' car park of the hospital. I half slid, half fell from the back of the bike in my haste to dismount. My legs wobbled and my heart thumped from the exhilaration of the journey and the proximity of his body. Every cell in my body was wired and buzzing with heightened sensitivity. I pulled off my helmet and handed it over.

'Thanks for the ride. I hope you don't get fined for driving through the bus lane.' To my relief my voice sounded normal; it was not the high-pitched squeak I had expected to hear.

He tugged off his helmet and smoothed down his unruly gold-brown hair with his free hand. 'You should have told me you were on your own and planning to take the bus.'

My heart did this strange lurch as I looked into his green eyes, while my mouth dried and the summer air seemed to stick at the back of my throat.

'Oh, it wasn't a big deal. Simon had to go home because he's, um . . . got a heavy day tomorrow.' Mentioning my fiancé's name seemed to break the spell. I smoothed my thumb across the back of my engagement ring for reassurance.

Drew fell into step beside me as we made our way inside the hospital, cutting his usual long, loping strides to match my short legs.

'I didn't realise you still had a bike.' I kept my eyes fixed firmly ahead and looked for the signs to Marla's ward. I wanted to peep across to look at Drew's face but I was still shaky from the effects of riding with him on his bike so I decided not to risk it.

'Yeah, I got it when I arrived back in England. Like old times, having you ride pillion with me again.'

Heat scorched into my cheeks as I broke my resolve and peeped at him. I knew from the curve of his mouth that he had shared the same memories as I had on the journey here.

'Not quite the same.'

We were at the entrance to the ward. I dropped my gaze from his face to study the toes of my canvas wedge shoes.

His fingers were warm beneath my chin as he lifted my face and looked into my eyes. 'No, I guess you're right. It's not quite the same.'

I lost the ability to breathe with the touch of his hand against my skin and the intensity of his expression.

'We need to go inside.' I struggled to get my words out. This was all wrong. I was so over Drew. I was engaged to another man and living with him, too.

'I'll come with you.' He dropped his hand. I sucked in a breath and tried to rally my thoughts before heading for my mother's cubicle.

Marla lay propped up in bed, her face almost as white as the NHS pillows that supported her. An intravenous infusion line ran from the back of her hand via a strange blue machine to a large clear plastic bag of fluid that dangled from a shiny metal stand next to the bed. Her lovely long hair lay tangled and dark against the linen.

'Marla?' I kept my voice low. Her eyes were closed and I wasn't certain if she was asleep.

Drew took two dark-blue plastic stacking chairs from the pile by the door and carried them across to her bedside. I sat down gingerly on the edge of the one nearest Marla and slipped my hand beneath her palm, careful not to disturb any of the tubes and wires.

Her eyelids fluttered open. 'Azure.' She gave me a small smile.

'How are you?' Anxiety clenched at my heart. She looked so frail and vulnerable.

She squeezed my fingers. 'I'm okay. Tired. I think they put something in this contraption.' She lifted her other hand and gestured very slightly towards the blue machine.

'Have you seen the surgeon yet?' I'd cast my eye over the bundle of notes attached to the clipboard at the foot of her bed, but hadn't really understood anything.

'He's coming round tomorrow. He said it went okay.' Her eyelids closed again, making her long black lashes fan against her pale face. It seemed strange to see her without the long, handcrafted earrings she usually wore. I stroked her fingers, naked and thin without their usual chunky rings and accompanying wrist ornaments.

'We won't stay long tonight. I'll call again in the morning.' I tried hard to swallow the huge ugly lump that had formed at the back of my throat, making me sound choky.

Marla opened her eyes again. 'I'll feel better tomorrow when I can meditate.' She twisted her head a little on the pillow to look at Drew. 'Thanks for looking after Azure.'

I tried to ignore the small stab of resentment about the fact that she thought I needed looking after – and that Drew, not Simon, was the one she thought should do it.

'No prob. What else are friends for?' He smiled at her and she settled back.

Within a few minutes it was clear she was asleep.

There seemed little point in staying any longer. Drew re-stacked the chairs by the ward entrance while I spoke to the nurses at the desk. They couldn't tell me anything other than that Marla's procedure had gone as planned and I was welcome to call them at any time.

'Are you okay?' Drew asked as we walked back along the corridor towards the exit.

'Yeah, it was just a shock seeing her like that.' I blew my nose on a tissue I'd found in my bag. I hoped Marla would have started to recover and look better tomorrow.

'I'll give you a ride home.' Drew's voice was gentle as he walked beside me.

I couldn't help but feel a bit guilty at the way my spirits lifted and my body responded to the idea of riding pillion once again with Drew. When we reached the powerful bike and he handed me the helmet, I had the same sensation I used to get at the fairground on the roller coaster as it inched its way up to the top of the climb right before it hurtled down the track.

Drew sat astride the machine and waited for me to climb on. I hopped on the back and gripped the metal bar behind me as he started up the engine. My pelvis cradled the curve of his buttocks on the black leather saddle and the tops of my thighs warmed with the heat from his legs.

The traffic had thinned as Drew threaded his way out of town and back down the smaller side roads to the coast. The sky had turned a pale translucent blue, streaked with pink and orange. We drifted past emerald-green hedgerows studded with large yellow wildflowers and tiny pink-and-white daisies while in the distance the sea lay flat and azure, topped with white-sailed boats.

Drew pulled to a stop on the common overlooking the bay, lifted his visor and turned to face me. 'Fancy an ice cream?'

My stomach did a mini somersault. We were back at one of our old haunts, a place where, in the past, we'd walked hand-in-hand as we looked out at the boats and ate vanilla cones topped with chocolate flakes.

I shouldn't be there. But I lifted my visor. 'Okay, why not?'

D rew dumped his helmet on the bike and strolled over to the ice-cream van. I took off my helmet and put it next to his before tidying my hair with my fingers. He strolled back towards me a few seconds later holding two cornets.

'You still like sprinkles and a flake?' He handed me an ice cream topped with both.

'What do you think?' I licked the top of my cornet and relished the sweet, cold, creamy taste.

'Just checking.' He smiled and bit the top off his flake.

We ate in silence for a few minutes, standing next to the bike and looking across the common towards the sea. Two young boys were attempting to get a brightly coloured kite airborne, an elderly woman walked an equally ancient-looking Labrador, and a courting couple walked arm-in-arm towards a bench further down the path.

'Why did you stop here?' I waited for his response. Seeing the lovers cosy up together to watch the sunset, the same as Drew and I had done so many years ago, made me feel uncomfortable all of a sudden. Their intimacy stirred too many personal memories.

He didn't answer immediately, but took another bite of his ice cream and crunched thoughtfully on the cone.

'Why not? I knew you were upset after seeing Marla and you always used to like coming here.' He popped the last of his ice cream into his mouth.

I nibbled the edge of my cornet, savouring the flavours. Simon liked Häagen-Dazs served in a glass sundae dish with a silver spoon. I couldn't remember him ever buying me an ice cream from a van.

I stopped thinking about Simon and returned to the problem that was at the forefront of my mind. 'Do you think she'll be okay?'

'I'm sure she'll look better tomorrow when she's got the anaesthetic out of her system. If I know Marla, she'll soon bounce back.' Drew looked at me.

'You know she thinks the reason she's ill is because there are things she's left unfulfilled? You know, poor energy flow and stuff like that.' I knew I could speak to Drew about something like this and he'd immediately understand. Simon would probably snort and look at me as if I had grown an extra head.

'Maybe she's right.' Drew shrugged. 'There are a lot of things science can't easily explain.'

The young boys had managed to get their kite into the air and it soared, scarlet and navy against the pale pink sunset. The logical teacher side of me knew Drew was right, but the rebellious teenager inside, who hated being the odd girl with the weird mother, wanted to reject his response.

I concentrated on my ice cream. Marla was safely through the surgery and I was grateful for that, but I would have to wait until tomorrow to find out more.

The elderly woman and her dog had disappeared from view and the kite dived down to crash-land on the grass. It felt strange being here with Drew after all this time.

'Where did you go after we broke up?' The question popped suddenly from my lips; it was something I had always wondered about. I'd received three postcards after he'd gone. I'd kept them for years in an old biscuit tin inside my wardrobe. Two were from America and one had come from Phuket. I'd read them so often that it was surprising there was any ink still visible. Not that they'd said much – in each one he'd told me it was hot and that he was having a good time and that was all. For a few years I'd believed he would realise he'd made a mistake and come back.

'All over, really – America, Asia, Australia . . .' His jaw tightened and I got the impression that not all his experiences had been memorable for the right reasons.

'I got your postcards.' I don't know why I felt the need to say that, but my ice cream seemed to be having a strange loosening effect on my tongue. Perhaps it was a sugar rush.

The corner of his mouth quirked upwards. 'I should have written you letters.'

'Why didn't you?' All around us grasshoppers chirped as the sky grew darker with the onset of night.

'We wanted different things, Zee. We still do.' He fixed his gaze on the horizon as the sun slipped slowly into the sea. The ice-cream man pulled down the shutter on his van ready to drive away.

'Then why are you back? I mean, you could have gone anywhere, stayed anywhere, but you came back here even though you still want something different.'

Like me, Drew didn't have much family. His father wasn't around much when Drew was growing up. The man would appear, stay for a few months and then be gone, only to resurface a year or so later. Drew had lived in a rented cottage on the other side of town with his mother and his younger brother, Gavin. His mum had died a couple of years ago and I didn't know what had happened to Gavin, whether he still lived locally or whether he'd moved away. Marla had never said.

Drew dug his hands into the pockets of his jeans and raised his shoulders in a slight shrug. 'I had my reasons.'

I wondered if his pretty blonde girlfriend might be one of his reasons but although I longed to ask I couldn't quite get up the courage. After all, it was really none of my business.

A gust of wind skimmed across the grass, rustling the leaves of the nearby trees and silencing the grasshopper chorus. The boys with the kite had gone and my arms prickled with goose bumps in the cool evening air.

My bag vibrated against my hip. I guessed it was

probably Simon wondering where I was. 'We should head back.' I checked my phone.

Where R U? How's M?

Simon's text reminded me that I had no business wondering what Drew's reasons were for returning home, and that it wasn't a good idea to have agreed to revisit one of our old trysting places either. I dropped my phone back inside my bag and picked up my helmet ready for the ride home.

'Simon?'

I nodded.

'You're cold.' Drew lightly skimmed his finger along my arm, his touch sending sparks of electricity into the sensitised flesh.

For that instant his gaze met mine. I struggled to identify the emotions that flickered in his eyes and disappeared before I could be certain of what I'd seen.

'Climb on, I'll take you home.' He pulled on his helmet and sat astride the bike to turn on the engine. I put my helmet on, too, and hopped on behind him, the throb and roar of the powerful engine vibrating beneath me as we travelled the short distance back to the cottage in the gathering darkness of the summer night.

Drew killed the engine in the narrow street outside Marla's front door. Lights shone down in the harbour and the faint sounds of music from one of the pubs drifted up towards us.

I handed him my helmet. 'Do you want to come in for coffee?'

He pulled his helmet off so he could hear me better. His hair glinted dark gold in the light from the street lamps. 'I don't think so. You probably need to call your fiancé.'

'Thank you for the lift.' He was right – I should call Simon and tell him all about Marla.

'No prob. See you tomorrow.' Drew put his helmet back on and rode off towards the waterfront, swiftly disappearing from sight around the corner, the fading sound of the bike's engine the only evidence of his presence.

I was woken the next morning by Jethro mewing piteously outside my bedroom door. The light that filtered through the batik-patterned curtains at my window seemed suspiciously dull and the gulls were less vocal than usual. I wondered what it was like outside. Jethro streaked into the room the moment I opened the door and installed himself on the end of my bed with deep throaty purrs of satisfaction.

I left him to it and stumbled downstairs to switch the kettle on. Outside the window the air was thick with one of those warm summertime sea mists that hug the coast when the conditions are right. With luck the sun would grow warm enough to burn it off.

Last night I'd called Simon after Drew had gone. He had the Xbox plugged in and was busy shooting things when I rang. I told him how poorly Marla appeared and although he made soothing noises I guessed his mind was more on his game score than on what I was saying.

It hadn't seemed like a good idea to mention my outing with Drew, so I didn't. Simon has a deep jealous streak and although it was hardly a crime to ride on someone's motorbike and go for an ice cream, it would only have made him uneasy.

While I waited for the kettle to boil I rang the hospital. A nurse informed me that Marla had spent a comfortable night, though I was willing to bet that Marla's definition and the nursing staff's definition of comfort were probably slightly different.

The phone rang as I was pouring boiling water on my teabag. The unexpected noise made me jump and I narrowly missed scalding myself.

'Marla, is that you?'

I didn't recognise the voice.

'No, I'm sorry, she's not here right now. This is her daughter, Azure. Can I help you?' I wondered if it was one of the shop's suppliers or one of Marla's therapy clients, although the latter were usually female and the caller was male.

There was a silence on the other end and I thought he'd been cut off. 'Hello, are you still there?'

'Yes, I'm still here.' The voice sounded strange, hesitant almost, as if I'd thrown him by saying who I was. 'Do you, er . . . know when she'll be back?'

'Hopefully in a couple of days. Shall I get her to ring you?' I picked up the little pad of recycled paper that lived next to the phone and hunted around for a pen.

'No, it's okay. I'll call back.' The man sounded almost panicky at my suggestion and, before I could ask for his name, he'd rung off, leaving me with the dial tone buzzing in my ear.

'That was odd,' I told Jethro, who had slunk into the kitchen at the sound of the fridge door opening.

I poured some milk into his dish and finished making my tea. It wasn't so much what the caller had said that was strange, but the way he'd reacted to me. He clearly hadn't expected to speak to anyone but Marla and had sounded nervous and strained from the outset. I decided he was one of Marla's therapy clients; I'd ask her about him if she felt up to talking when I visited after work.

The ever-charming Katya was already outside the shop when I arrived to open up. Fran usually worked on Mondays but she intended going up to the hospital during the afternoon visiting session.

'How is Marla?' Katya demanded to know. I hadn't even got the key in the lock. She didn't bother with a 'good morning', or a 'what about this mist?'

'The hospital says she's comfortable.' I pushed open the door and rushed inside to turn off the alarm.

'When will she be home?'

I turned round and almost fell over her, she was so close behind me.

'I'm not certain. It might be tomorrow.' The staff hadn't said anything to change what Marla had been told originally about her stay, so I assumed that if she felt better today they would go ahead as planned with her discharge.

Katya pursed her lips as if dissatisfied with my

answer. 'Then I shall visit her when she is back at home,' she announced.

Oh joy. So I would have the pleasure of Katya's company at the cottage as well as at the shop. 'I'm sure she'll be pleased to see you,' I offered.

She fixed me with a hard stare as if to accuse me of sarcasm before heading for the stockroom so she could start to replenish the shelves. Two deliveries of new stock arrived in quick succession, which kept us pretty busy with pricing and unpacking for a couple of hours.

The sea mist that covered Fore Street like a diaphanous veil made for a slow start to the business day; most of the holidaymakers appeared to have opted for a leisurely breakfast instead of some shopping. After the last of the new stock was finally stored away, the shop door opened and Drew strolled in.

He wore the same ancient denim jeans topped with a green T-shirt which matched his eyes. Against the tinkling, feminine background of the shop he appeared starkly masculine and attractive. 'I thought I'd call in and see if you've heard how Marla is this morning.' He leaned a hip on the shop counter.

Katya immediately found a reason to come over and tidy the racks near the till.

'They wouldn't tell me much,' I replied. 'They said she was comfortable, that's all. Fran's going this afternoon. I plan to go tonight.' I was conscious of Katya listening in on our conversation for all she was worth. My pulse had picked up as he'd approached the counter and I could feel myself growing hotter and more flustered.

'I'll give you a lift over,' Drew offered.

'No, it's okay. I can get the bus,' I stammered, making him raise his eyebrows in mild surprise.

'It's no problem. I'll call at the cottage at half past six.' He straightened up and turned to leave.

There was no point in protesting. He made his way out of the shop, leaving Katya radiating animosity at me from her position next to the resin pixies.

The sun failed to materialise for most of the day, leaving the mist clinging to the buildings along the street and making the passers-by appear like ghostly wraiths from another time. Thankfully, the phone at the shop kept ringing with enquiries from Marla's friends – or 'the coven', as Simon called them.

Katya had put some ghastly tinkly music on the shop music system that had me wanting to hang myself with a dreamcatcher by mid-morning. It was so bad that I was even glad to see Fran when she appeared to ask if there was anything she should take to the hospital for Marla.

'I've got organic grapes and freshly squeezed apple juice.' She rummaged through her homemade quilted bag, dumping oddly shaped parcels on to the counter.

'She should be home tomorrow, Fran.' I half expected to see her produce an aspidistra plant in a pot, à la *Mary Poppins*.

'Oh, I do hope so. It's better to be prepared just in case, though, don't you think? I wondered if perhaps my iPod with some meditative music might be nice?' She scrunched her eyes up at me from under her 1980s Bonnie Tyler-style hair.

'I'm not sure. Why don't you ask her when you get there?' I had no idea what kinds of things people usually took to hospitals when they visited. I'd never been inside a hospital before Sunday, when Simon and I had taken Marla in. On TV and in books the popular choices were always grapes or flowers. The hospital didn't like flowers, though. The sister had told us when Marla was admitted that they were a bacterial hazard. Marla hadn't been impressed.

'I suppose so.' Fran's face brightened and she started to repack the contents of her bag.

'I think Marla will like your gifts. You are very thoughtful,' Katya butted in.

Fran beamed at her and guilt immediately washed over me. It hadn't occurred to me to take anything last night, not even the obligatory grapes. I'd assumed that, as Marla wasn't going to be there for long, she wouldn't need anything. Now I felt like a crap daughter again.

'I'll call you when I come out to let you know how she's doing,' Fran offered.

'Thank you, Fran.' Katya gave me another hard stare, as if to imply that I hadn't offered to tell her about Marla's progress. I drew on the stress-management techniques of my teacher training to try not to let her wind me up.

Fran ambled off to get the bus to the hospital. I tried my best to persuade Katya to go out for lunch but she informed me she had a packed lunch and would eat her food in the stockroom. The tension knot between my shoulders felt as large as a boulder by the time my break came around.

I left Katya to her own devices and stepped out into the misty street. It had crossed my mind that I didn't know Katya well enough to leave her alone with valuable stock and money in the till. Then again, I reasoned that Marla and Fran obviously trusted her and that Drew seemed to know her, too. It wasn't very likely that she'd seize the moment to raid the shop and do a runner in the time it took me to eat a sandwich.

The nearer I got to the harbour the thicker the mist grew, clinging damply to my skin and hair. The statue of William of Orange loomed up at me and I hurried past the tourist information office to the café. There were very few people on this side of the harbour, although I could make out some brightly coloured cagoules over by the Sprat and Mackerel pub.

Once at the café I ordered a latte and a panini before snagging a free table by the window. I couldn't see much but at least I was away from the shop for half an hour.

No one was trying to sell boat trips or fishing sessions today. The mist had defeated everyone, and even the replica of the *Golden Hind*, Sir Francis Drake's famous ship, which was moored at the harbourside, stood forlorn. The waitress arrived with my order and I tucked in, staring at the swirling whiteness outside the window. Occasionally someone would pass by only to be swallowed up by the mist within a few paces.

I nibbled on my panini, savouring the taste of the

melted cheese and thick Devonshire ham. I would have to make time for a run later if the fog cleared, otherwise Simon would start making cracks about muffin-tops and poking my belly with his well-manicured finger. He was very keen on my staying slim; for my birthday he'd given me a gym membership. I would have preferred a book token. As if on cue, my phone vibrated on the tabletop with the arrival of a text.

Call Mum re church, S.

Evelyn had been hinting about Simon and me booking our wedding at the pretty little church near their house. It was 'the' place to get married and was supposed to be very popular. One of the other teachers at school had told me you had to have been christened to get married in church. This might cause a problem if it were true, since Marla was a pagan and as a baby I hadn't been anywhere near a font.

I'd only ever been inside a church once and that had been for Granny Millichip's funeral over in Ireland. She'd been a big church attender. I'd kind of hoped we could get married abroad somewhere. I'd even got some brochures and left them for Simon to look at.

We hadn't actually set a date for the wedding. I'd gathered a stash of bridal magazines and information on weddings in Cyprus but that was as far as I'd got with any kind of planning. Evelyn, however, had made no secret of her desire to be a grandmother and had been pushing us for a date ever since Simon had placed the ring on my finger.

I took a sip of my latte and stared out into the fog. I

didn't feel like calling Evelyn and discussing churches, especially as I didn't know how Marla was doing. Personally, a visit from Fran would make me feel worse instead of better, but she was Marla's friend and her heart was in the right place. I wondered what Marla had told Katya about me. She'd never mentioned Katya when I'd made my duty phone calls home. All she'd said was that she'd got some help in the shop.

When I'd first gone into teaching I'd quickly decided that I preferred primary school children to stroppy teenagers. Two days of working with Miss Attitude-on-a-Stick seemed to confirm that my decision had been a wise one. I knew she had a thing for Drew, but I couldn't see how, even if she knew we'd dated nine years ago, that would cause her to be jealous of me now. Besides, Drew had his blonde girlfriend, the one I'd seen him with at the bistro.

As if by instant magic I glimpsed Drew walking past the café, deep in conversation with the blonde woman. At least, I assumed it was her: it was hard to be certain as I looked through the veil of mist. I strained my eyes trying to see where they were headed and if they were holding hands. Jealousy started to gnaw at my insides so I silenced it with the last bit of my panini. Where had that emotion sprung from? I was engaged to Simon, planning my wedding, and about to call my fiancé's mother about booking a church, for heaven's sake. I should not be puzzling over my long-ago-ex-boyfriend's new squeeze.

I wiped my greasy fingers on a paper napkin and

contemplated my mobile phone. It was no use; I knew if I didn't call Evelyn then she would definitely call me, and I preferred to get it over with sooner rather than later. I found her number in the contact list and pressed the call button.

'Azure, dear, I was just about to call you.' I moved my mobile a little further away from my ear. Evelyn has one of those voices that carries, probably from her years as the star of her local light operatic society.

'Simon sent me a text, something about the church?' It suddenly struck me that fixing a date for my wedding might not be a bad thing. Seeing Drew again and spending time with him had stirred up all kinds of strange emotions. Perhaps some certainty and definite plans for my future would help me feel more settled again.

'Yes, wonderful news. Mrs Patterson heard from Mrs Laine that Judith Morgan's daughter, Rachel, has called off her engagement.' She paused for breath and I tried to figure out what all that had to do with me and Simon and why it was good news.

'It means St Peter's has a date free in July next year,' she continued. 'You know how booked up it is. I knew you wouldn't mind, so I rang the vicar as soon as I heard. Velma Martin wanted it for her son, Dale, but I managed to get in first. So you and Simon are pencilled in for the twenty-fourth of July.'

'Oh.'

July was a good time as it was the end of term, and a summer wedding would be nice, wouldn't it?

'Jonty wanted me to ask you first, but it was too good an opportunity to miss. A few minutes later and Velma would have pinched it; you have to move quickly on these things. Simon was thrilled when I called him.' Evelyn paused, presumably to give me a chance to demonstrate how thrilled I was too.

'That's wonderful, thank you, Evelyn.' Perhaps when the stunned and steamrollered sensation wore off I'd feel suitably grateful.

'Oh, it's going to be lovely. You know, if you'd like me to come with you when you try on your wedding dresses, you only have to say the word.' She paused again and then carried on: 'Or perhaps your mother might want to go with you for that.' The last part was said in a slightly doubtful tone, as if she really didn't think Marla would be interested.

Wild horses couldn't make me go shopping for my wedding dress with Evelyn, but I couldn't say I'd given much thought to Marla going with me either. Marla didn't really take much interest in clothes unless they were tie-dyed or vintage, so maybe Evelyn had a point. 'I'm sure she will when she's feeling better.'

'Oh, of course.' Evelyn sounded a bit crestfallen. 'Jonty and I always wanted a daughter, you know, but after Simon it just wasn't to be. I'm so looking forward to seeing you and Simon tie the knot.'

I wasn't quite sure how I was meant to respond to that. 'I'll have to go, I'm afraid, I'm needed back at the shop.'

I rang off and drained the last of my latte. It was official: I would be getting married on 24 July next year at St Peter's church. The news of a wedding date would probably set my mother's recovery back by a good fortnight. It looked as if I'd have to find out about this christening thing, too. Did they christen people my age? I hadn't a clue.

The mist had started to lift as I walked back to the shop, with pallid sunshine breaking through the gloom. A tall, thin youth pushed past me in the shop doorway as I went to go in. He disappeared off along the street before I could get a good look at him. He certainly didn't look like someone who would normally be a customer of a crystal shop.

The place was deserted.

'Is everything all right, Katya?' I asked. She looked a bit flustered and her eyes were a little pink.

'Yes, why would it not be?' She sniffed as she answered and turned her back to me, pretending to straighten up a tray of mood rings.

'The man who just left seemed to be in a hurry. I wondered if everything was okay.'

'Yes, of course. He was lost and wanted directions, that is all.' A tell-tale line of pink crept along her cheeks and I was sure she was lying but for the life of me I couldn't think why.

'Fine.' I decided not to probe further; she certainly wasn't going to tell me anything more. I wondered if he might be her boyfriend and I was determined to find a pretext to check the till just to be on the safe side.

With the mist retreating, trade picked up as more tourists ventured into the town, lured by the promise of weak sunshine. Fran rang shortly before lock-up time to tell me that Marla was doing well.

'She seemed quite perky. I told her you were coming tonight. She can't wait to see you.' Fran's mobile sounded crackly and from the traffic in the background I assumed she must still be on the bus.

'Okay. Thanks, Fran.'

'Is Katya there?'

I handed the phone to my assistant, who had come to stand at my elbow the minute I'd said, 'Hello, Fran.'

I moved across the shop to give her some privacy. After a few minutes she finished the call and I resumed cashing up.

'Marla will be home tomorrow,' Katya announced. 'I will visit her after work.'

If Marla did come out tomorrow, I'd arranged with Fran that she would look after the shop while I'd stay at home with Marla. Katya would work with Fran to give me a chance to catch up on chores and to care for my mother. I had hoped, despite Katya's earlier threat of visiting the cottage, that I'd have a day without her. She clearly had other ideas.

I called Simon when I arrived home from the shop.

'Great news about the church, huh?' He was obviously as thrilled as his mother had said he was.

'Yes, so we're on – twenty-fourth of July.' I wished I felt more excited. It was a perfect date and a lovely-looking church.

'Mum did well, didn't she? Bet Dale's mother is pretty sick about it,' he crowed.

'Where are you?' I wondered if he was back at the flat. I pictured him leaning back on the leather settee, gloating at having got one over on the unknown Dale.

'Um, just getting changed. Promised Phil a game of badminton.' His voice went muffled as if he had pulled something over his head.

'Who? Phil-from-the-office Phil?' The man was about twenty stone: Simon would murder him.

'Yeah, he's on some sort of health kick.'

'Watch he doesn't have a heart attack.' I tried and failed to picture Phil on a badminton court.

'Have you given Marla the good news about the wedding yet?'

'No, I'm seeing her tonight. Fran went this afternoon, she said she looked better.' I could hear Simon rustling something.

'Maybe we'll get lucky and she won't come.' He laughed. 'I'm joking, Zee, of course you'll want your mother to come.'

'Not funny, Si.' He probably did hope she wouldn't attend if it was a church wedding. That would leave a dozen friends from work on the bride's side and six million members of Simon's extended family and Evelyn's social connections on the groom's. Fun.

'Zee, really, I'm kidding. Listen, got to go. Call you later. Bye, babe.'

I dropped my phone back in my bag, feeling distinctly disgruntled. Okay, more than disgruntled. My mother was seriously ill and Simon as usual was being his normal tactless, insensitive, selfish self.

Jethro came and twined himself round my legs. 'And I suppose you're hungry?' I asked.

I got a piteous mew for an answer so I filled his food bowl and left him to it while I headed for the shower to freshen up before Drew arrived to take me to the hospital.

My conversation with Simon had left me emotionally jangled and out of sorts. His story about playing Phil at badminton had sounded pretty thin, too. An uneasy feeling crept up my spine the more I thought about it. I took my time in the shower and fixed myself a jacket potato for supper, hoping to silence my disquiet with carbohydrates.

I heard the roar of Drew's motorbike outside as I loaded the washing machine with towels. Jethro followed me along the hall to the front door to greet Drew like an old friend. Usually he took one look at Simon and disappeared.

'Come in, I'll go and get my bag.' I held the door open.

My bag was on the floor next to the sofa, where I'd dropped it before calling Simon. I hurried along the hall, conscious of Drew close behind me.

'How's Marla doing? Did you hear from Fran?' He seemed to fill the small room and I could smell the fresh, clean scent of his soap mixed with the leather of his jacket.

My fingers fumbled with the catch on my bag and it

dropped to the floor, scattering its contents all over the floor.

'Yes, she said she was much better this afternoon.' I dived for my favourite lipstick just as Drew reached out for it too. His fingers brushed against mine, sending a tingle of electricity into my body as he handed me the small silver tube. Drew's gaze met mine for a brief moment and I could tell he'd felt the same thing. This wasn't good – not good at all. He had a girlfriend, and I had a date set for my wedding.

'We should get going.' Drew straightened up.

'Yes.' I couldn't look at him as I dropped the offending lipstick back inside my bag.

My fingers shook as I fastened my helmet and climbed on to the back of his bike. Desire, hot and unwanted, flared in me as his body made contact with mine. We roared off along the narrow streets and I prayed we wouldn't hit much traffic on our way to the hospital. I wasn't sure I could take much more of being pressed so close to him.

The car park was busier than it had been on our last visit and Drew parked in a small space at the end of a row. Despite the cooler air I still felt uncomfortably warm as I dismounted. As if by mutual accord, we didn't speak as we made our way through the entrance and along the corridors to Marla's ward.

To my relief, Marla was sitting cross-legged in the centre of her bed and no longer attached to any kind of medical equipment. Her face lit up as Drew and I entered the room.

'Azure, darling!' She unfolded herself and kissed my cheek before embracing Drew with equal affection. 'Drew, sweetheart. Oh, you're just the people I wanted to see.' She sat back on her bed.

'How are you?' Under the neckline of her pale-blue kitty-print pyjamas I could see medical tape and what appeared to be gauze.

'I'm fine, the consultant says I can go home in the morning as soon as my medication is ready from the pharmacy.' She smiled at me as Drew returned with the blue chairs we'd sat on the night before.

'Fran said you seemed better. She rang the shop on her way home.' I noticed grapes in a bowl on top of Marla's locker and apple juice in a glass.

Marla patted my hand. 'She's a good friend.'

'Have they said what other treatment you'll need?' Drew asked.

This was the sixty-million-dollar question. If the tumour had spread more than they thought then she would need chemotherapy.

'Well, they'll need to get the biopsy results to be certain, but it looks like a short course of radiotherapy once I've healed.'

I released the breath I'd been subconsciously holding. 'That's good, isn't it?'

Marla sat up a little straighter on the bed, her clear blue gaze solemn as she looked at me and Drew. 'It's marvellous, but it's not everything, darling.'

Uh-oh . . . I had a bad feeling about where this conversation was headed.

'I've been doing a lot of thinking. Remember I told you why I thought I'd developed this problem in the first place?' Her grip on my fingers increased in intensity.

Drew sat with his arms folded across his broad chest, waiting for her to explain. I nodded, remembering our conversation about the imbalance of her ch'i, down by the harbour before she'd come in to hospital.

'I discussed it with Fran this afternoon too,' she continued. 'I need to rebalance in order to heal and prevent further problems.'

'Well, a holiday with some rest would do you good,' I suggested, although I had a feeling that wasn't what she meant.

Marla leaned forward and took hold of both my hands. 'Darling, I need to address those areas of my life that I've neglected or left unfulfilled. It's important.'

Drew shifted his position on the plastic seat. 'What do you need to do?'

I couldn't believe he was encouraging her.

'I've made a list. Drew, would you look inside the top of the locker and find my notes?'

I gave him a murderous look as he moved to obey my mother's instructions. In my opinion, Marla needed to focus on her radiotherapy and conventional medicines to get well. But I knew my mother – once she got an idea fixed in her head that was it, and I didn't want anything to jeopardise her recovery.

'Is this it?' Drew held up a green paper towel covered with Marla's spidery scrawl.

'Read out the list,' Marla instructed, still holding tightly to my hands.

Drew raised his eyebrows slightly and glanced at me before reading from the scribble on the towel. 'One: find and make reparations with Chris. Two: watch the sun rise over the Serengeti. Three: dance in the Mardi Gras festival in Rio de Janeiro. Four: appear on stage with a rock band at a major festival. Five . . .' He stopped reading and looked at Marla and then at me before continuing. 'See that Azure is happy in her life choices.'

I pulled my fingers free from her grasp. 'Well, you can cross number five from your list. I'm perfectly happy with my life choices. Simon and I set our wedding date today, it's the twenty-fourth of July next year at St Peter's church in Simon's home town.'

Marla didn't blink. 'Then I'm happy for you, darling.'

'Good.' How dare she still think she could order my life for me, simply because she didn't like Simon?

'Who's Chris?' Drew asked. His eyes were as cold and flinty as emeralds when he looked at me and I knew he disapproved of my outburst.

'He's my father.'

The expression on Drew's face changed to one of sympathy.

That particular item on Marla's list had shaken me. She hadn't spoken about him for the last few years. When I'd been younger she'd spun all kinds of stories about how wonderful he was, standing up to protest against the government and stuff. She'd painted a picture of him as uncrowned king of the eco-warriors; an heroic, almost mythical figure.

We'd had a conversation once after my eighteenth birthday when she'd asked me if I wanted to try and find him. I'd thought about it for a while and refused. I would have liked to meet him but I had this fear that he wouldn't live up to the picture of him which I had in my head. One flaky parent was enough. I didn't think I could bear it if I found out he was odd, too.

'This list represents unfinished business in my life. Chris falls into that category. The next three are promises I made to myself that are unfulfilled. The fifth is up to Azure Dawn.' She looked directly at me.

I shrugged. I had no intention of being sucked into an argument I knew I could never hope to win. Marla was always right, even when she wasn't. She would simply open her wide, blue eyes and go all mystic on me, claiming that the runes or the spirit of the crystal had guided her.

'Do you know where Chris is?' Drew asked, handing the paper towel to Marla.

'I've been meditating a lot lately and I believe the time is right for fate to redirect him into our lives,' she said.

Well, that was fine, it should be a snap to find him. I could sense Drew watching me, trying to gauge my reaction to all this. He knew better than anyone how I would feel about tracing my father because of his own family history and everything we'd shared together in our teens.

'Azure, you do understand why I have to fulfil this list, don't you?' Marla asked.

Actually, no, I didn't understand. I'd never really understood. I liked certainty, security, stability and knowing black from white. Marla lived with maybe, perhaps, serendipity and a million shades of grey. Everything I'd decided I didn't want.

'Do whatever you feel you have to do – just promise me you'll complete the treatment your consultant gives you.' I knew she'd made up her mind and I had a horrible sensation that, just like my childhood, I was about to be dragged along for the ride.

'Thanks a bunch.' Rationally, I knew I shouldn't be taking my irritation with Marla out on Drew but, irrationally, he happened to be there. Plus, he knew my thoughts about tracing Chris, never mind all the rest of the crap on Marla's list.

'And you're mad at me, why?' He swiftly caught me up in the hospital corridor as I huffed my way towards the exit, fresh air and sanity.

'You know why. You were encouraging her.'

Outside, a misty drizzle clouded the sky. Soft, fine rain clung to my hair and skin. I wanted to leave, turn back the clock, and return to Simon's nice, orderly flat and my calm, uneventful life.

Drew caught hold of my arm, forcing me to stop. 'Zee, I know you're angry but this sounds like something Marla feels she has to do.'

'Fine. Great. Then she can go ahead.' I tried to

extricate myself from his grip. 'Please take me home.'

He studied my face as if trying to decide what to do. 'Okay.' He relinquished his grip.

I clambered back on to his bike and we drove off towards Brixham. The rain fogged my visor and unshed tears added to the blurriness of my vision. My head ached with trying to sort through all my emotions. Worry about Marla and how she would cope with radiotherapy. Anxiety about this sudden decision she'd made to find my dad – and on top of that, a wedding that was less than a year away.

We pulled to a halt in front of the cottage. The back of my jacket was soaked and the damp had seeped through into my shirt, making it stick to my skin.

'I don't suppose you fancy a coffee?' I handed Drew his spare helmet. I didn't expect him to take up my invitation; I'd made the offer more to be polite than out of any desire for his company.

'Sure, why not?' He rode the bike up under the cottage window and kicked the stand down into place before following me inside.

'Go through to the kitchen. I need to go and change.' I scampered off upstairs.

There weren't masses of clothes left in my wardrobe. I'd only brought the bare minimum with me as I hadn't been expecting to stay. I could hear Drew clumping around downstairs as I stripped off my wet shirt and jeans to pull on an old tracksuit that I kept for lounging around in. Simon hated it. He said it made me look fat.

I ran a brush through my hair and fastened it up with

a clip before rejoining Drew in the kitchen. He'd taken off his black leather biker's jacket and draped it over one of Marla's chairs. The kettle had boiled and two mugs of organic fairtrade coffee stood steaming on the worktop.

'Thanks for making coffee.'

He raised one shoulder in an offhand gesture. 'Are you still mad at me?'

I slumped down on a chair and picked up my coffee, cradling the mug between my hands. 'No, not really.'

He pulled out the chair opposite mine, the one with his jacket on the back, and sat down. His knee brushed against mine in the confined space beneath the table.

'I know you always said you didn't want to find your dad, but maybe Marla has a point. It would be a kind of closure, an end to the not-knowing.'

'And maybe it would open up a whole can of worms. We don't know anything about him. Marla met him while she was travelling and got pregnant with me really quickly. He stayed around for a few months after I was born and then he left.' I felt cold despite the heat radiating from the coffee.

'They were young. People make mistakes, Zee.'

Something in his tone told me that he spoke from personal experience, as though he had mistakes in his past, too. I wondered exactly what had happened to him while he'd been travelling.

'He could be anywhere. He could be married, in prison, have other children.' I didn't know how I would feel if it turned out that I had half-brothers and half-sisters somewhere.

'Wouldn't it be better to know?' Drew asked.

'I just think it's a complication she could do without. She needs to get well, have her treatments and get the all-clear first. Then, if she wants to go gallivanting off all over the place and contacting people from her past, she can.' The words tumbled out of my mouth all in a rush. I was still annoyed that Marla thought I was incapable of making good life choices for myself, even though Drew had tactfully not mentioned the fifth item on Marla's list.

'Marla isn't stupid. She knows she has to have the radiotherapy, but that doesn't stop her from doing the other alternative stuff that makes her happy.' He took a sip of coffee.

'Maybe it might stop her meddling in my life.' I knew I sounded as rebellious and angry as I was nine years ago, but I couldn't stop myself.

Drew placed his mug back on the worktop and surveyed me with a level gaze. 'Why do you think she's so concerned about you?'

Something in his expression made me uncomfortable. 'I have no idea. But she doesn't like Simon.'

Drew stood and picked up his jacket, ready to leave. 'Marla likes everyone, she always sees the best in people. Have you ever wondered why she doesn't like him?' He pulled on his coat, his thick corn-coloured hair curling up over the collar. 'Think about it, Zee.'

I stayed in my seat for a long time after Drew had gone. I thought of all the things I'd wanted to say while he was still there. Like how my relationship with Simon was none of his business and how I wished everybody would butt out and trust me to make decisions for myself.

Apart from Evelyn and Jonty, not a single person had congratulated me on setting a wedding date or been excited or pleased about it. Okay, so I'd only told Marla and Drew, but it would have been nice if one of them could have made the effort. Instead, my mother had greeted my announcement with her usual calm and Drew had simply said nothing.

I slept badly that night. I dreamed I was walking down the aisle in a big, meringue-style wedding gown. Evelyn and Jonty were seated in the front pews smiling at me while Marla, dressed in black, sat at the back of the church. When I got to the altar my groom turned around, but it wasn't Simon – it was Drew, looking at me with his dark green eyes. He took hold of my hand and I turned around to see where Simon had gone. Evelyn and Jonty had vanished and Fran was there, throwing rose petals while Katya glowered at me. Then Drew bent his head to kiss me . . .

When I woke up, the baggy cotton T-shirt I always slept in was drenched in sweat and my pulse hammered in my ears. The room was already warm and early morning sunlight had picked its way around the edge of the curtains. I propped myself up against my damp pillows and took a sip from the glass of water I kept by my bedside.

My engagement ring chinked against the glass, reminding me of the dream. My heart rate settled a little as I lay there with my eyes closed, listening to the sounds of the town waking up to start the day. I was certain that, should I be daft enough to confide in Fran, she would be able to analyse my dream for me. Not that I had any intention of doing so.

I could figure most of it out for myself. Yesterday's events had obviously been on my mind when I'd fallen asleep and that was why I'd dreamed of the wedding. The part I didn't understand was why – in my dream – I'd been happy to see Drew and had wanted him to lift my bridal veil and kiss me.

Coming back to Brixham was really messing with my head. Before I'd returned I'd been perfectly happy living with Simon, teaching my class and generally puttering around very nicely in my own little world. I enjoyed my job and I had good friends amongst my colleagues, but now everything felt all discombobulated and weird. I shouldn't be feeling attracted to Drew when I was engaged to Simon. It was just plain wrong.

I finished my water and decided to go for a run before ringing the ward to find out when I could collect Marla. When she'd first been admitted Drew had offered to borrow a car to take me over when it was time for her to come home but as I wasn't sure how long it would take for them to let her out I'd declined the offer.

My tracksuit was still draped over the chair where I'd slung it the night before. I tugged it on quickly before I could change my mind. Having a shower could wait till I got back, since I would get even more stinky and sweaty while I was running. I stuffed my hair into a ponytail, pulled on my trainers and set off.

The streets were virtually empty, with just a few locals out walking their dogs or collecting a paper from the newsagent's. I jogged down Broad Steps towards the harbour, enjoying the feel of the early morning sunlight on my face. I headed past the small boats and along the path by the exclusive new waterfront apartments with their bijoux balconies and floral window-boxes.

The sun on my face grew hotter as I ran along the breakwater wall that stuck out into the sea like a giant arm. Eventually I reached the end and, as I paused to catch my breath, I looked back to town and admired the view. I jogged up and down on the spot to relieve the first signs of a stitch building up under my ribs.

A small sailboat tacked across the open water, making for the harbour. I watched its progress while I stretched out my hamstrings ready for the jog back to the cottage. As the boat drew nearer I realised that it was Drew who had his hand on the tiller, while a young lad dealt with the sail. When we had been together, Drew had taught sailing and surfing at one of the local sail schools.

Memories bubbled up of sitting on the sands watching Drew in his wetsuit riding the breakers. He used to take me out in the boats, laughing at my complete lack of nautical knowledge. Then we'd drop anchor way off shore in a small bay and make love in the boat on a pile of towels while the waves slapped against the sides. For a moment I was back in my past, back when I'd been secure and happy.

The boat headed in through the entrance to the marina. I gathered my wits, tightened my ponytail, and set off back along the breakwater towards the town.

Drew spotted me as I neared the narrow jetties where the smaller boats were berthed. He'd stripped off his T-shirt and wore only an old faded pair of khaki cargo shorts as he jumped on to the jetty to secure the boat.

'You're out early,' he called.

'I thought I'd fit in a run before bringing Marla home.'

He strode up the gangway to join me on the path. Perspiration gleamed on the tan on his shoulder muscles from where he had been working, and a faint line of dark hair bisected his abdomen, leading down like an arrow below the waistband of his shorts. Oh boy, he looked good. I wondered what he looked like naked now that he was older and clearly more developed. Suddenly it wasn't only the exercise making me breathless. My face felt as if it was on fire from exercise and embarrassment at the direction my mind had taken.

'Sun's getting warm already.' From the twinkle in his

eyes I knew that he had picked up on my thoughts.

'Yes. It looks as if it'll be a better day than yesterday.' I started to edge away, conscious of my ratty hair and lack of make-up.

'Tell Marla I'll call round to see her later.'

The young lad who'd been on the boat came up the gangway towards us and Drew turned his head to acknowledge him.

'I'll tell her. I'd better get going.' I took advantage of his momentary diversion, turned on my heels and jogged away, fighting the urge to look back for one more glimpse. So much for a run helping me to get my head sorted out.

Compelled by guilt at my lusting over Drew's half-naked torso at the harbour, I called Simon as soon as I got back to the cottage.

'Zee, is everything okay?' He sounded out of breath.

'Fine. Are you all right? Did Phil give you a better game than you thought last night? You sound out of condition,' I teased him, while I tried to eliminate the picture of Drew looking extremely fit from my memory.

'What? Phil? Um . . . no. Just rushing around getting ready for work.'

My uneasy feelings from our last conversation resurfaced and I glanced at my watch. Normally Simon would have been gone by now. In the background I could hear a woman talking. 'Hey, you're late. You'd better turn off the TV and get going.'

The background noise stopped. 'Yeah, I, um . . . overslept. I'll call you later, okay?'

Simon didn't normally bother with TV before work; he must be out of sorts. Unless it hadn't been a television that I'd heard. My dormant sixth sense kicked up a notch and I hoped I was mistaken.

'Okay, bye.'

I'd already placed the phone back on the hook before realising he hadn't said he loved me. Come to think of it, I hadn't said I loved him either. I wasn't sure what that meant except – no – I wasn't going to go there. I pulled my hair free from its ponytail band, ready to hit the shower. Perhaps we were getting a bit complacent in our relationship. That could explain why my hormones went into a mad tango every time I saw Drew.

I stood under the warm jet of water in the shower for a long time while I tried to work out my feelings. I loved Simon and we were going to get married, so why did seeing Drew again make me feel all kinds of emotions that I didn't expect? Inconvenient, lustful emotions that clutched at my insides. It was all wrong.

By the time the taxi arrived to take me to the hospital to collect Marla, I felt better. My shower and a fresh croissant for breakfast had helped me pull myself together again. I'd decided that if Simon came down for the weekend and I had some time with him, then my emotions would settle back into their rightful place again. It must have been the TV that I'd heard and maybe he had played badminton with Phil. Perhaps the sooner I could get him to come and stay the better it would be.

At the hospital, I found Marla with her belongings

packed, perched cross-legged on her bed, waiting for me to arrive. The nurse came over with her prescription, a small bundle of letters and some information leaflets as I picked up her bag. I took charge of the letter for her GP and the one with her follow-up appointment for the radiology department. Marla had never been very good at keeping appointments and I intended to ensure that she kept these ones.

'You seem a little distracted, Azure. Your aura appears troubled.' Marla squinted at me as she slid into the back seat of the cab.

'I'm sure my aura is fine.' I closed the door and walked around the back of the taxi to get in the other side.

'It doesn't *look* fine.'

I gritted my teeth. 'Really, I am absolutely and totally fine.' I cast around frantically in my mind for something to distract her with, as I knew she would keep trying to get me to talk all the way home.

'Someone phoned for you yesterday. I meant to ask you about it. It was a man; he didn't leave his name, so I assumed he must be one of your therapy clients.' Relieved at having remembered something, I settled back in my seat.

'A man?' Marla frowned.

'He asked for you by name.'

She shook her head. 'Sorry, darling, I can't think who it could be.'

'That's odd. I got the impression he knew you.'

'Well, I expect if it's important he'll call again. I do

hope it wasn't the press. I've kept this hospital business low-key.' She tucked a strand of her long dark hair behind her ear, making the bangles on her arms jingle together.

'Katya, Fran and Drew all plan to visit you today. You won't let them tire you out, will you?' She might look more like herself now she was out of the hospital, but there were faint shadows beneath her eyes and the sunlight picked up small silver threads in her hair. I hadn't given any thought to the media being interested in Marla but, as she was well-known locally and often appeared in the papers and on the radio, it would be a natural assumption.

'I'm sure they won't be tiring. Dear Katya, what a blessing that child is.'

'A blessing' wasn't the description I'd have applied to Katya, although it was typical of Marla that she always saw the good in people. Drew's words of the previous night popped back into my head. It was strange that she had never said good things about Simon.

'It's nice to have Drew back. He's been so supportive.' A gentle smile played around the corners of her mouth and I knew she wanted me to respond in some way.

'Yes, and his girlfriend seems very pretty.' I was determined to squash any matchmaking mischief that Marla might have in mind. But a part of me wanted to find out more about the mystery blonde he appeared to be dating. Not that it was a big deal or anything, just curiosity.

Marla peered at me and her smile broadened. 'Your aura is lightening up. Drew doesn't have a girlfriend at the moment. You must have seen him with Serena – he's been doing some work for her at the sail club.'

'It didn't appear to be a purely "working" relationship.' Marla obviously didn't know everything. I vaguely remembered Serena from school; she'd been younger than me and I could have sworn she used to be a brunette. Her parents had been quite wealthy, owning one of the larger houses in the better part of town. We had never moved in the same circles so it was no surprise I hadn't recognised her.

She gave me a satisfied look. 'You and Drew always appeared so well suited. It was a shame things didn't work out between the two of you.'

'Marla.' I gave her a warning glare. Her meddling had to be nipped in the bud. My emotions were all over the place as it was without her stirring them up.

She raised her hands in appeasement. 'Darling, it was simply an observation, that's all. After all, you've set the date with Simon now.'

Her comment should have made me feel better. But it didn't.

'Oh dear, your aura is darkening again.' She shook her head as the cab squeezed along the narrow street to the cottage and halted by the front door. 'I hope it wasn't something I said.'

12

I paid the taxi driver and installed Marla in the courtyard on a comfy shaded seat while I sorted out the stuff she'd brought back with her from the hospital. Before I'd even carried her salad and glass of fruit juice outside to her, the doorbell had rung. Fran stood panting on the steps.

'Whew, it's hot! I can't stop long as Katya's on her own in the shop.' She wheezed the words out without pausing.

She puffed past me, leaving behind a faint trace of musky body spray and mothballs.

'Fran! How lovely, I didn't think you'd make it till later.' Marla greeted her warmly from under the big green parasol I'd wedged over her favourite corner of the courtyard. 'Come and sit down. You'll stay for a quick lunch?'

Fran sank on to the spare lounger while I headed back to the kitchen for more juice and an extra plate of salad. I sliced extra cucumber and tomato as snatches of their conversation drifted in through the open kitchen window. They say eavesdroppers never hear well of themselves but it wasn't as if I was actively trying to listen, so I paid no attention to the first few mentions of my name. It wasn't until Drew's name cropped up that I deliberately stopped chopping so I could hear more clearly.

'Have you discussed your plans with Azure?' Fran's voice carried clearly to where I stood.

'Drew has an idea of what I've got in mind, but you know Azure . . .' Marla dropped her voice.

I poured an extra glass of juice for Fran with shaky fingers. Whatever crackpot wheeze Marla had dreamed up, it sounded as if Drew was in on the plans.

'Is she still with the other one?' I heard Fran's question even though she'd lowered her voice to match Marla's.

I resisted the urge to open the fridge door and scream my frustration into the salad drawer. Instead, I banged the salad plate and Fran's drink on to a tray and carried them outside.

'Thank you, Azure.' Fran's face coloured as I placed the food down on the small white-painted cast-iron table. She could probably see from my expression that I knew they'd been discussing me.

'Azure and Simon have set a date for their wedding; July next year.' Marla smiled gently at me.

'We'll send you an invite, Fran.' I must have sounded snippy because a tiny frown wrinkled Marla's brow. Playing Florence Nightingale wasn't my thing; my mother had barely been home an hour and already I'd made a mess of things.

'I love weddings; I've got a hat.' Fran's face brightened as she tucked into her salad.

I tried to imagine a hat-bedecked Fran at my wedding meeting Evelyn and Jonty, along with the esteemed members of the local light operatic society, and failed miserably. Even Marla smiled as she assured Fran that she would look lovely.

Fran didn't stay long as she was worried that Katya might be overrun with customers in her absence. I saw her out and wandered back through to the courtyard to clear away the plates.

Marla had tilted her lounger back and closed her eyes. At first I thought she'd gone to sleep but as soon as I began to move the crockery she looked straight at me.

'Leave those for a moment, darling, and come and sit with me.'

Reluctantly, I left the plates on the table and took the seat Fran had so recently vacated.

'You should get some rest,' I told her. Marla appeared pale and the fine lines around her eyes and mouth seemed to be accentuated by the afternoon sunlight. 'Do you need one of your painkillers? The nurse said you were to take them if you started to become uncomfortable.'

She shook her head. 'Oh, do stop fussing. I'm perfectly fine. I'll rest in a moment. I want to talk to you first.'

I had a horrible sinking sensation that probably I wasn't going to enjoy the conversation. Ever since I'd been small Marla had insisted on having 'talks' with me in the belief that it would draw us closer together. It hadn't worked – at least, not for me. Instead, I'd become adept at not discussing my emotions and feelings with her; a tactic that I'd carried on into every relationship I'd ever had.

'I can understand that you're upset about my need to contact Chris.' She was using her therapist voice: the soothing, understanding tone she used with her clients when she told them something they weren't going to like.

'No, I don't think you do understand.' My voice sounded flat and emotionless, a complete contrast to how I felt inside.

Marla sighed. 'Your father is the only man I've ever really loved, Azure. You know that.'

I did know that. There had been other men in my mother's life from time to time. She was an attractive woman. But I'd heard about them rather than seen them; Marla had never taken any of them seriously enough to want to introduce me to them. However, when I'd entered my teens Marla had thought that I was old enough for her to confide in. She'd been concerned that I might hear rumours about her dates and had promptly shared more than I had ever wanted or needed to know about her love life.

I nodded. She kept her dark blue gaze fixed on me.

'Then you'll understand that I have to find him again. Just lately I've felt as if he's very close to me. Almost as if he's searching for me, too.'

'And where does Drew come into all this? I heard

Fran – there's more going on here, isn't there?' I met her gaze head-on.

'I mentioned to Drew that there were things in my life that were out of balance. He agreed to do what he could to help me restore equilibrium, that's all.'

'And what if I said I didn't want you to find my father?' I folded my arms across my chest. 'Finding Chris will affect more than just *your* life.' Despite my best efforts my voice wobbled.

Immediately Marla took my hands in hers. 'I don't think it will make any difference if I physically look for him or not. I have this feeling that he's going to re-enter our lives regardless.'

Marla napped on the sofa in the lounge after our talk, while I cleared away the lunch things in the kitchen. Katya arrived shortly after the shop had closed, clutching a bunch of yellow carnations.

'Oh, that's so kind of you. Isn't that sweet of Katya, Azure?' Marla exclaimed as if they were a bouquet from the best florist in town instead of a £2.99 supermarket special. I found a jug Marla had acquired years ago from a jumble sale and muttered something non-committal while Katya made herself at home in my favourite armchair.

Once they were ensconced with a tray of herbal tea I made an excuse about needing to fetch something from the supermarket and escaped from the cottage. Heat still sizzled from the pavement as I walked slowly down the hill towards the sea. The crowds of daytrippers had thinned by the time I reached the quayside.

I bought myself an ice cream and sat down on the nearest bench to call Simon on my mobile. It was odd that he hadn't called me during his lunch break. Normally he was constantly texting me to see where I was, what I was doing and what I'd been eating. I took a big lick of my cornet and decided he had probably been kept busy all day if he'd gone in to work late.

My call went straight to his voicemail. I left a brief message and popped my phone back in my bag so I could concentrate on my ice cream. It occurred to me that I had been eating far too much of the stuff lately, a sure sign that I was stressed.

'Penny for your thoughts.'

Drew dropped down on to the bench next to me. It creaked ominously under his weight. I'd been so intent on my texting and my food that his arrival had taken me by surprise.

'I'd forgotten what a small place this town is.' My heart raced as he casually draped an arm along the back of the bench behind my shoulders.

He glanced around at the cafés and shops. 'Yeah, I guess it is.'

Something in his expression made me add: 'You couldn't wait to leave it not too long ago.'

'It took me a long time to work out it wasn't this place that I was trying to leave behind.' His gaze was fixed on the sea and his tone was sober.

I wasn't sure what he meant, although I suppose it could have been me he'd been trying to leave. Memories of the day we'd ended our relationship welled up in the back of my mind where I'd shut them away all that time ago.

We'd been walking along the beach at Paignton. It had been early evening, as it was now. The sands had been quiet with only a few stragglers strolling at the water's edge while the music from the funfair on the green had drifted down to us. I knew if I closed my eyes I would be able to smell the candyfloss from the stall on the walkway and hear the swish and boom of waves breaking on sand instead of the quiet slap of the sea against the harbour wall.

I'd been holding Drew's hand, talking about the future and all the things we could do together once I'd finished my teacher training. In my excitement I hadn't noticed that he hadn't agreed to anything I'd said. I'd rambled on and on about finding a flat together and work opportunities for him.

Then he'd dropped the bombshell. He was leaving, he had plans too. Plans to travel, to see the world and experience life outside Brixham. I knew when he asked me to go with him that he didn't expect me to say yes.

'Zee?' Drew's voice interrupted my reverie and I could see he'd been speaking to me for a while.

'Sorry, I was miles away. I don't know what's the matter with me today.' My face heated up as I told the fib but he didn't challenge me.

'Is Marla up to a visit?'

'I expect so. Fran came at lunchtime and Katya is there now. I'm sure she can fit you in for a few minutes.'

'Zee, I know this can't be easy, but Marla really does need you.' He dropped his hand on to my shoulder and gave it a gentle squeeze.

My heart thudded at the contact, even though it was casual. 'I know, and I want to be here for her. It's just – well, she's Marla.' It was a rather paltry explanation but I knew that Drew, more than anyone, would have some idea of what I meant.

'I know.' He gave me a gentle hug and desire tugged at my stomach.

I jumped to my feet, spilling the melting remains of my cornet on the ground beneath the bench in my haste to get away. 'I'd better get back.'

Drew remained sprawled out on the bench; the corner of his mouth quirked in a smile. 'You're in a hurry.'

'I don't want Marla to get too tired.' My excuse was feeble and he knew it. He was aware of exactly why I'd shot up like a scalded cat and for some reason, probably male ego, he found it amusing.

'Okay. I'll come with you.' He roused himself from the bench, still smiling.

'People will talk if they keep seeing us together.' Totally the wrong thing to say, but it was what popped out of my mouth.

'What people?' Drew strolled alongside me, his long legs easily matching my pace as I tried to hurry away back up the hill towards the cottage.

'Just people.' I grew more flustered with every step I took.

'Oh.'

I could hear the suppressed laughter in his voice.

'It's not funny. I have Simon to consider and you have Serena.' The hole I was digging grew another mile deeper. Now he'd think I was sufficiently interested in his love life to have found out the name of his girlfriend.

We'd reached the foot of the stone steps leading up to Marla's house. Drew placed his hand on my arm, forcing me to stop and face him.

'Serena is a business associate; we work together. She's not my girlfriend.' His green eyes looked deep into mine.

'Yes, well . . .' The words died on my lips.

His mouth was inches away from mine and I knew his feelings were the same. For that one brief moment I thought – no, I *wanted* him – to kiss me.

He released my arm and took a step back. 'Maybe you have a point. People might talk.'

13

I couldn't get up the steps and inside the cottage fast enough. If I could have persuaded the ground to open up and swallow me whole then I would have done so. Drew followed, keeping up with me with easy, loping strides.

Katya met us in the hallway, her dark eyes darting suspicious glances between my red face and the amused creases around Drew's mouth. 'I was about to leave,' she announced. 'Marla is looking tired.'

While she looked at Drew I was in no doubt that her comment was aimed at me. Guilt immediately kicked in. I pushed the door to the lounge open a crack and peeped in to see Marla lying back on the sofa with her eyes closed.

'Maybe you should come back tomorrow,' I suggested to Drew.

Katya's face immediately lit up, as if she'd just won the lottery. 'You can walk with me back down to town.'

'Is Marla okay?' Drew asked.

'I think she's probably worn herself out.' I pulled the lounge door closed, aware that we were all whispering in the hall.

Katya slipped her hand round Drew's arm. 'We will go. I will ring tomorrow,' she announced.

'Will you be all right?' Drew asked.

My heart gave a small squeeze of pleasure that he was concerned about me. 'Sure, why wouldn't I be?'

Katya tugged him towards the front door. Deep inside my handbag my mobile began to ring. 'That'll be Simon.' I delved inside it, trying to get to my phone before he got transferred to the answer service.

Drew didn't say anything. He didn't have to; his expression said it all as I closed the door behind him and cat-who-got-the-cream Katya.

I slid my phone open and waited to feel a warm, reassuring rush of affection at the sound of Simon's voice. Instead, a hard knotty lump sat on top of my stomach as I tried to suppress the memory of the mixture of pity and bafflement that had been in Drew's green eyes when I closed the door.

'Zee, did you take my blue suit to the dry-cleaner's?' Simon's tone was brusque. My heart crashed down to my feet.

'No, you said to wait till they put a special offer on as you didn't need it for a while.' I couldn't believe he had asked me about dry-cleaning. I mean, didn't he miss me a little bit? Wasn't he in the slightest bit concerned about how Marla was?

'Damn.'

'Why, did you need it?' Perhaps he'd had a bad day at work.

'No, it's nothing, I've got the grey one. How's Marla?'

I leaned against the lumpy white plasterwork of the hall wall. 'Healing, but tired. She came out just before lunch.'

'Have you any idea when you'll be coming back yet?' he asked.

'Si, she's only been home for a few hours. It *is* cancer – there will be follow-up treatment.' Irritation at his lack of sensitivity sharpened my voice.

'I know, I'm sorry. I miss you, that's all.' He sounded contrite and my heart melted a little.

'Okay, I'll forgive you.' I waited for him to tell me he loved me. In the background I heard the doorbell buzz and the line crackled in my ear.

'Listen, I don't know if I'll be able to get away to join you in a couple of weeks like we'd planned. Work is horrendous, so it looks as if our holiday is off till September.'

'But Simon, I'll be back at school then.'

'I know, I'm sorry. Maybe we can go abroad in the half-term. We could go to Phil's villa in Portugal.'

'Simon!' I didn't want to go to bloody Portugal and spend a fortnight as a golf widow. I needed him now, here, with me.

'Got to go, babe – pizza's here.' He ended the call without even saying a proper goodbye, leaving me staring at the phone.

Marla shuffled into the hall and leaned against the

doorframe for support. 'I thought I heard Drew.'

'He popped in quickly to see how you were. I thought you were napping so he left with Katya.' I shoved my mobile back in my bag, and hung it up on the hall stand.

'I am a bit tired,' Marla admitted.

'Go on up and have an early night. I'll bring you a drink.' She did look as if she'd had enough for the day. Normally Marla didn't look her age at all. It had always irked me when I was a teenager that people who didn't know us had mistaken her for my sister instead of my mum.

To my surprise she didn't argue but headed towards the foot of the narrow stripped-pine staircase. 'That sounds nice. I've some camomile tea in the kitchen.'

'I'll put the kettle on.'

Marla lay on her bed propped up by a mountain of cushions. Street noise drifted in through the open sash window. The voile drapes fluttered in the slight breeze, making her crystal wind chimes tinkle like fairy bells. At first I thought she'd fallen asleep again as I slid her favourite china cup and saucer on to the rattan table next to her bed.

Her eyelids fluttered open. 'Come and sit with me for a while.'

Obediently I took a perch on the end of her bed. It looked as if I'd been snookered into another one of her 'talks'.

'You should sleep.'

She adjusted the cushions behind her head. 'If I fall asleep now I'll be up at five.'

'Shall I get you something to eat?' I wasn't in the mood for another one of Marla's tête-à-têtes.

Ever since I'd taken Marla's phone call at the school I'd had a sense of my world slowly starting to tilt and wobble. It was like being trapped in the hall of mirrors at a funfair where familiar objects and people had become distorted. Simon appeared to be behaving oddly and every time I met Drew I reverted back into a hormonal frenzy that left me blushing and stammering like an idiot.

Marla shook her head. The faint movement disturbed the sequinned edge of the cushion behind her head, causing tiny pinpoints of reflected light to dance across the whitewashed ceiling of the bedroom.

'I'm not hungry. It's nice to have you home for a while, even though it's taken something like this to bring you back.' She motioned vaguely with her hand towards her breast.

'You knew I was going to come for a couple of weeks anyway.' It was true – Simon and I had planned to stay with Marla for a holiday during my six weeks away from school. Although, in fairness, I don't suppose we would have spent much time in the cottage, or with Marla. Simon had been talking about heading into Cornwall for the surfing, but this had been before his work had become so busy. Now it looked as if he wouldn't get any time off until September, which was no use to me as the new term would have begun by then.

'I know, but it's nice to have time when it's just you and me, like the old days.' Marla patted my hand.

What she actually meant was that it was nice not to have Simon around. I wondered whether he really was busy at work, or whether he just didn't want to come down if it meant he couldn't go off and do what he wanted because I had responsibilities to Marla and to the shop.

'I suppose it is.' To my surprise I found myself agreeing with her. It would be good to have the opportunity to do things together again. I suppose that sometimes I forgot the good things about my childhood and focused on the negative, annoying aspects instead.

'It was kind of Katya to come and see me. You will look after her in the shop, won't you, Azure? She's had a very difficult life for such a young girl.'

I was conscious of Marla's direct blue gaze fixed on my face. 'I don't think Katya likes me very much.' There was no point in lying to her. My mother's uncanny instincts could detect an untruth a mile away.

Marla sighed. 'It's not that she doesn't like you, she's simply very wary of trusting people until she gets to know them. She's a little cautious.'

'I think she resents me being here, and she definitely has a thing for Drew.'

Marla arched an eyebrow and I knew what she thought.

'I am *not* jealous. I'm engaged to Simon, remember?'

'I remember,' she sighed. 'Katya came to England with her older brother a couple of years ago. I don't know what happened to her mother. Her father was an alcoholic and, from what I've pieced together, he drank himself to death. The brother, Pieter, is rather a bad lot. He works on building sites and plays gigs with a band but all the money goes on drink and drugs. Drew tried to help – apparently he knew Katya's brother through a friend of his who is in the band. He managed to get Katya a bed at a B&B. after she was evicted from the flat she'd been sharing with Pieter. Non-payment of rent. Pieter had taken off and she was all on her own.'

'That's awful.' It certainly went some way to explaining Katya's behaviour.

'Not surprisingly, she thinks of Drew as her gallant knight on a white steed.' Marla smiled at me.

I had once thought of Drew in that way too. That had been back in the days when I'd been the geeky stranger at school, new to the area and with the weird mother and no friends. But then my gallant knight had ridden off into the sunset on his motorbike, leaving me in his dust. I'd decided then that I'd had it with that kind of lifestyle. I wanted someone who was Mr Nine-to-Five, someone who liked visiting garden centres at weekends and who would never ever abandon me in favour of a kibbutz in Israel. Someone just like Simon.

'Where's her brother now?' I couldn't help feeling more sympathetic towards Katya now that I knew her story. It must have been hard being alone in a foreign country with little or no money when she was so young.

Marla picked up her tea and took a considered sip. 'I'm not sure. He reappears from time to time, usually to try and scrounge some money from Katya.'

The light in the room had changed whilst we'd been talking. Through the filmy drapes I could see the sky had turned pinky-gold above the tiled rooftops of the town.

'You really should get some rest. The district nurse is calling in tomorrow. I don't want her to tell me off for not looking after you.'

Marla replaced her cup on its saucer. 'It'll probably be Tina, she won't say anything.' She adjusted her position on the cushions. 'I thought I heard you on the phone earlier?'

'You did, it was Simon. He doesn't think he can get away from work for a few weeks.' I fiddled with the long silky tassel attached to the corner of one of the pillows, threading the strands through my fingers.

'I see.' She didn't say anything else. She didn't need to.

'We'll probably go abroad during October half-term, when you're better.'

Again, she didn't reply. Perhaps she might have done after a few moments, but the phone started to ring and since the landline was in the kitchen I had to get up and sprint downstairs before whoever it was could ring off.

'Hello?'

'Could I speak to Marla Millichip? This is Lee from Radio Funshine. We've heard that Marla is ill and our listeners would like to know—'

I hung up before he could finish speaking. It hadn't occurred to me until Marla had mentioned the press that other people would want to know about her private business. I had assumed that most of their interest would be because she was such a public figure locally and because of her work in crystal therapy. It was weird how people appeared to think that alternative therapists were somehow immune to everyday illnesses and afflictions and that if they did become ill they could cure themselves.

I barely had time to gather my wits when the phone rang again. This time it was the local paper. I gave a 'no comment' reply and hung up. No doubt when Marla had recovered she would make her own statements about her health, but I didn't think it was appropriate right now when she'd only just come out of hospital.

Jethro wrapped himself round my feet and purred hopefully. I'd just made it over to the fridge to find his fish when the phone went again. I braced myself to deal with whichever hapless reporter might be on the line this time.

'Could I speak to Marla, please?' the male caller said in reply to my 'hello'.

'I'm sorry, she's not available right now.' I'd heard the voice before. I was sure it was the man who'd called the other night when I'd been on my way to the hospital. I couldn't place his accent but he didn't sound local.

'Do you know when she'll be home?'

'She may be around tomorrow lunchtime. You could try then or, if you want to give me your name and number, I could ask her to call you when she's free.'

There was a slight pause before he responded to my

suggestion. 'No, it's okay. It's waited this long, it'll keep a while longer.'

He finished the call before I could ask him anything else. Marla had told me she couldn't think who he might be, but he clearly knew her and had unfinished business, by the sound of it.

I slept badly again that night. When I did fall asleep I dreamed about Drew and the time we'd been together, but then his face had morphed into Simon's and I'd woken up. I should have called Simon back to talk about the holiday, that's probably why I kept dreaming about him and Drew. That, and the great chunk of amethyst crystal I found in the drawer next to my bed. I knew that amethyst was supposed to enhance your dreams and help you see things more clearly. I detected my mother's meddling.

Marla was already in the kitchen when I made my way downstairs.

'Azure, darling, I was about to bring you a nice cup of tea.'

I squinted at the kitchen clock, wondering if I'd over-slept. 'Marla, I'm supposed to be here looking after *you*, remember? It's only six o'clock, you should still be resting.'

She waved her hand dismissively. 'Pooh, I'm rested enough. Now, what are your plans for today?'

I took the mug she offered me, hoping it would be a

nice cup of PG Tips, preferably with milk and one sugar. It wasn't – from the smell and hue I assumed it was a cranberry and orange herbal mix, Marla's favourite flavour for early mornings.

'The nurse is coming to check your dressing. Fran and Katya are running the shop, although I'll need to pop down to do a banking run. Other than that I'm here to take care of you.' I took a sip of my drink and decided I'd stick to coffee while I was staying at home.

'Great, that will give us time to get started on my list,' Marla announced as she flitted across the kitchen to collect muesli and a bowl from the cupboard.

The cranberry and orange tea I'd just swallowed tried to stage a comeback from my stomach. 'How can you work on your list? You certainly aren't going to be able to trot off to the Serengeti for a while yet.'

Marla calmly ladled soya yoghurt over the top of her muesli. 'I know that, darling, but there are other items on there that we can work on in the meantime. I rang Drew when I got up and he said he'd be happy to come and help. The more brains the better, don't you think?'

'Marla, you can't go phoning people this early in the morning. Drew was probably still in bed.' A sudden picture of Drew in bed, bare-chested amid rumpled sheets, popped unbidden into my head.

'Don't be silly, he's always up early. He said he'd stop by after his first class finishes.' She sprinkled a handful of blueberries on top of the yoghurt.

'Class?'

Marla raised her spoon. 'I think it's you who needs

more rest. His boating classes, of course. I told you he had a job teaching at the sail club.'

'Oh yes, I'd forgotten.' While Marla was busy with her breakfast I managed to tip the rest of my fruit tea down the sink. I planned to brew myself a cup of strong coffee later. If Drew was coming over I figured I would need it.

I left my mother to finish her breakfast and headed back upstairs to have a shower. It didn't look as if Marla was about to be dissuaded from her crazy list idea any time soon and I knew Drew wouldn't help me try to talk her out of it.

The shower woke me up but didn't do much to relieve the feeling of doom that threatened like a thundercloud whenever I thought about Marla's list. I blow-dried my hair, pulled on a pretty pale-blue summer dress and decided I'd call Simon.

'Hi, it's me.'

There was a small pause and then a female voice said: 'Huh?'

I looked down at my phone, thinking I'd accidentally pressed the wrong button and called one of my colleagues, but Simon's name was clearly displayed on the screen.

'Simon?' I said when I put my mobile back to my ear. There was the muffled sound of a phone being passed across and a snatch of conversation.

'Hi, Zee.'

'Who just answered your phone?'

It was seven in the morning; normally at this time

Simon would be eating Crunchy Nut Cornflakes and telling me to stop by Marks & Spencer on the way home to pick up something for supper.

'Oh, that was only Elaine.'

'Elaine?' I didn't know any frigging Elaine. Who the hell was she, and why was she in our flat answering Simon's mobile?

'She's new at the office. Turns out she lives down the street so I said I'd give her a lift in to work.'

'Right.'

He knew I didn't believe him, but I wasn't there, so just possibly he could have been telling the truth. Except the muffled background sounds of a woman's voice, the playing badminton with Phil, all started to make sense. Yeah, right – a herd of flying pigs had just been cleared for take-off.

'Zee, sweetheart . . . honestly, I'm doing her a favour, that's all. There's nothing in it, I swear.' Simon put on his wheedling voice.

'Don't lie to me, Simon.'

'Sweetheart, really, she means nothing . . .'

'Liar!' My initial hurt and burning anger was subsiding rapidly into an all-too-familiar and painful heartworn weariness.

'Zee, really, it's nothing . . .'

'Okay, fine, whatever. Call me later.' I wasn't in the mood for his crap. If I challenged him further, he would deny everything and I'd be accused of being paranoid and jealous. I would end up being the one who felt guilty for suspecting him of any wrongdoing. Even though I knew my earlier instincts had been proven right.

I know it says in all the women's magazines that good relationships are built on trust and, normally, I'd go with that. It's just that Simon has previous offences on the not-exactly-being-faithful front.

He'd dated tons of girls before me. In his office building he had quite a reputation as a ladies' man. Of course, I discovered this later once we were dating, when one of his exes cornered me in the ladies at his office Christmas party. Only, according to her, she wasn't quite an ex. She claimed he'd been shagging her in the stationery cupboard after everyone else had gone home.

I dumped him but he kept calling, sending me flowers and cute fluffy bears with big pink bows round their necks. After a few weeks we got back together. He swore undying fidelity and, like a fool, I believed him. At least that was until I caught him taking down the office receptionist's particulars on top of his desk one night when he was supposed to be working late.

Then there had been the incident with the girl at the sandwich shop. That had been when Simon first proposed, after I'd found the naked pictures she'd sent him on his mobile. He'd sworn she was stalking him and that nothing had happened. He'd simply been flattered by the attention and had never reciprocated any of her advances. I knew in my heart it was lies but I'd wanted to believe him. Then, at Christmas, he'd given me my engagement ring and asked me to move in with him.

If he'd been in front of me right now I wasn't sure how I would have reacted. Slapped his face? Burst into tears? I'd cried too many tears over Simon in the past. Now his actions left me feeling dazed and numb.

I'd never told Marla any of this. She would have disliked him even more than she already did and would have been on the phone every two minutes, offering advice. She would probably have read the runes for me or got one of her Druid friends to cast a charm. Instead, I'd confided in Megan, the temporary supply teacher at work. She'd helped me drink a cellar-load of Chardonnay and eat my way through a tub of Ben & Jerry's finest ice cream – cookie dough flavour.

So why was I still with him? I suppose I'd convinced myself that he'd changed. Getting engaged was a commitment, a serious step. We were living together and there had been no sign of any other women for over six months, a record for Si. All his other relationships had been fleeting and he'd never asked any of his past girlfriends to move into his flat or taken them to meet his parents. Surely, that proved that what we had together was special?

I guess the other reason, though I hated to admit it, was that I knew the worst about him. I knew he'd cheated but there were no other nasty surprises. Oddly, he was completely reliable and predictable in absolutely everything else – even the way he liked to have sex. I'd had enough upheavals and unpredictable incidents throughout my childhood and teenage years to last me a lifetime, but with Simon my only unknown was when he would cheat again.

All the same, it didn't bode well for our future if

I'd only been gone for a few days and already another woman was in our flat and answering my fiancé's phone.

My mobile rang. I glanced at the screen, expecting it to be Simon with a grovelly 'forgive me' plea of innocence speech, but instead Evelyn's number flashed up at me. I turned off my phone and tossed it down on the bed. Now was not the time to discuss wedding dresses.

'Azure, Drew's here,' Marla called from down in the hall.

I'd been so preoccupied with my call to Simon and my thoughts that I'd missed hearing the doorbell. Anger and hurt in equal measures began to tumble about in my head and I wished I could have stayed safely upstairs in my room for a few minutes longer. I swiped some lip gloss hastily across my mouth and fluffed my still slightly damp hair before making my way back downstairs to the kitchen.

With any luck Marla wouldn't notice that anything was wrong, though this was unlikely with her gift for reading auras, but I could always hope. I wished I could be that certain of Drew, but he had always been as quick as my mother to pick up on my moods.

Drew leaned on the worktop as I entered the kitchen, his arms folded as he watched Marla bustling about. He wore a faded T-shirt that enhanced the green of his eyes and fitted snugly across the broad muscles of his chest. His dark blond hair was damp and curled at the nape of his neck. He smelled of the outdoors and of man.

Marla pulled a recycled paper notepad from the kitchen drawer and started to rummage for a pen.

'Morning, Zee. Want a coffee?' Drew pulled a clean mug from the shelf and placed it next to the one he'd already prepared for himself.

'Thanks.' I tried not to mind that this was *my* mother's kitchen and that I was supposed to be the one offering him coffee, not the other way round.

'Darling, have you seen a pen?' Marla scooped the contents of the junk drawer on to the worktop and started sorting through the heap.

'There's one in the lounge. I'll go and get it.' I hated disorganisation. Usually, whenever I came home for a visit, I would surreptitiously reorganise some of my mother's clutter. Escaping into the lounge would also give me a breather. The shock from the realisation that Simon had cheated yet again had started to dissipate, leaving behind a sore, hollow feeling in my chest. If I'd been on my own I would have been having a good sob by now. I located Marla's favourite pen, the gold-coloured one with the red sparkly crystals round the top, and took it back into the kitchen.

'Thank you, darling.' She beamed at me as I handed it to her. 'Shall we go into the front room? We'll be more comfy in there.' She picked up her notepad and led the way.

Drew's eyes had narrowed when I'd walked into the room and I knew he'd noticed that something wasn't right.

'Are you okay?' Drew's whisper tickled my ear as we

followed my mother, carrying our coffees as we went.

'Yes, of course, it's just this whole list business.' That wasn't a total lie – Marla's crackpot list did concern me, but even though I'd convinced myself in the past that I was completely immune to Simon's weakness for other women, his inability to stay faithful to me still really hurt.

Marla settled herself in the armchair, her cheeks pink and eyes aglow with excitement. I took a seat on the sofa and Drew joined me. Heat simmered from his thigh through the thin canvas of his board shorts and my flimsy summer dress, sending a testosterone telegram into my bloodstream.

I shifted my position to try and create a gap between us. My efforts to make it appear as if I were merely making myself more comfortable failed, because Drew immediately adjusted his position to close the gap again. The curve on the corner of his lips told me that he knew exactly why I'd moved.

'This is so exciting.' Marla picked up her pen.

I wished there was something stronger than coffee in my mug.

'Have you heard back from any of the people you'd contacted about tracing Chris?' Drew leaned forward and picked up his drink.

What people? When had Marla had time to contact anyone about tracing my father since leaving hospital? And how come Drew knew about it and I didn't? Why was I always the last person to know anything?

'You've already started trying to find him?' I asked.

Marla didn't even have the grace to blush. 'I made a

few enquiries before I went into hospital. I found a few numbers from the old days and made some calls. Nothing major.'

'And you knew?' I turned to Drew.

'Only found out just now, while you were still upstairs.' He held up his hands in a defensive gesture, warding me off with his mug.

'Humph.' I glared at both of them.

'No one actually knows where Chris is now, but the old network is still going, so they plan to pass the word along.' Marla happily twirled her pen. The tiny red stones embedded in the top glittered in the morning sun, sending tiny ruby drops of light all around the room.

My coffee roiled in my stomach as the prospect of finding my father took another step closer to becoming reality. Drew briefly placed his free hand on top of mine, giving me silent reassurance that he understood how I felt.

'Now, the next thing on my list is the concert.' Marla frowned and tapped her pen against her cheek.

'I think I can help you there.' Drew placed his drink down on the table before shuffling forward to retrieve a folded piece of paper from the back pocket of his shorts. He passed it to Marla.

She unfolded the flyer and read out loud: 'The Flying Monkeys.'

I'd heard of them. They were this year's hot ticket.

'They're playing the end-of-summer concert at the Eden Project. The drummer owes me a favour.' Drew settled back in his seat with a grin.

I wondered how Drew knew the band.

'Oh, we could camp at a site there for the weekend! Get the whole experience. It would be like old times.' Marla did a happy wiggle but winced when she caught her wound.

'I'll give him a shout and get things sorted out.' Drew smiled at her.

'Marla, I really don't think you can go dancing on stage at a rock concert, let alone camping, in just a few weeks' time. You might not be well enough.' Honestly, Drew should have more sense than to encourage her.

'Nonsense, I'm sure I'll be fine. The hospital said I would have a few weeks to heal and then I could see the radiologist but that shouldn't stop me from having a little holiday.' She waved her pen airily as she dismissed my concerns.

'I don't think you're taking this seriously.'

'Azure, darling, you take life seriously enough for the both of us! You can come with me as my minder. Then you can be certain I'm not overdoing it. Drew will be there too, won't you?' She looked at him for confirmation.

Much to my annoyance he nodded in agreement.

'Marla . . .' I tried to protest.

She closed her notepad with a snap and clipped her pen to the cover. 'Fabulous, it's all going to be so much fun.'

I was stopped from saying anything else by the arrival of the district nurse. Marla had been right, it was Tina. She lived a couple of streets away and was four years older than me. She hustled Marla upstairs to the bedroom, leaving me sitting on the sofa with Drew.

'This is like old times,' Drew observed, the corner of his mouth tilting up in a wry smile.

I stood and picked up Marla's discarded cup as if tidying was my sole reason for moving away from him, even though we both knew it wasn't.

'You shouldn't encourage her. How is she going to be well enough to dance on stage with the Flying Monkeys – even assuming that a really cool rock band will want a woman in her late forties making a fool of herself during one of their gigs?'

His smile disappeared and his eyes took on a hard, flinty expression. 'Marla is one of the coolest people I know. She's not stupid about her health. Who made you Queen of the Universe, Zee? You always have to file everyone away in a neat little box and it kills you when they want to break out.'

His accusation stung, so I retaliated. 'Would you have wanted your mother looking like an idiot in front of thousands of people while she tried to recapture some long-lost youth she never had?'

He got to his feet. 'If it had made her happy and if I knew she had a life-threatening illness, then yes, Zee, I wouldn't have minded one bit.'

His words hit me like a slap in the face. I stared at him, realising what I'd said.

'I'm sorry,' I whispered. How could I have said something so thoughtless? Drew's mother had died when he was eighteen.

'Zee, I'm sorry too. That was harsh.' He took a step towards me.

Was that really what he thought? Tears stung my eyes. It wasn't even nine thirty and already my day had gone from bloody awful to pure nightmare. First Simon, then Marla, and now Drew had turned on me.

'I don't know why I bother. I get everything wrong.' My words came out in a sort of gulping sob and I turned tail to seek refuge in the kitchen.

'Don't do the whole girly tears thing on me. You know I hate it when you cry.' He followed me to where I stood next to the sink, trying to regain my composure.

'I'm sorry, Zee. I shouldn't have said all that stuff. She's your mum and I know you want what's best for her.' He placed large, gentle hands on the tops of my arms and turned me round to face him.

'No, maybe you had a point and I was thoughtless and horrid. It's just that I'm having a bloody awful day.' I closed my eyes as Drew wrapped his arms round me and held me close the way he'd always done when we were together. I could smell the faint tang of the sea mixed with his cologne.

'Hey, it's too early to be having a bad day,' Drew teased.

I shook my head, messing up my hair by ruffling it against his T-shirt.

'No, it's not. You don't understand. It's—' I managed to stop myself in time. Before I could blurt out everything about Simon and Evelyn and Chris and . . . well . . . everything.

'What?' Drew moved back a little so that he could see my face. A small frown creased his forehead.

I took a step away from him, extricating myself from his embrace. 'Nothing. It doesn't matter. Forget I said anything.'

Drew leaned his hip against the kitchen counter, his hands in the pockets of his shorts. 'It's clearly something, Zee. You've been weird ever since you arrived home and it's more than just spending time with Marla that's done it.'

'Knock, knock! Azure, are you in here?'

The kitchen door opened and Tina popped her head round, effectively ending my conversation with Drew.

'I've left your mum upstairs, she's having a bit of a rest. I've seen to her dressing and she says she's got all her appointments and things. I'll pop round again in a few days to do another check and see if the sutures have dissolved. Everything is healing really well. Marla's got my number if you need me.' She gave me a cheerful smile.

'Thanks, Tina. I'll see you out.'

I was grateful for the opportunity as I needed to put some space between me and Drew, but when I closed the front door behind her and turned round, I bumped right into him. My body instantly went on to red alert. So much for grabbing a few seconds' breather before I faced him again.

'I've got to get back to my classes,' he said. 'Will you have a chance to come down to the harbour later?'

'Maybe, I don't know. It depends how Marla is.' I got the feeling that if I didn't go down to meet him he would probably come to the house anyway.

'I'll see you later, then.' He reached his hand past my shoulder to open the door, his nearness sending tingles down my spine.

'Okay, later.' I gave in. If Marla insisted on going ahead with this concert idea I would need to find out more about it anyway. For now, though, I needed some space on my own where I could think about Simon and Marla and everything else that was going on in my life.

Once he'd gone, I crept upstairs to peep in on Marla. She was busy meditating with her rose quartz crystal and didn't notice me. I left her to her contemplation and, after collecting my mobile, I wandered back downstairs. As soon as I switched my phone back on I found I had six missed calls. Two were from Simon and four were from Evelyn. Simon had also left two voicemails asking me to call him and there was one from Evelyn demanding to know why my phone was switched off.

Automatically, I did it again. I had no idea what I wanted to say to Simon and Evelyn could get stuffed. Every time Simon was unfaithful and I found out, we'd have the same old discussion. He'd apologise, buy me gifts, make rash promises, and would somehow make it seem like it was my fault he'd gone off and bonked someone else. Hence the need for me to stay in shape, dress appropriately, keep the flat exactly the way he liked it, et cetera. Marla called it playing 'Simon Says'.

Jethro strolled in through the open back door and gave me a disapproving stare. 'What are you looking at?' I couldn't even get a break from the cat.

Drew had called me Queen of the Universe. All I needed was a set of rules to follow so I could try and control the chaos that had haunted me all my life. When Simon was guilt-tripping me he accused me of being a control freak. Maybe I was, I didn't know. I simply wanted some certainties in my life. Was that too much to ask? I guess I even thought of Simon's cheating as a constant and if I wanted to be all analytical and Freudian about it, then maybe, subconsciously, I'd thought that if I was thinner, tidier and prettier, it would all stop.

Jethro sat down on his haunches and began cleaning his front paw with neat movements of his small pink tongue.

'Life must be much simpler if you're a cat.'

He ignored me, choosing instead to stroll by with his nose in the air. He headed for the lounger, obviously having decided to catch the morning sunshine outside in the courtyard. I followed after him, pausing to lean on the open doorframe. I closed my eyes as the sun warmed the skin on my face, teasing my eyelids with golden promises of a bright, sunny day.

For a moment I envied Marla her ability to switch off and meditate. She'd tried to teach me to do it when I was younger, claiming it would help me with exam stress. It was no use. I'd tried to focus and let my thoughts go free but, instead, my mind started finding more things to stress about.

She'd never given up trying to get me to use crystal therapy, hence the chunk of amethyst in my bedside drawer. Marla had always hoped I'd be intuitive like her, and inherit her interest in the world of the psychic and the unexplained. It had soon become apparent, however, that Jethro was more intuitive than I was. Marla had simply given a sad little smile and said that I took after my father.

The doorbell rang, shattering my moment of reflection. I staggered down the hall, blinking as I went, trying to refocus my eyes after having closed them for so long.

'Can I help you?'

I didn't recognise the middle-aged man on the doorstep. He didn't speak, just stared at me. A strange prickly sensation started creeping over the back of my neck as I looked into his eyes.

'Azure?' he said.

Panic rushed through me and I tried to close the door.

The stranger was a fraction of a second faster than I was and stuck his foot in the gap. A torrent of swear words coloured the air.

'What's going on? Is everything okay?' Marla came hurrying down the stairs. '*Chris?*'

The man stopped cursing and hopping around, holding his toes.

'Marla?'

Oh God.

'Is it really you?' Marla swayed on her feet and both the stranger and I reached out at the same time to steady her. She raised her hands and backed away from both of us.

The man – my father – winced and took a step towards her. 'I phoned a couple of times but then I thought I might as well call round and see if I could find you.'

The colour started to return to my mother's cheeks. 'You'd better come inside.'

We trooped into the kitchen. I'd only ever seen two good pictures of my father. One was a grainy black-and-white press cutting, yellowed around the edges from when he'd led a protest march to stop a bypass being built somewhere in Essex. The other was an old Polaroid of him and Marla when she'd been pregnant with me.

I took a seat opposite him at the breakfast bar and stared at him, trying to see the resemblance between those images and the man currently sitting in my mother's kitchen. In the pictures he'd been a skinny youth of nineteen with long, thick, dark hair, dressed in a T-shirt and ripped jeans. Now he was a balding thick-set man in a neat suit, only the studs in his ears and the tattoo peeking out above his collar indicating his more colourful past.

'Tea?' Marla offered, her composure apparently fully restored.

'Sit down, I'll make the drinks.' I suddenly became aware that I was supposed to be looking after her, not the other way around.

'It's been a long time,' he said, looking at my mother.

'Yes.' She sat next to him, her gaze fixed on his face.

'You look as beautiful as ever,' he murmured.

I brought in the drinks and retook my seat. I had a million and one questions buzzing inside my head. Where had he been? What did he do? Why had he never kept in touch? I mean, what kind of man walks away from the woman he says he loves, leaving her in a squat with a six-month-old baby? I wished I'd slammed the door harder.

Marla touched the side of his face, resting her fingertips lightly on his cheek. 'I knew you were coming.'

'I heard from Zippy and Fuzz that you were looking for me. I soon found out where you were. You've made quite a name for yourself.' He didn't seem perturbed by her actions.

'Where have you been?' Marla asked.

Ha! Good question – only I wanted to know where he'd been for *all* of my life, not only the last year or so. I waited to hear what he had to say.

'Here and there. I spent some time inside. They got

me for criminal damage at the anti-nuclear protest for cutting the fence and damaging the gates. When I came out, you'd been moved on. Skinny George offered me some work in France, fruit-picking and stuff.' He glanced at me. 'When I came back to England I asked around and couldn't find you. Someone said you'd gone to Ireland with Azure. I thought you'd made it up with your mum and that I definitely wouldn't be welcome there so I ended up going to sea. I got some work on the cargo ships.'

Marla sighed and lifted her hand away from his face. 'Are you still travelling now?'

He shook his head. 'No, I settled back on land a couple of years ago. I drive a bus now in Basingstoke.'

Hysterical laughter bubbled in the back of my throat and spilled out, startling the cat from his comfy position outside on the sun lounger. Chris, the great freedom fighter and protest leader, was a bus driver.

Marla gave me a sharp look.

'Sorry.' I hiccuped to a halt.

'I took Azure over to Ireland to see my mother when you didn't come back and I got desperate. She turned me away. Luckily, I met up with a group travelling back to England, to Kent. We tagged along. After that we moved around quite a lot until my mother died. She didn't leave a will and Azure and I were her only relatives. There was enough for us to settle here and I took a lease out on the shop.'

'Did you ever meet anyone else?' His attention was firmly fixed on my mother.

'No one special. How about you?'

To anyone who didn't know her, the question sounded casual, almost disinterested, but I knew she had her heart pinned on his answer.

'No, no one special, I was at sea for so long. I never spent much time in any one place.'

An awkward silence fell. I picked up my mug and a shaft of sunlight hit my ring.

'You're all grown up and engaged?' Chris looked at my hand.

'She's a teacher at a primary school in Bristol. She's getting married next July,' Marla explained. The sun seemed to vanish as she spoke and a shiver ran up my spine as if someone had walked across my grave.

16

Chris's congratulations on my engagement washed over me; meanwhile, Marla answered most of his questions about where I worked, how I'd met Simon, and all the broad details of the last twenty-plus years of my life. I couldn't seem to focus. It was all too unreal: Chris being there and everything that had gone on earlier . . . I felt numb.

'Listen, I'm popping out for a while. It'll give you two some time to catch up.' I got up from my seat. I needed to get out of the house and give myself a chance to think.

I grabbed my phone and bag and bolted from the house. My feet automatically headed for the harbour. All around me tourists were busy browsing in the shops, eating ice creams and generally enjoying their holidays. I moved amongst them with my life in bits.

Once I reached the seafront I walked away from the popular area, down past the new apartments and out to where it was quieter. I walked right to the end of the promenade and leaned against the railing. The sea stretched out in front of me, calm and blue. A couple of ships sat on the horizon.

I wondered what it had been like for Chris, moving from place to place with only the sea surrounding him for days on end. Had he ever been lonely or thought about me and Marla? Had he wondered where we were? How we were?

I pulled my phone out of my handbag and switched it on. More missed calls, mainly from Evelyn. I was surprised she hadn't tried the house number. Then again, she probably didn't want to risk Marla picking up the call and having to make conversation with her. Evelyn had a lot in common with her son in that neither of them got on with my mother. I could kind of understand their view, but Marla *is* my mother, and while I can criticise her I don't think they can.

There were no more voicemails. I wasn't sure how I felt about that. Part of me was relieved that I didn't have to listen to more of Simon's lies, but my pride was a little hurt that he couldn't be bothered to try. Maybe he took my forgiveness so much for granted that he, too, was simply going through the motions.

I wondered when Simon's first bouquet of flowers, complete with love note, would arrive. It was all so predictable and I realised I didn't want it any more. Without stopping to think about the consequences of my actions, I hurled my phone into the sea and watched it disappear beneath the waves with a satisfying plop.

For a brief, heady moment I considered taking off my engagement ring and hurling that into the sea, too. But then sanity returned and I realised that although it might provide me with some instant satisfaction, it wouldn't solve anything. It wouldn't solve the problem of whether or not I was prepared to remain engaged to Simon, to forgive him one more time and carry on with the plans for our wedding. Neither would it solve the quandary I was in about the feelings I got every time I was around Drew.

People were walking along the promenade towards me. I straightened up and started back along the seafront towards the town. At some point I would need to call into the phone shop and buy a new mobile, but right now all I wanted was a handmade waffle cone filled to overflowing with vanilla ice cream that was made with real Devonshire clotted cream. If it came topped with a chocolate flake and raspberry sauce then so much the better.

As my pace quickened with the lure of the ice-cream stand on the quayside, I spotted a small flotilla of yellow and black kayaks on the water. My eyes automatically searched for Drew. Sure enough, he was there, clad in his wetsuit and watching his young pupils practise rollovers. Serena was there too, her bright blond hair glowing healthily against the dark grey-blue of the sea. Something like jealousy gnawed at me as I forced myself to look away and moved on towards the café area.

I joined the queue at the ice-cream stand behind the pensioners, the loved-up couples and the harassed-looking mum with three kids. I wondered how Marla and Chris were getting on with their reunion. I couldn't think of Chris as my dad. If I'd met him on the street before today I wouldn't have known him.

I'd watched the mushy shows on TV – they usually appeared at Christmas – when a man in a naff knitted jumper reunited families from all over the world who hadn't seen each other for years. Everyone always cried and hugged. I'd often thought of what it must feel like to be one of those people. Now I knew.

Come on down, Azure Dawn Millichip, and meet the father you haven't seen for twenty-nine years!

'Small, regular or large?' the vendor asked.

I'd reached the front of the queue.

'Large vanilla with everything, please.'

Bugger Simon and his obsession with my calorie intake. I needed sugar. It wasn't every day you met your father for the first time in for ever.

I collected my cone and ambled along in the sunshine. All the benches were taken and the harbourside was a hive of activity. The kiosks where the local boatmen sold tickets for their trips were bustling and small children dangled lines hopefully over the harbour walls while crabs wriggled about in buckets at their captors' miniature feet.

Looking back out over the water I noticed that the kayaks had made their way to the steps leading from the promenade where I'd been walking earlier. The children had gathered on the ramp that led into the water next to the steps and were busy peeling off their helmets and collecting up their oars.

Drew stood next to Serena; even at this distance I could make out her blond hair and his tall frame. I turned away quickly, spilling a sticky blob of raspberry sauce on my sundress. Drew meant nothing to me. I had to sort out what I planned to do about Simon. It was ridiculous to be obsessing about an ex – make that a long-ago ex – when I had other, much more pressing worries.

With my ice cream finished I trudged slowly back up the hill to the cottage. The sun beat down on my head and I wished I'd put on my suncream before I'd gone out; I could feel my nose and the tops of my shoulders reddening in the heat. The streets grew quieter the higher I climbed and the air shimmered and danced under the midday sun.

I let myself into the cottage, listening out for the sound of conversation. Everywhere was quiet.

'Marla?' I called out.

She poked her head into the hall. 'Oh, you're back. Chris has just gone.' She looked a bit pale and I hoped she hadn't been overdoing things while I'd been out. I shouldn't have left her for so long.

'Go and sit down, I'll fix you some lunch.' I hustled her back into the kitchen.

Marla drifted out into the courtyard and sat on the lounger that was shaded by the big parasol.

'You look done in,' I said.

'I'm fine, really.' She swung her feet up on to the rest in an easy, graceful movement. 'More to the point, how are you?'

'I'm okay. It was a shock when I opened the door and realised who he was.' I turned slightly and pretended to arrange the salad on to plates so she couldn't see my face.

'I don't just mean with Chris turning up.' Her voice

carried clearly through the open door. 'You were arguing with Drew.'

Damn, I hadn't thought she'd heard us.

'It wasn't an argument. It was a difference of opinion, that's all.' I sliced up the last of the quiche and added it to the plates.

'It sounded like an argument to me.'

'Well, it wasn't. I'm meeting Drew later.' I placed her lunch plate on a tray and carried it out to her.

'Azure, I do wish you'd stop holding me at arm's length all the time. I only want you to be happy – that's all.' She looked up at me, her deep blue eyes filled with concern.

'Okay, fine, I give in. I had a fight with Simon earlier, too.' I took a seat on the chair next to her.

She heaved a deep sigh. 'I'm sorry. Do you want to talk about it?'

'There's not much to say. I need to take some time to work things out.' I shrugged my shoulders and stood up again to get my own lunch from the kitchen.

'Evelyn called to speak to you while you were out.'

'Oh, did she say what she wanted?' Great, it must be something *really* important if she'd used the house number. Not that I had any intention of talking to her until I'd sorted out how I felt about her son.

'No, she didn't stay on for long. She said she couldn't get you on your mobile.' Marla gave me a quizzical look.

'I threw my phone into the sea.'

One good thing about having a mother like Marla is that she's very hard to shock. She simply said, 'Oh, I see.'

I walked into the kitchen and picked up my lunch. Jethro spied an opportunity and leapt on to my vacated seat, his yellowy-green eyes daring me to dislodge him. I collected a fork from the drawer and glared back at the cat.

Marla smiled at my expression. 'I'm not even going to ask why you threw a perfectly good phone into the water.' She tugged at the cushion beneath Jethro, tipping him neatly on to the floor. He gave us both a disgusted look and stalked away back inside the house with his tail held high.

'What do you want me to say to Evelyn if she calls again?' Marla asked as I resumed my seat.

'I'll talk to her if I'm in.' I nibbled a carrot stick from my plate.

'And Simon?'

'Him too.'

I didn't want to drag Marla into my quarrel with my fiancé. With any luck he wouldn't call me again for a couple of days. Once he realised my phone was out of order he'd probably get the message that I was seriously upset with him. Then again, he could be remarkably obtuse and not really notice at all. By the time we actually got around to talking, he would probably manage to twist everything round so that it was all my fault. Then he'd expect me to cajole him back into a good mood.

'Hmm.' Marla clearly didn't think much of that idea.

I finished my quiche and decided to change the subject. 'By the way, I took quite a few press enquiries yesterday from the local radio and the papers.'

Immediately a tinge of guilty pink coloured her cheeks. 'Um, I've dealt with all that. Fran's given them a statement.'

'Really?' Heaven help the press if Fran gave them anything. It would take them for ever to wade through the waffle. I almost felt sorry for them.

Marla busied herself clearing her plate and it dawned on me that there must be more to this press statement than she'd let on.

'The press won't be bothering you again, then?'

'Um, not exactly.'

I gave her the same glare I'd used on Jethro. 'Spill.'

'Well, I sort of promised I'd do an on-air interview on Friday. They were very interested in the Flying Monkeys concert thing.' She put her cutlery neatly down on her empty plate and avoided my gaze.

I made a mental promise to kill Drew when I saw him later. 'What did you tell them? Drew hasn't even said anything to his friend yet, and you don't know for certain that you'll be well enough to go to a concert, never mind to sleep in a tent overnight.'

'Oh pish, those are just details, darling. I'll be as fit as a flea by then. Tina says I'm healing nicely and I've only got to have a teensy bit of radiotherapy. Besides, you'll be there to keep an eye on me.'

'I think you should talk this plan over with your consultant first. Why would the radio station be interested in you being at the concert, anyway?' I knew I was clutching at straws by hoping that her doctor would veto her plans. Marla was unlikely to listen to him even if he said no to the whole dancing and camping trip.

Marla swung her legs off the footrest and started to get up from the lounger. 'Um, they might want me to do a special live broadcast and maybe some interviews.' She managed to slide past me and into the kitchen while I sat there with my mouth open.

'What do you mean, "a special live broadcast and maybe some interviews"?'

'Nothing definite. It was mentioned, that's all.' She rinsed her plate noisily under the tap. 'It would be fun, though, don't you think?'

Fun wasn't quite the word I had in mind. Tiring, madness, exhausting and totally not a good idea for an ill woman, were more the kinds of things I was thinking. It also occurred to me that if I didn't manage to dissuade Marla from going ahead with her concert plans then I was stuck with a weekend of camping. Camping in a tent – at a rock festival – with portaloos, insects and a blow-up airbed. All things I hated.

And my mother thought this would be fun.

17

Fran arrived shortly after she closed the shop, so I left her chatting with Marla while I ventured back down towards the sea to find Drew. I'd changed into a clean sugar-pink sundress with spaghetti straps. I told myself it was because I'd dropped ice cream down the one I'd been wearing earlier, and not because this particular dress was quite flattering to my figure.

Excitement mixed with apprehension fluttered in my stomach as I reached the harbourside. Marla had told me the time his class finished and where he was likely to be afterwards. It was hard to shake the thought that meeting up with Drew like this was somehow a bit wrong. Almost as if I were planning to cheat on Simon the way he'd cheated on me.

I loitered along the promenade looking for Drew. It was like going back in time to when I used to wait for him before our dates, straining my eyes for the first glimpse of him strolling towards me. I'd felt the same mixture of emotions back then. Excitement, apprehension and that deep, dark undercurrent of naked desire.

As if my mind had conjured him up, I saw him. He was further along the walk near the top of the slope that was used by the boating school. His tall frame made him stand out amongst the clusters of tourists. I had started to walk towards him when I realised he was with Katya.

Her dark head was bent close to his blonder one as if they were sharing some secret, private conversation. I watched as she gesticulated with her hands while she talked. My feet slowed as I drew closer. I was near enough now to see the expression on Drew's face darken and become serious as Katya continued to talk. Her pale face looked strained and confused.

I hesitated, unsure if I should interrupt what was clearly a quite intense discussion. At that moment Drew lifted his head and saw me. Katya followed his gaze and scowled while I remained a few feet away, uncertain whether to join them. Drew murmured something in Katya's ear, and she gave me one last dirty look before walking off, flouncing past me as if I smelled nasty.

'You came.' Drew smiled at me. 'You look nice.'

'I'm sorry if I interrupted something.'

He shook his head. 'It's nothing.'

I hitched my bag a little higher on my shoulder, feeling as awkward as a teenager again. 'I'm not sure why I'm here.'

He took a few steps forward to stand in front of me, his eyes locked on mine. 'Aren't you?'

He stroked a gentle finger along the curve of my cheek, tucking a stray tendril of hair behind my ear, and my heart squeezed. Heat built in my stomach and I knew then that I was on very dangerous ground.

'Um, shall we walk?' I stepped back.

Amusement mixed with some other undefined emotion flitted across his face before he fell into step next to me and we began to stroll along the path leading away from the town.

'My father showed up this morning right after you left.'

Drew halted and stared at me. 'Shit, you've really had a crap day today. How did it go?'

I shrugged. 'So-so. I shut his foot in the door because I was so shocked to see him and then it all got too much. I left him talking to Marla and got out of the house.'

The corner of his mouth quirked. 'I won't ask why you tried to cripple the bloke.'

We resumed walking once more, Drew fitting his easy long-legged stride to my shorter steps.

'It was weird, I've only ever seen a few snapshots of him and he doesn't look anything like he did in the pictures.'

'What's he doing now? Where has he been?' Drew asked.

'At sea, working on cargo ships, and lately he's been driving a bus in Basingstoke.'

Drew laughed out loud, sobering when he saw my expression.

'Yeah, I know.'

'I'm sorry. How's Marla taken it?' We'd reached the

end of the walk. Drew sat down on the wooden bench at the end of the path and waited for me to join him.

'She seems happy. It was a big shock for her too, even though she said she'd sensed him near her for a while.' I perched on the very end of the bench, taking care to leave space between Drew and myself.

'Are you going to see him again?' He stretched out his legs as if settling in for a long chat.

'He wants to see me.'

Drew stayed silent for a moment.

My life was a total mess. Until Marla's call I'd been happily engaged to Simon and daydreaming about my wedding. My mother had been doing her own thing and my father had been out of the equation altogether, someone I never thought about.

But now . . . Marla had all kinds of outrageous plans, most of which seemed to involve me; my engagement was hanging by a thread; and the father I hadn't seen for almost thirty years had suddenly pitched up out of nowhere.

Drew looked at me. 'You don't have to see him if you don't want to, Zee.'

'I know, but I'm not even sure what I *do* want any more.' A part of me was curious to get to know him a little. Marla had always said that although I physically resembled her, I was like Chris in my ways.

'What does Simon say about it?' An indefinable expression crossed Drew's face as he asked the question.

The flesh on the top of my arms goose-pimpled as a sudden breeze blew in from the sea. 'I haven't told him.'

Drew frowned. 'Don't you think you should? Hell, it's not every day something like this happens.' He straightened up and moved along the bench closer to me.

Tension crackled in the air between us like electricity. My tongue welded itself to the roof of my mouth as I looked into his green eyes.

'I . . . we . . .' I couldn't find the words to explain before I was in his arms and he was kissing me.

He tasted every bit as good as I remembered. All male and all Drew. Automatically my body curved into his, my breasts pushing against the firm muscles of his chest as I wrapped my arms round him and pulled him in towards me. It felt so right, so good, as his lips blazed a trail from my mouth along the curve of my neck towards my breasts.

'Damn it, Zee, we shouldn't be doing this.' He pulled away from me and got to his feet, walking off to lean on the rail overlooking the sea.

Shameful heat burned through me. I was no better than Simon. 'We should forget this ever happened.' I rubbed at the tops of my arms, suddenly cold again without the heat from Drew's body.

'Just tell me why you're marrying him, Zee,' Drew demanded, turning round to face me once more.

Tears stung at the back of my eyes. A few days ago I would have said it was because I loved him but now I didn't have an answer. I couldn't speak.

He watched me for a moment, then shook his head. 'Forget it. We'd better head back.'

I picked up my bag from the bench and silently fell into step beside him as we started back towards the town, being careful to keep a gap between us as we walked. This time I had to hurry in order to match Drew's pace and by the time we reached the tourist area by the statue, I was out of breath.

Drew's hand on my arm stopped me in my tracks. 'Wait here.'

He released me and headed off towards the pub. At first I couldn't see what had drawn his attention until I noticed a small knot of youths. There seemed to be some kind of argument going on as there was a lot of jostling and pushing. Drew strode towards them, picking up pace, and I wondered why he felt the need to get involved until I saw Katya in the middle of the group.

People were giving the protagonists a wide berth while a few others lingered to watch what was going on. One of the men looked vaguely familiar and I tried to think where I'd seen him before. Drew reached the group and put his arm round Katya, moving her to the side. Immediately, the tall skinny guy, whom I thought I recognised, took a swing at Drew.

My heart lurched into my mouth as he blocked the blow with his arm. Acting swiftly, he brought up his other hand to connect firmly with his attacker's nose. His assailant hit the floor like a bag of flour and the rest of the group backed away from Drew. They grabbed the injured youth and hauled him to his feet as Drew led Katya away from the scene across the road towards me.

I hurried towards them, my heart beating like a drum with fear. Drew could have been knifed or something – and what on earth was Katya doing in the middle of it all?

As I reached them I could see tears pouring down Katya's face, her make-up streaking down her face as she sobbed. I glanced over to where the group had been but they had melted away like shadows in the height of the midday sun.

'What happened? Are you okay?' I looked at Drew and then at Katya.

Drew's face was like thunder and from the set of his jaw I knew he was fighting to keep his temper under control.

'Who was that?' I pressed.

Katya clung to Drew's arm like a limpet, her shoulders shaking with the force of her sobs.

'That delightful scumbag is Katya's brother, Pieter.' He ground the sentence out.

Katya let out a stream of some incomprehensible language that I assumed was Romanian or Hungarian or something. I wasn't really sure where Katya was from.

'So, what was going on?' It must have been something awful judging by Katya's reaction and the way Drew had waded in.

'He wanted money for drugs.' Drew smoothed Katya's hair and murmured reassurance in her ear. 'I hate to ask this, but could Katya come back to Marla's for tonight?'

I knew my mother would have no problem in letting

Katya bunk down at the cottage. I'd grown up with a succession of strange people coming and going in whatever accommodation we'd been in.

'Sure.' I thought it best not to ask why she couldn't go back to her lodgings.

Katya clung to him even more tightly, shaking her head at his request. I wasn't sure why she would be reluctant to stay with my mother unless it was because I was there too. Or maybe I was being mean and she was concerned about Marla's health.

'Pieter might cause trouble at her digs. It would be better if she were somewhere safe and there isn't room in my flat,' Drew explained.

Katya tugged on his arm. 'Police.' She nodded her head towards the town and I spotted two uniformed officers making their way towards the pub.

'Let's go.' Drew led the way with Katya still holding on to him for grim life.

When we arrived back at the cottage, Fran was still in the courtyard with Marla. A bottle of wine stood open on the table. Marla sprang to her feet as soon as she saw Katya's tear-streaked face.

'Oh, darling girl, whatever's happened?'

Katya immediately relinquished her hold on Drew to sob on Marla's shoulder; fortunately, she chose the uninjured side. Fran came clucking round her like a ruffled mother hen with her chick while I retreated to the kitchen with Drew.

'What was the fight about?' I kept my voice low so that they wouldn't hear me outside.

Drew glanced out the door to where Katya was now installed on a lounger being hugged by Fran. 'Pieter wanted money. Katya had given him all the spare cash she had earlier. That's what we were talking about when you met us. Katya thought he'd gone but then he decided he needed more money so he . . .' Drew pushed an angry hand through his hair. 'He was trying to sell her to one of the other men you saw, in lieu of his drug debt.'

My mouth dropped open in shock. I'd read about this sort of thing in the papers but I never imagined it might happen so close to home.

'Katya might act tough, but she's just a kid.'

'Poor girl.' I glanced outside at the women huddled together in the courtyard. Suddenly my problems seemed quite small in comparison.

'Marla will take care of her.'

I looked up at Drew and realised how close together we were. I could feel the faint heat from his body and smell the scent of his skin. Awareness prickled down my spine.

'I know she will, but I need to take care of Marla at the moment, too.'

The corners of his mouth quirked upwards. 'I wish you luck with that last part.' His face sobered again. 'I'm going to see someone I know who might be able to help me find out where Pieter's gone. Just be careful opening the door to anyone tonight, okay?'

I nodded, apprehension creeping through my veins. I didn't want any trouble at the cottage. Marla could do without the stress.

'Good girl.' He leaned forward and his lips brushed the top of my head before he started off down the hallway.

'Be careful,' I called as the front door closed behind him.

18

Marla and Fran were still outside clucking around Katya, all unaware of Drew's plan to try and track down Pieter. I hoped he would be okay.

'Has Drew gone?' Marla drifted in through the back door.

'He went to see if he could find out where Pieter went. I don't know why; it didn't seem like a very sensible idea to me.' We both kept our voices low so our conversation wouldn't carry outside, but there was no point trying to keep it from Katya.

'Katya said there was a fight.'

'It wasn't really a fight. There was some jostling then Pieter swung at Drew, but Drew got in first and knocked him to the floor. The next thing I knew was that the police were heading towards us and Pieter and his friends had vanished.'

I looked out through the open door. Devoid of her usual layers of mascara and eyeliner, Katya appeared much younger than her years. Her long dark hair hung loose over her shoulder as she stroked Jethro.

Marla followed my gaze and shook her head. 'I can't

believe he was trying to pimp her out. If I could get my hands on him . . .' She broke off as Fran entered the kitchen.

'I'd better be off. I think Katya could do with a nice cup of tea, some camomile might help calm her down.' Fran blinked at us hopefully through her flicked-up fringe. I wondered if she purposely hadn't noticed that hairstyles had changed since 1986.

'I'll put the kettle on.' I suited my actions to my words while Fran gathered her things together, ready to leave.

'Zee will go down and work in the shop tomorrow. Katya can stay here with me,' Marla announced as she handed Fran her cardigan.

I busied myself with mugs and teabags. It would probably be better if Katya stayed at the cottage. If Pieter were to appear at the shop, he wouldn't know me. I doubted very much if he'd had any chance to take notice of me before Drew had decked him. Plus, if I were at the shop, there was less chance of any kind of trouble.

Marla showed Fran out and I carried a mug of herbal tea out to Katya in the courtyard. Jethro rolled back on to his stomach at my approach, narrowing his green eyes in annoyance at having his petting session disturbed.

'Fran thought you might like a drink.' I offered her the mug.

'Thank you.' She took the tea and stared down into the steamy depths, her pretty face the picture of misery.

I fiddled around, collecting up the empty wine glasses. 'I'm sorry about what happened, you know, with your brother.'

She shrugged her shoulders and a tear slid down her cheek. 'I have been very unkind to you before, Azure, I am sorry.'

'That's okay. I understand.'

Marla re-entered the courtyard, her bare feet moving silently across the faded flagstones. 'You're safe here. You can stay for as long as you need.'

Jethro leapt down from the lounger to rub against her legs as she crossed to where Katya sat with her head still bowed.

'He was not always like this. He owes much money for drugs and he has nothing left to trade now.' She dashed her free hand across her cheek.

Inside the house the phone began to ring. Marla ignored it and took a seat next to Katya. I left them to it and hurried inside to answer the call.

'Zee, I've been calling you all day.' Simon's voice cut across my hello.

My heart fell into my shoes. I didn't want to have this conversation right now. All day long I'd tried to push thoughts of what I intended to say to Simon to the back of my mind.

'This isn't a good time to talk.' Guilt flooded through me. If I loved Simon, I would be desperate to talk to him, to straighten things out between us; I wouldn't have been kissing another man only hours earlier and wanting him to take me to bed.

I heard Simon sigh. 'When *will* be a good time? You've been ignoring my calls and messages. I don't know what silly idea you've got in your head about me and Elaine, but I swear there's nothing going on between us. She's just a colleague.'

I swallowed my annoyance as a great wave of exhaustion washed over me. I didn't have the strength to argue with him.

'Zee, are you still there? I promise there's nothing going on. She picked up my phone and answered without thinking. She has the same model as I have.'

I listened to him make lame excuse after lame excuse and with every word he uttered I knew it was over. I couldn't delude myself any longer.

'Simon, please, I really can't discuss this right now. I know you're sleeping with her. I think it's probably better if you don't call me for a while. Oh, and by the way, don't try the mobile, it's at the bottom of the sea.' I wondered if there was any wine left in the bottle Fran and Marla had been sharing earlier.

'What? You're crazy, you don't know what you're saying. It was a one-off thing – it meant nothing; you know I love you. This is all your mother's doing, isn't it?' The anger in his voice carried down the line.

'It's got nothing to do with Marla. This is all about you and your inability to keep the zipper on your fly closed whenever a new girl crosses your path. I'll talk to you when I'm good and ready and now isn't that time.' I banged the handset back down on the cradle and turned to see Marla and Katya eyeing me warily from the doorway.

'Could you find the spare bedding from the airing cupboard, darling? Katya can sleep on the sofa in the front room,' Marla suggested.

I knew they must have heard the tail end of my conversation with Simon but thankfully neither of them mentioned it. I went upstairs and found pillows and a lightweight hand-crafted quilt for Katya.

Neither of them referred to my loud phone conversation that evening. Instead, we all ended up in the lounge watching a repeat showing of *Midsomer Murders* and ignoring my outburst.

I woke early the next day to a cracking headache and the sound of gulls fighting on the rooftop, as well as a delivery guy from the local florist standing on the front step clutching a bouquet. The flowers were from Simon. I guessed he'd probably ordered them before we'd spoken on the phone yesterday evening. I couldn't bring myself to bin them so I stuck them in a bucket in a cool corner of the courtyard while I went to find a vase and take some painkillers for my headache.

They were beautiful flowers, but I couldn't face having them in the lounge where I'd have to look at them all the time. Their presence would feel like a constant reproach.

I decided to grab a piece of toast before heading off to the shop. Katya was still fast asleep on the sofa when I left. Somehow she'd even snored her way through the florist hammering on the door with Simon's bouquet. I propped a note for her and Marla up against the toaster, fed Jethro, and closed the front door quietly behind me.

It was another beautiful blue-sky summer morning. The streets were still empty of people as I made my way down the Broad Steps. I reached the shop early and fumbled in my bag for the keys.

Overhead I heard the rumble of a sash window being opened. 'Hey, Zee.'

I looked up to see Drew looking down at me. His thick, dark corn-coloured hair stood up in spikes around his head and a night's growth of stubble adorned his chin.

'Morning. I thought you usually had a class at this time of day?' His sudden appearance had thrown me completely. I'd physically resisted the temptation to take the longer route to the shop via the seafront so I wouldn't look for the flotilla of boats that would mean Drew was on the water.

'Serena gives me a day off every now and again for good behaviour.' He grinned at me and my stomach gave a flip of excitement.

'When were you ever good?' I slotted the key in the door, hoping he hadn't noticed the blush that had swept over my cheeks.

'Do you really want me to answer that?' he teased, and the heat in my face grew at the suggestion in his tone.

I unlocked the shop door. 'I'm going inside.'

'Open the internal door and I'll bring you a coffee,' he called.

My hands shook as I entered the shop and deactivated the alarm. Once the lights were on I unlocked the doors at the rear of the shop that led to the stockroom and up to Drew's flat.

I busied myself with balancing the float in the till and tried not to keep glancing towards the back to look for Drew. Fran was due to arrive soon and I wanted to have everything ready before she did.

'Breakfast delivery.' The back door opened and Drew entered, balancing a cardboard tray in one hand with two tall, lidded disposable cups. In his other hand he held a bakery bag. Dressed in long khaki shorts and a bright blue sailing-club T-shirt, he looked as if he'd rolled out of bed and into the first clothes he'd found. He looked all male and totally beddable.

I shook my head and tried to focus on sorting the float in the till. My heartbeat zipped up a notch as Drew came near and placed the cups and bag on the counter.

'Coffee and a Danish.' He popped the lid off one of the cups and the lovely aroma of freshly brewed caffeine tantalised my senses.

'Ninety-eight, ninety-nine . . .' I counted the last of the pennies into the till.

'Apricot or raisin?' He rustled the bag open and held it so I could see inside.

'What makes you think I want one?' I closed the till drawer and tried to act casual, as if he always turned up with breakfast for me.

The corner of his mouth curved upwards. 'Because you love Danish pastries.' He plucked the apricot one – which he knew was my favourite – from the bag and waved it in front of my nose.

'Stop it, you're sprinkling crumbs everywhere.' I tried to glare at him.

He stopped moving the pastry around and held it a couple of inches away from my mouth. 'Go on, then, take a bite.'

Something in the tone of his voice, and the hint of a challenge in the green depths of his eyes, sent a thrill of excitement running up my spine. Without taking my eyes from his I leaned forward and took a bite of the delicious, sweet pastry.

'Mmm, good.' I chewed and swallowed, still without breaking my gaze.

I saw the pupils of his eyes dilate slightly and felt the soft sigh of his breath against the warm skin of my face.

'You have a crumb on your mouth,' he murmured and leaned in to kiss the corner of my lips.

The shop bell chimed and Fran coughed theatrically as we sprang apart like two naughty children who'd been up to no good.

'Morning!' She smiled at us. 'How did you get on last night? Did you find Pieter?' She addressed her questions to Drew.

I'd forgotten he'd gone to find Katya's brother.

He straightened up and took a sip from one of the coffee cups. 'No trace of him in his usual haunts, he seems to have gone to ground. It's probably best if Katya keeps away from the shop for a couple of days in case he comes round to try and make trouble.'

'I think you're right,' Fran agreed.

Drew pulled the raisin Danish from the bakery bag and took a bite. Fran frowned as crumbs dropped on to the shop counter.

'I don't think you should eat those in the shop,' she reproved and headed through the back door to place her bag in the stockroom.

'That told you,' I murmured. I wasn't sure if I was upset or pleased that Fran had interrupted us. It was embarrassing to be caught smooching by my mother's friend, especially when the man kissing me wasn't my fiancé. Not that I was even very clear about whether or not Simon was still my fiancé. His ring was still on my finger but I knew that I needed to see him to cut the tie between us once and for all.

Drew just grinned and ate the rest of his pastry in three clean bites. Fran clattered her way back into the shop. I guessed she wanted to give us plenty of warning in case we were doing anything else naughty.

'I'd better get a duster and clean this up.' I frowned at the flakes of pastry on the counter. My heart rate had settled down into something approaching normal, although my mouth still tingled from the gentle pressure of Drew's lips: I couldn't go on like this much longer. I didn't know how he felt about me but I knew that whatever happened I couldn't go ahead and marry Simon even if Evelyn had booked the church.

'I'll catch you ladies later.' Drew picked up his coffee and headed for the front door. He strolled out into the morning sunshine, lifting his arm in a lazy farewell wave as he passed the window.

'He's such a good boy,' Fran sighed.

A memory of Drew's mouth on mine and the hard length of his body pressed against me flooded into my mind. I knew *exactly* how good Drew could be and I wanted that again. A shaft of sunlight fell across my engagement ring as I moved, sending tiny sparkles around the shop.

First, though, I had to break up with Simon.

The day passed surprisingly quickly with a mix of tourists and Marla's regular customers calling in to the shop. Fran and I took turns to go out the back for lunch as the shop never grew quiet enough for either of us to go into town for a sandwich. I called Marla at midday and she informed me that Katya had cleaned the house and was busy cooking her dinner.

The rush finally died away at five as the tourists left to get ready for their evening meals at the local guesthouses and hotels. Fran straightened up the shelves and displays while I reconciled the cash in the till ready for the next day. I was about to ask her to turn the sign on the door to 'closed' when Pieter barged into the shop. His nose looked bruised and sore from where Drew had landed his punch.

'Where is my sister?' He thumped his fist down hard on the counter. His face twisted with anger and he leaned forward till he was only a couple of inches from my face.

'She's not here.' I was surprised that my voice sounded so calm. I'd expected it to come out as a squeak.

'But you know where she has gone. She is not at her rooms.' Little flecks of saliva landed on my face as he spat the words out in a heavy foreign accent.

I wanted to back away but there wasn't much room behind the till. I couldn't see Fran and I wondered if she'd gone to get help, though who she'd find I had no idea, unless she'd slipped out the back to try to find Drew.

'Look, she's not here, now please leave before I call the police.' My voice wavered on the last few words. I didn't have my mobile and the shop phone was out of my reach.

'I do not care for the police. I demand to know where Katya is gone.' He thumped the counter again, making the tape dispenser and a pot of glitter pens next to the till vibrate with the force of his action.

'I can't help you, she isn't here!' My heart raced ten to the dozen at the anger in his eyes. I hoped he wasn't about to hit me.

Without any warning he snatched up one of the snowglobes from the counter and hurled it against the wall, missing my head by inches. It smashed into a million pieces and I flinched as tiny shards of plastic and droplets of water rained out at me.

'Tell me where she is!'

He glared at me and I noticed the red rims round his eyes and the tiny burst blood vessels. His breath stank of cigarettes and stale beer.

Where the hell was Fran?

'She's not here.' I dragged the words out in a kind of whimper.

Outside the shop I heard a warning chirruping sound, like someone cupping their hands around their mouth to imitate a bird call and Pieter leaned back from the counter.

'I come again. Tell Katya I find her.' With that he disappeared through the front door and vanished out on to the street.

I sank down on to the carpet behind the counter, my legs refusing to support me any longer. My whole body felt shaky and I thought I might be sick.

'Azure!' The bell over the shop door chimed and Fran called my name.

'Here.' I couldn't stand up. The carpet was damp with water from the broken snowglobe and bits of plastic were sticking in my legs.

Fran came panting across the shop, accompanied by a large man wearing a bloodstained apron and carrying what appeared to be a sizeable meat cleaver.

'I went for help. This is Morris from the butcher's.' Her round face glowed pink from exertion – she must have run all the way down the street and back again.

'Are you okay, my love?' Morris extended his hand to help me to my feet.

'Just shaky.' I leaned against the counter for support.

'He di'n't hurt you?' Morris enquired in a heavy West Country accent while Fran flapped around and fetched me a glass of water from the back room.

I shook my head. 'No. Really, I'm okay. Thank you for coming.'

The glass chattered against my teeth as I forced myself to take some calming sips.

Fran saw Morris out and bolted the door behind him.

'I was really scared. I didn't know what to do so I went to get Morris,' Fran explained. 'Look at this mess! What happened?'

'He – he threw one of the globes. It just missed me.' I tried not to think of what else he might have done if Morris hadn't made an appearance.

'I'll get a dustpan. It's a good job Morris was still in his shop.' Fran clucked around me, clearing up the mess of broken plastic.

I concentrated on my breathing, trying to calm my racing heartbeat. 'He certainly did the trick. Pieter must have had someone keeping watch outside in the street and when they saw you coming back he left.'

'Ooh, it's made me go all of a doodah. Do you think he'll come back?' She glanced nervously through the window as if expecting Pieter to reappear like a pantomime villain.

'I hope not.' I decided not to tell Fran that he *had* threatened to return. She'd get all worked up and demand armed security every time she sold a wind chime. She'd also stress out Marla. I wasn't sure what I would be able to tell my mother or Katya without frightening them.

A sudden rapping on the glass of the locked front door startled both of us.

'It's Drew.' Fran hurried across to let him in.

My pulse kicked back up a notch as he entered the

shop. From the look on his face he'd heard what had happened. Brixham was a small place and news travelled fast; it would be a matter of seconds for the update to go from the butcher's to the rest of the street.

'Zee, are you all right? What happened?' He folded his arms across his chest and waited for my answer. He didn't look happy.

As soon as I'd finished explaining he let loose a string of expletives that brought the pink back into Fran's cheeks.

'I'll sort this out.' He slammed out of the shop without any further explanation.

Fran's face crumpled and tears slid down her cheeks. 'Oh, Zee, he won't get hurt, will he?'

I gave her a hug. 'I hope not, but I'm sure he knows what he's doing.' At least, I *hoped* he knew what he was doing. Pieter might be younger and scrawnier than Drew but he seemed to have a gang of dodgy blokes around him and if they outnumbered Drew he could really be in trouble. Fran didn't look convinced by my answer.

We closed up the shop and set the alarm.

'I'll walk home with you – it'll be safer that way and I can call in to see Marla,' Fran insisted. I hoped she wouldn't; I wanted to give Marla and Katya the gentler, less scary version of what had happened. Fran special-ised in making dramas out of crises, although, to be fair, it *had* been pretty dramatic.

All the way back to the cottage I felt edgy. I kept hoping Pieter wasn't watching me from somewhere to see where I lived. The last thing I wanted was for him to turn up at the cottage.

Marla and Katya were out in the courtyard. It looked as if Marla had been occupying herself by teaching Katya how to read tarot cards, judging by the number of them that were spread across the table.

Fran immediately launched into a recital of Pieter's visit, while I went and helped myself to a glass of juice from the fridge. When I stepped back outside I could see that Katya had paled and even Marla appeared shaken.

'Let's hope Drew can get things sorted out,' Marla said.

'I am so very sorry. I do not think I should stay here.' Katya rose from her chair as if poised to flee straight away.

'Nonsense,' Marla said firmly. 'Where else could you go? You're safer here than anywhere.'

Fran nodded in agreement. 'Marla's right. Drew will sort things out and you'll be back to normal in no time.'

I wasn't clear why my mother and her friend were so confident about Drew's ability to handle the obnoxious Pieter. I mean, Drew's a pretty tough guy and while I was aware that he could handle himself physically, Pieter was a nasty piece of work.

'Your card reading was good, Katya, positive things are going to happen for you,' Marla added.

I bit back a sigh. Marla does give amazingly accurate forecasts with her tarot readings but you can't plan your life on the turn of a card. We'd been there, done that and worn the T-shirt. My mother had spent most of my child-hood basing our various moves around card readings and messages from the crystals received through meditation. I'm not sure, now I look back, how successful they were. I mean, who can say what would have happened if we'd made different choices, done other things?

Fran nodded again, blinking her agreement through her fringe like a badly groomed Afghan hound.

'Maybe we should go to the police,' I suggested.

Marla gave me a look. She'd never been too fond of the police. Most of her interactions with them had ended with her being evicted from various properties or being arrested for obstructing a police officer.

'No police.' Katya appeared equally perturbed by my suggestion.

'It might land Drew in trouble,' Marla pointed out. I supposed she meant the fight.

I took a sip of my juice. I couldn't think of anything else to suggest. Either Pieter would show up again, spoiling for trouble, or he would do as he'd done before: drop out of sight. He might be looking for Katya but Drew had said there were people who were looking for Pieter, too.

'I'm sure we'll hear from Drew soon,' Marla said as she gathered her cards together and shuffled them. 'Talking of hearing from people, Simon's mother rang this afternoon, she wanted to speak to you.'

'Oh?' The niggly ache I'd woken up with that morning restarted in my left temple.

'I told her you were working at the shop. She didn't sound terribly pleased.' Marla continued to shuffle her cards, her face carefully expressionless.

Katya and Fran exchanged glances. Clearly Marla had given them her opinion of Evelyn on other occasions.

'Well, then, she'll just have to be displeased.' I was beyond caring what my erstwhile mother-in-law-to-be happened to think about anything. No doubt Simon had probably told her what a silly girl I was being.

Fran jumped up from her chair. 'Oh dear, I hadn't noticed the time. I must go, there's a lovely talk tonight at the village hall on identifying garden pests and I really want to go.'

Katya followed her inside to see her off while I sank down on her recently vacated chair.

'Darling Fran,' Marla mused and peeked at me from under her lashes. 'Let me do a reading for you.'

'Marla, you know I don't like all that sort of thing.' I eyed the cards in her hand as she lovingly stroked the worn edges with her thumb. But I couldn't help feeling curious. Everything in my life was topsy-turvy right now; perhaps it wouldn't do any harm. The readings were only for fun, I told myself, and I could use a little fun.

'Cut the cards.' She held them out to me.

I was aware of Katya rejoining us, perching on the worn stone step between the kitchen and the courtyard. The cards were warm in my hand. Marla used an old set of Russian cards, hand painted in blacks and golds. I knew what I had to do – think of the question I wanted answered, concentrate on it, cut the cards, and return them to my mother.

I passed them back.

'The relationship spread?' Her question was

perfunctory as she slipped into her role as seer, concentrating on the task at hand.

She dealt cards from where I'd made the cut into a letter H shape, frowning at them as she did so. Then she read the first card. 'Coins, reversed. You see yourself as jealous and selfish.'

I swallowed. I guess that one could be true.

'Six of cups reversed – how you see your partner. Hmm . . . plans that are failing.' She glanced up at me. 'How you feel about your partner? Knight of coins reversed. Stagnation, inertia, and limits set by dogmatic views.'

I fidgeted uncomfortably on my seat. It seemed this reading was likely to prove a touch too accurate for comfort. Simon was certainly dogmatic.

'What stands between the two of you is the six of clubs: good news and advancement.'

I was surprised it didn't say Simon's latest piece of skirt, but I knew there was more than a hint of truth in the cards. Simon's quest for promotion, more money and a better position had caused a lot of strain on us. His desire for me to look and behave like the perfect corporate wife all linked in with our problems.

'How your partner sees you, page of coins reversed. Rebellious, illogical, wasteful, and failing to see the obvious.'

I bit my lip. I suspected Simon did think exactly that.

'Ace of cups reversed represents what your partner feels about you. Change, erosion, and unrequited love.' Marla frowned. 'The centre card, representing the question or issue you face, is the hierophant reversed. This indicates susceptibility, frailty and renunciation.' She leaned back in her chair.

A silence fell over the courtyard. The cards, it seemed, had spoken. Even they agreed that my relationship with Simon was doomed. Renunciation . . . I wondered who was renouncing whom. Me, for wanting to end my engagement, or Simon, because he couldn't renounce other women?

Jethro squeezed past Katya and padded into the courtyard, pausing to stretch in front of me before jumping up to settle next to Marla.

'Maybe we should all have some supper,' she suggested, reclaiming her precious cards and restoring them to the small handcrafted cedar box in which she kept them.

'I will cook,' Katya announced and scrambled to her feet.

I smiled my thanks at her as she disappeared inside the kitchen.

'Have you spoken to Simon today?' Marla asked. 'I noticed you've received some flowers.'

I glanced over at the vase of beautiful expensive blooms, still stuffed in the shady corner of the courtyard next to the bucket. I hadn't wanted to take them into the cottage, yet I hadn't been able to bring myself to throw them away either. 'No, there isn't much point. I think I need to go and see him, maybe after this weekend, if you feel okay, and Katya's able to go back to work in the shop.' I hated the thought of confronting Simon but it had to be done. I needed to pack up my things and return his ring.

'Of course, I'm sure everything will have settled down by then and I'm feeling better every day.'

I tried to give her a smile.

'You've made a decision then, about you and Simon?' she asked, her eyes filled with concern.

'Yes. It's over. I'm not getting married.'

Even as I said the words a small cloud of unhappiness lifted from my shoulders.

20

Drew didn't ring or visit that evening. I'd really thought he would, if only to tell us whether he'd found Pieter and convinced him to keep away from Katya. Thankfully, Evelyn didn't call again, either. After we'd eaten supper Marla went for a shower and an early night as she had her radio interview the next day. Katya stayed in the courtyard reading a magazine on holistic therapy and painting her toenails purple, and I went to my room.

I thought long and hard before I slipped Simon's ring from my finger and placed it carefully in a dark blue jeweller's box I found in a drawer. I suppose I should have kept it on until I spoke to him face-to-face, but that felt hypocritical. My finger looked strangely naked without my big glittering diamond, but inside I felt much happier, almost relieved that the decision had been made.

The ring had been beautiful but it wasn't a style that I would have chosen for myself. It always seemed too big, too ostentatious – and, like Simon himself, I suppose, intended to impress. It had always got in my way at school when I helped the children with art projects or cookery. Left to myself I would have picked something neater and less showy.

I decided Monday would be a good day to go and see Simon. If Marla stayed well, then I could take the train back to Bristol and pack my belongings. There wasn't much of mine in the flat, anyway; just a few books, my clothes, and that was all, really. Most of my possessions were still here in storage, in Devon. Simon hadn't felt there was much room to take everything when I moved in and, of course, it would have ruined his minimalist décor.

I stowed the ring in the drawer of my bedside locker next to the amethyst crystal that my mother had placed there. Amethyst, the revealer of dreams . . . The truth about my relationship had been in plain sight for a long time but I'd chosen to be blind to it. I wondered how Simon would take the news that our engagement was over. Perhaps he, too, might feel relieved.

The next day dawned with ominous dark grey skies and the distant growl of thunder. I left Katya blow-drying Marla's long dark hair with the diffuser ready for the arrival of the interviewers from the radio station and the press photographers. Marla promised to call me if Pieter showed up. She also said she wouldn't overdo things with the press, but I'm sure she had her fingers crossed behind her back when she made that 'promise'.

The wind picked up as I hurried down Broad Steps towards the town, making me glad that I'd pulled on trousers and a top instead of a sundress. I couldn't help looking about me as I walked, wondering if Pieter or his cronies were about to pop out and harass me to try and find out Katya's whereabouts.

Morris gave a friendly wave from behind his counter as I walked past his shop. Fran was already waiting for me outside the Crystal Palace. I glanced up at Drew's window, but there was no sign of movement. Thunder rumbled again and a few large splashes of rain fell like wet pennies on to the pavement as I unlocked the door and deactivated the alarm.

'I reckon we're in for a good old storm today,' Fran observed as she headed for the back room to deposit her bag.

As she spoke, lightning illuminated the shop and a large crack of thunder sounded overhead.

'That sounded close.' I switched on the shop lights and hoped Drew wasn't out on the water with the boat school. I knew that once outside the harbour walls the waves would quickly grow choppy in a storm.

Outside, the rain started in earnest, drumming down on the pavements with a force that made the droplets bounce back up again as soon as they landed. The few people who'd been out and about rapidly dispersed and overhead the thunder rolled around the bay, growling and snapping like a wounded dog. The boatmen by the harbour wouldn't sell many trips today, that was for sure.

I checked the float in the till while Fran vacuumed the shop floor. The storm continued to rage overhead and I wondered how many customers we were likely to get if the rain continued.

'It's like the middle of the night out there.' Fran switched off the vacuum and peered out at the rain that streamed down the large pane of glass in the window.

I joined her next to the display of carved jade elephants and we watched the trickle of water in the gutters grow and run like a small river as the drains struggled to absorb the volume of rainwater. Lightning flashed briefly, illuminating the street, and all the lights in the shop went out as thunder cracked like a cannon hard on its heels.

Immediately, several of the shop alarms higher up the street began to wail.

'Darn, the power's gone down.' Fran squinted out of the rain-spattered window trying to see which shops were affected.

'I think our morning cup of tea is out of the question for a while.' I tried to make a joke of it, but standing in the dark and empty shop with the deepening gloom outside felt eerie, to say the least.

'Good job we've no customers; the till won't work without power.' Fran wound the cable back around the vacuum and prepared to push it back into the store cupboard.

I wrapped my lightweight cotton cardigan a bit more firmly around me and shivered. 'Do you think it'll be long before it's back up and running?' I followed her to the back of the shop.

'Hard to say, but it usually comes back quickly.' Fran had her head in the cupboard, so her answer sounded muffled.

A sharp knock on the shop door made me jump; it was loud even above the drumming of the pouring rain and the growling storm. A familiar figure stood outside, trying to shelter under the meagre ledge while he waited for someone to unlock the door for him.

'Drew.' I hurried to unfasten the latch.

He slipped inside the shop and stood dripping on the mat. His hair, darkened by the rain, was plastered to his head and his shirt and jeans clung damply to his body. He shook his head, sending tiny drops of water splashing outward before wiping his hands across his face. 'It's a bit damp out there.' He grinned at our shocked expressions.

'Oh dear, I'll get you a towel,' Fran said. She trotted off to rummage in the cupboard in the back room.

'Where have you been?' My body had inexplicably heated the moment I'd seen him peer in through the wet glass.

He took the small red-and-white-checked hand towel Fran had retrieved from the kitchen and rubbed at his hair. 'The boat school. We managed to get the kids back on land before the storm kicked off – luckily we were only in the harbour this morning; it was too dangerous to risk the open water.'

'I thought you might have called round last night, to say what had happened with Pieter.' I kept my arms folded and tried to ignore the lick of desire in my stomach as he peeled off his sopping wet shirt and rough-dried his torso.

His hands stilled briefly before he continued to dry himself. 'I tracked him down in Torquay. At the moment you can rest easy, since he's managed to get himself arrested.'

'Arrested?' Fran and I chorused in unison.

'Yep. Custody's probably the safest and best place for him to be right now. He's got some seriously disgruntled people on his tail.'

The shop lights flickered and pinged back to life.

'Oh, lovely! I'll put the kettle on; you could use a cuppa to warm you up, Drew,' Fran called over her shoulder as she disappeared into the kitchen area.

I shifted uneasily from foot to foot and tried to ignore the tantalising trickle of water that had crept from his damp hair and started to run down the muscular wall of his chest. 'How do you know all this?'

Drew lifted his head and his eyes met mine in a level gaze. 'You don't want to know.'

My lips dried and my pulse hammered in my throat as I considered the implications behind his words. 'Drew, you aren't mixed up in anything . . . well . . . shady, are you?'

When we'd been together he'd always sailed close to the wind and I suspected that he'd had adventures while he'd been travelling that I'd prefer not to know about. He shared my mother's unfavourably jaundiced opinion of the law.

His broad smile lit up his face, making his eyes spark with mischief. 'Nothing you need to worry about.'

I relaxed my arms and smoothed imaginary lint from the front of my cargo pants.

'You're not wearing your ring.' Drew's hand reached out to clasp my wrist, holding my hand still as he studied my bare fingers.

I snatched my hand free, thrusting it into my pocket. 'No.'

He raised an eyebrow, I assume at the abruptness of my movement and my reply, but he didn't ask anything else.

'Tea's up,' Fran carolled as she carried a small tray with three mugs on it in from the kitchen.

'Thanks, Fran.' I took a mug from the tray, glad of the diversion. Neither Marla nor Katya had commented on my naked finger when I'd left the house, although I knew from Marla's face that she'd noticed it was missing.

Fran slid the tray on to the counter and picked up Drew's wet shirt from the floor. She clicked her tongue in disapproval. 'I'll put this in the sink till you go upstairs. Honestly, you treat this place just like a hotel.'

'Cheers, Fran.' He draped the towel round his neck and claimed a mug. 'How's Katya taking all this?'

'It's hard to say. She's been very quiet.' She'd probably opened up far more to Marla than she ever would to me. I'd been feeling a lot more kindly towards her since I'd seen her brother in action. I couldn't imagine how awful and alone she must feel in a strange country with no friends and with her only relative prepared to betray her for money.

'I'm glad she's got you and Marla.' Drew took a sip of his tea.

A small glow warmed me deep inside because he thought I'd been helpful towards Katya. The way things had been going lately I felt as if I'd been more of a liability than a help to anyone.

'Looks as if the storm's passing.' He nodded towards the window and I realised the rain had slowed. The sound of the thunder seemed more distant and it looked like it had grown brighter outside.

'We might even get some customers.' I sensed the tension building up between us again. It wasn't there in anything we said or did, it was simply there: an unspoken animal attraction.

'I'd better go and change. Could you open the internal door to save me going back outside?' He finished his tea and stood the mug back on the tray.

'Sure.' I walked through the back room with Drew following behind me.

Fran passed him a carrier containing his wet shirt before heading back into the shop ready to open up.

'Thanks for the tea, Fran,' he called.

She raised her hand in acknowledgement as the door closed behind her, leaving Drew and me together in the small space leading to the stairs up to his flat.

My hands shook as I selected the key to unlock the internal door. The combination of the confined space and a semi-naked Drew was having a strange effect on me. Unsurprisingly, I dropped the keys. We both dived at the same time to rescue them from the tiled floor.

Our hands met as we reached for the keys together, and my heart skipped at the contact.

'Sorry, I'm such a klutz, the thunder and lightning's made me jumpy.' I tried to stop myself gabbling.

Drew took the keys from my hand, selected the right one and slotted it into the lock.

'So, you and Simon . . . is it over?' He kept his hand on the keys, preventing me from snatching them back and escaping.

Heat seemed to radiate from his bare chest across the small space between us. 'I think so.' It was all I could do to force the words out through lips that had suddenly become dry.

'I thought you had the church booked, the whole nine yards?' His voice was gentle.

'We do – we did. I don't want to talk about it. I haven't even had a chance to speak to Simon yet.' My face heated.

Drew frowned. 'You mean you've dumped him and he doesn't know?'

'No. It's not like that. Look, it's complicated. I'm going back after the weekend to collect my things and to talk to him.' Without thinking, I placed my hand on top of Drew's in a feeble attempt to get to the keys.

My skin tingled as it made contact with his; I almost expected him to move away, convinced he must feel it too.

'Zee, this isn't anything to do with you and me, is it? The other night?' he asked.

I shook my head, unable to make the break from that

tantalising electric connection between us. 'No, this is to do with me and Simon. There were things going on before I came back here.'

His fingers moved beneath mine, sliding from the keys to hold my hand in his.

'So, you're a free agent again?' He caught hold of my other hand stroking my finger where my ring had been.

I nodded. There was no way I could lift my head to look him in the face, because I was too afraid of what my eyes might reveal.

In that split second, with his hand on mine, the truth hit me. I was still in love with Drew.

21

'Azure, phone!' Fran called from the counter in the front of the shop.

Drew released my hand and I stepped back, too shocked by the realisation that all my old feelings for him were still there under the surface to say anything.

His lips brushed mine and I tasted him briefly against my mouth: warm, male and pure Drew.

'See you later.' He slipped away through the door leading up to his flat.

'Azure!' Fran called again, jolting me out of my daze.

I hurried back through to the shop floor.

'It's someone called Evelyn.' Fran passed me the phone making an 'I don't know who this is, but I don't like her' face as she did so.

'Azure, I've been calling and calling to try to speak to you. I did leave a message with your mother but I know she's not terribly reliable.' Evelyn launched into her speech as soon as I'd muttered a brief and wary 'hello'. I rolled my eyes at Fran, who grinned sympathetically at me in reply. Knowing my soon-to-be-ex-mother-in-law-to-be, I guessed she'd probably been ordering Fran about in her mission to get hold of me.

'Now, I have no idea what's going on between the two of you, but poor Simon is so upset.'

'Evelyn . . .' I tried to squeeze a word in as I had absolutely no wish to listen to her views on 'poor Simon'.

'He seems to think you've got some silly notion in your head that he's been seeing some other girl,' she ploughed on, completely ignoring me.

Tension tightened along my jaw and my teeth started to hurt where I had them clenched together.

'I do hope you're not going to let some trivial misunderstanding spoil everything. Simon is so distraught, he's hardly eating. I said to Jonty, that with all the trouble I'd been to in making sure you could have the church instead of Velma Martin's Dale, there must be some mistake.'

'Evelyn!' I shouted down the phone, finally succeeding in getting her to shut up. 'Any problems that are going on are solely between me and Simon.' After this, there was a pause that lasted all of a microsecond.

'Men will be men you know, Azure; they often have little foibles.' Her coy tone implied that they were an alien species to be excused from shagging everything in sight because they couldn't help it. 'Normally, I wouldn't dream of interfering, but he's *so* unhappy and if the vicar hears any rumblings then, as I said to Jonty, you'll lose the date at the church.'

Well, tough cookies – I couldn't believe she still thought I was going to marry Simon. 'Then he should have thought of that before he jumped into bed with his latest tramp. I happen to think that the inability to stay faithful is hardly a little foible and you can tell the vicar and Velma Martin that the wedding is most definitely off.'

I banged the handset back down on the phone, cutting off Evelyn's shocked gasp at my outrageous rudeness. My hands were shaking and I felt sick with nerves. I couldn't believe I'd actually spoken to Simon's mother like that.

Fran stared at me, her mouth hanging open in surprise. Before either of us could speak, the phone rang again. I couldn't pick up the receiver; my legs were barely strong enough to support me after my conversation with Evelyn.

Fran snatched up the phone and I prayed it wasn't Simon's mother calling back for round two. 'Hello? Oh, hi! Okay. Mmm-hmm . . . Yes, I'll tell her.' Fran hung up. 'It's okay, you can relax, that was Marla. She said to tell you that Chris is coming for dinner tonight.'

I nodded in acknowledgement and leaned against the counter for some support.

'Thunderstorms do strange things. It's all those ions being released back into the atmosphere,' Fran said, by way of an explanation for the last ten minutes.

Ions, right . . . that must be what it was. Nothing else could explain the way my emotions were bouncing around all over the place.

'Shall I make you another drink? You look dreadful, Azure.' Fran peered through her fringe at me, concern showing in her pale blue eyes.

'No, really, I'm fine. Evelyn managed to rub me up the wrong way, that's all.'

Fran gave a cluck of disapproval with her tongue. 'I shouldn't think there are many people she doesn't annoy. Ringing here and ordering me about like *her* off that telly programme, you know. What's her name? *Mrs Bucket!* Proper brass neck she's got, if you ask me.'

Her obvious indignation made me smile. 'I know, but I still shouldn't have spoken to her like that. It isn't her fault that Simon is, well . . . how he is.' I didn't want to elaborate on his unfaithfulness, but I was sure Fran had probably guessed the source of the problems between us from what I'd said to Evelyn.

Fran looked at me for a moment as if she was about to say something. Instead, however, she clamped her lips firmly together and turned away to rearrange the displays of carved elephants.

The day dragged. Intermittent showers and the continuing growls of thunder meant that the town was quiet. I took the opportunity to get a new mobile phone from the shop further up the street and spent the afternoon trying out the new games and testing the ringtones.

Although playing mindless games on my phone had distracted me from thinking about Evelyn and Simon for the afternoon, it hadn't stopped me fretting about Drew. Plus, as if I hadn't got enough to worry about, there was still dinner with my errant father to get through, and Katya lodging in our front room.

We shut up early, and after I'd deposited the takings

at the bank I stocked up on some groceries for Marla. The mist had closed in again while I'd been loading up my basket with eggs and teabags. I slogged back up the hill to the cottage with the damp air clinging to my skin and the smell of wet earth in my nostrils.

Katya was in the kitchen stirring a big pot of something on top of the cooker. The air was redolent with the scent of tomato and basil.

'Where's Marla?' I hoped my mother hadn't tired herself out by talking to the press and doing her radio interview.

'Upstairs; she is resting in her room.' Katya continued to stir the contents of the pan.

'I got some groceries.' I dumped the bags down on the counter and started to pack the contents away in the cupboards and the fridge. 'Was Marla okay with the interviews? She hasn't worn herself out?'

Katya raised the spoon to her lips to taste her cooking. Apparently satisfied, she dropped the spoon in the sink and placed a lid on the pan. 'She is fine. I take good care of her, so now she is resting.'

'Thanks.' I closed the fridge door and folded the empty carrier bags so they could be reused.

'She is excited about tonight. I cook for you all to thank Marla for letting me stay here.' Katya turned the heat off under the saucepan.

'That's kind of you.' Whatever was in the pan smelled quite nice and I'd been wondering with some weariness if I would have to cook that evening. I didn't know what kind of food Chris liked or anything. Actually, I told myself I didn't care what Chris liked – he was a stranger to me, even if he was my dad.

'I leave this now. There is rice to go with it and I have put cake in the fridge. I am going back to my rooms tonight, now Pieter is not going to cause me a problem. If he is locked up, then I can go home,' Katya announced.

'Are you sure that's what you want to do?' I could see why she couldn't sleep on our sofa indefinitely, but I didn't want her to feel pushed out.

'It is for the best. Tonight Marla and Chris will have a nice meal with you and Drew. I will be at the shop tomorrow to work with Fran.' Katya picked up her bag and walked towards the hall.

'Drew's coming to dinner too?' I detected the heavy hand of my mother playing Cupid.

Katya nodded. 'Marla wanted him to meet your father.'

'But aren't you going to stay? I mean, you've cooked the meal . . .' Panic started to rise inside me like a tide. It was bad enough that I was being pushed into spending time with my father but if Drew was thrown into the mix as well, then I wasn't sure how I would cope. It was typical of Marla to drag Drew into this, the only surprise was that she hadn't asked Fran along too.

Katya shook her head, her face solemn. 'No, I have much to sort out. I will see you tomorrow.'

She turned and let herself out of the house, leaving me to contemplate a cosy evening *en famille*. Well . . . family plus Drew.

Marla was asleep on her bed when I popped my head in to see how she was. I left her to continue her nap and went to my room. The mist outside the window made everything dark and gloomy so I switched on my bedside lamp to dispel the shadows. I picked up my brush to tackle the frizzy mess that the weather had made of my hair.

In the mirror I still looked the same as the girl who'd arrived only a few short days ago. The one who'd been merrily planning her wedding, ignoring all the signs that her relationship was built on foundations that were about as stable as the sand in Brixham harbour. That girl hadn't thought about her father in years, having written him off in her teens as a kind of urban myth. She also hadn't thought much about Drew.

I replaced my brush on top of the dresser and stared at my reflection. I didn't want to be in love with Drew. He was still as sexy and gorgeous as the last time I'd been head over heels in love with him, but all the reasons why we hadn't worked out as a couple before were still there today.

I picked up a tube of hand cream and squirted a blob into my palm. I worked the cream into my skin and along my fingers, massaging the lotion into the narrow, slim band of dry skin at the base of my ring finger where my engagement diamond had so recently sat. Drew didn't do commitment, he didn't do settling down or for ever . . . and I was a for ever kind of girl. I'd seen enough of what happened when you gave your love life up to fate and allowed things to drift on a hope and a dream.

There was a tap at my door and Marla entered, leaning against the frame. 'Chris is coming to dinner tonight,' she said quietly.

I forced a smile. 'Yes, Fran told me.'

She wandered into my room and started to examine the contents of the top of my dressing-table, picking things up and putting them down in slightly different spots. 'I asked Drew to come too. I thought it would be easier for you if there was a fourth person there.'

'Marla, please don't try and matchmake me and Drew.'

She put down my bottle of Curious and frowned at me. 'Darling, as if I would do anything of the kind. What will be will be between you and Drew.' She gave a tiny shrug of her shoulders. 'It's fate; you can't change it.'

I bit back the sigh that threatened to escape. 'Yes, but you don't have to try and help it along. I'm just ending my engagement to a man I thought I loved. I don't want any extra complications.'

Marla drifted across the room to perch on the bed next to me. 'Oh, Azure, darling, I am truly sorry that you and Simon didn't work out. You know I didn't like him but if he was what you wanted, then I would have been happy for you – eventually.' She patted my hand.

'Evelyn called the shop today. We had a big row and I told her about Simon cheating on me. It wasn't the first time.' Saying the words out loud didn't make me feel any better. Misery still stabbed me deep inside and I worried that Simon might have been right when he'd used me as an excuse for his previous cheating. Perhaps his inability to be faithful was my fault – perhaps it was because I wasn't thinner, prettier, better in bed.

Marla took my hands between hers. 'I don't suppose it came as that big a surprise to her. I think she knows full well what her precious son is really like.'

'You never liked Simon.' It was a statement, not a recrimination.

She sighed. 'His aura was all wrong and whenever I did readings to forecast the future for you it didn't come out well.'

'I'm going to see him on Monday. I need to collect my things and give him his ring back.' Her skin felt warm against mine and I grew calmer and stronger just from her being there with me.

'I wish I could come with you but Tina is coming to change my dressing, and before you say anything, it's fine. I don't need you to be here, it's just a quick check.'

'Okay, if you're sure. I'll be fine. I need to do this on my own. I'll catch the train and be back by the evening.'

She lifted her hand and smoothed my hair back from my face, the way she used to when I was small. 'It's for the best, darling. Better to find out now that you've made a mistake than to marry the wrong man and *then* figure it out.'

'And what if you're in love with the wrong man? What then?' I knew my question sounded bitter. It wasn't even something I'd intended to say. It had simply slipped out of my mouth.

Marla's deep blue eyes locked on to mine. 'I take it that by the wrong man, you mean Drew and not Simon?

What is meant, is meant. You'll see, everything will turn out as it should.' She smiled and stood. 'Now, we'd better get ready, the men will be here soon.'

She drifted out of my room, her bracelets tinkling as she walked. I sat for a moment and stared into my dresser mirror, summoning up the courage I needed to do what I knew had to be done.

Before I could change my mind, I took out my new phone and texted Simon.

Back Mon, C U at flat lunchtime. Z.

I turned my phone off as soon as I'd hit send so he couldn't try to call me back. Not that I thought he would anyway. No doubt Evelyn would have kept him fully informed as to my response to her call.

It was done. From Monday I would officially be a free agent again.

It was strange . . . I thought I'd feel heartbroken, but apart from being angry with myself for having been such an idiot, and embarrassed that everyone else seemed to have known that Simon was the wrong man for me, I mainly felt relief.

I heard Drew's motorbike rumble to a halt outside the cottage just as I was changing my earrings. Marla was already downstairs talking to Chris, who'd arrived a few minutes ago. I did a quick last-minute check in the mirror and made my way downstairs to open the front door. Marla was too engrossed with Chris to have ventured back down the hallway to let Drew in.

I'd struggled over what to wear. Part of me wanted to look sexy and desirable for Drew, while the other, more sensible part of me told me this was a bad idea. I'd compromised on my favourite blue spaghetti-strap dress that always appeared to do miraculous things for my bust, and covered up a bit with a fine, lacy-knit cardigan.

Drew tucked his bike on the inside of the double yellow lines that were intended to stop people from parking in the street outside the cottages. My excitement zipped up a level as he tugged off his helmet and flashed me his familiar lazy smile.

The cool misty air raised gooseflesh on my skin and I wrapped the front of my cardigan tighter round me.

'Hey.' He opened the pannier on the back of the bike

and retrieved a bunch of freesias, my mother's favourite flowers, along with a bottle of white wine.

'Hey, yourself.'

He walked the few short steps towards me and my heart started to race the way it always had when we were teenagers. Without Simon's great sparkly rock on my engagement finger I felt strangely vulnerable – and free.

'Has your dad arrived?' Drew halted in the doorway right in front of me, his voice low so his words wouldn't carry inside the house.

I nodded. 'He's in the kitchen with Marla. I haven't been in there yet.'

Drew's expression was sombre, 'Are you okay with this, Zee?'

'I have to be. Marla is so happy since he got back in touch; she's been like a little kid again. He's what she needs right now. Next week she has to go back to see the specialist and I don't know what they'll say to her. She's making all these plans but . . .' My voice trailed off.

I had to stay positive. When she'd left the hospital, they'd said that they thought things looked good, but this next appointment would give us the true picture. The lab tests would be back and we'd know what the next steps would be in Marla's treatment plan. If seeing my father again helped get her through her illness, then I would need to be supportive, no matter how I really felt.

Drew's eyes darkened. 'You know I'm here for you, Zee.'

'Thanks. We'd better get inside, get this show on the

road.' I stepped aside to let him in. I needed to put some physical space between us. Somehow one meaningful look from Drew made my insides go to mush: not a great thing when I was going to have to sit next to him all evening.

Marla opened the door from the kitchen into the hallway. 'There you both are, come through and get a drink.'

We dutifully filed into the small kitchen. Chris was already seated at the breakfast bar which had been laid up with cutlery, mats and glassware. My heart thumped in my chest like a hammer, I felt so nervous. I'd tried to tell myself that it didn't matter if I didn't like Chris or if he didn't like me, but somehow it *did* matter. Our first meeting hadn't been a howling success exactly, so this one needed to go more smoothly if we were ever to build any kind of father–daughter relationship.

Drew presented my mother with the flowers while I stashed the wine in the fridge.

'Well, isn't this cosy?' Marla handed me the flowers to put into a vase while she busied herself with making sure we all had a drink. Drew took a seat opposite Chris, and Marla made the introductions. Much to my relief, she passed Drew off to Chris as being the tenant of her flat and an old friend.

I went to the hob and put the saucepan of rice on to cook as Katya had instructed.

'Cheers, everybody. Here's to new beginnings and old friends.' Marla chinked her glass against Chris's and Drew's. I picked up mine and joined in, taking a large slurp of the red wine it contained before putting it back down again.

I'd noticed a tray of cheese and olives ready in the fridge, which Katya must have prepared as nibbles, so I took them out and placed them on the table. It suited me to keep busy while the other three made small-talk about the change in the weather and how delicious the olives were.

Chris and Marla were soon deep in reminiscences about the old days, discussing mutual friends and long-forgotten causes.

'Do you need a hand with the food?' Drew's voice rumbled low in my ear.

He'd left his seat at the table to join me by the window, where I stood staring out at the mist swirling lazily around the pots of summer bedding plants.

'No, it's all under control. Katya left instructions.' I glanced over to see Chris bend his head close to Marla's and whisper something in her ear that made her laugh.

'I think we're the gooseberries tonight,' Drew murmured, following my gaze.

'Looks like it.' I chugged back some more wine, every cell in my body aware of Drew's proximity to me.

'He seems an okay kind of bloke.' Drew took a considered sip from his own glass.

I shrugged. Maybe he was, maybe he wasn't.

Marla laughed out loud again and Chris joined in. The two of them were clearly lost in their shared past.

Katya's food proved to be very tasty, and with the help of several glasses of wine I managed to get through the meal – the lemon drizzle cake with clotted cream that we had for pudding helped soak up some of the alcohol. Drew and I stayed in the kitchen to make coffee while Marla and Chris went on into the lounge.

He sat at the breakfast bar, watching me as I spilled coffee granules all over the work surface. 'How much wine have you had?' He stood and took the spoon from my hand. 'Here.' He pushed a mug in front of me.

I watched the steam curl over the brim of the mug while he carried Marla's camomile tea and a coffee for Chris into the front room. The wine I'd consumed with dinner had softened my world nicely and I felt comfortably warm and sleepy as I perched on a kitchen stool and inhaled the aroma of decaffeinated Fairtrade Arabica beans.

Drew strolled back into the room. 'Do you want to go and join the lovebirds, or are you all socialised out for tonight?' He sipped his coffee, oblivious of the scalding heat of the liquid.

I shrugged. 'I don't know. Do you think I'll be missed?' All through dinner, Marla had been talking about going to the Eden Project and the Flying Monkeys concert. She'd shared her list with Chris, who appeared to think her plans were perfectly sensible. He'd even encouraged her, telling her tales about his travels in Africa. I'd plunged further into the Merlot with every statement.

It hadn't helped that, the whole time, I'd been acutely aware of Drew sitting opposite me, his green eyes shrewd and watchful of my every move.

'Marla's happy to have him back in her life,' he said.

I shrugged again. 'She never stopped loving him.' Tiredness weighed heavy on my eyelids. I wasn't sure how you could still have feelings for someone who'd left you high and dry for almost thirty years, especially when you'd had a child together. As the child concerned, I wasn't ready to be so forgiving.

'It's not like you to drink so much,' Drew persisted. He continued to watch me, his feet planted slightly apart, one hand resting in the front pocket of his jeans, the other hand cradling one of Marla's dark blue ceramic mugs.

I took a sip of my coffee; it slipped down my throat, dark and slightly bitter. 'Yeah, well . . . maybe I'm not myself right now. I seem to be doing all kinds of things that are out of character.'

Drew frowned. 'Does this mean you regret breaking your engagement to Simon?'

I let slip a hard little laugh. 'No, I feel stupid that I let it get as far as planning the wedding, but that's all. I guess I was in love with a dream.'

'Maybe you're not acting so weird after all. It was always about the wedding when we were together.'

His words cut through the muzziness in my brain. 'Is that what you thought when we were dating?'

He rested his mug down on the counter. 'Wasn't it the truth?' His eyes met mine, throwing out a challenge.

Okay, so back then I'd thought our relationship was special and that we had a future together. Why not? I'd been in love – wasn't that what people in love did? 'I thought we had something special. I thought we had a future together,' I said quietly.

'I asked you to come with me.'

His expression was blank. I couldn't read his emotions or decipher what was going on inside his head.

'Only because you knew I couldn't come. I had college to finish. I needed to get a job.' My hands were shaking and I risked spilling my drink, so I placed my mug carefully down on the counter.

'I offered to wait for you.'

My palms felt sweaty and I wiped them on my dress. I remembered that afternoon so clearly. Or did I? I didn't remember him offering to wait for me. All I recalled was him leaving.

'You left me. Three crappy postcards, that was all you sent. You never came back.' My heart twisted as I remembered all the times I'd waited for the post to arrive, eagerly scanning the mail for a card or a letter. The way I'd pored over the scant few words on each of those three postcards as if there was some clue as to when he planned to return.

Drew folded his arms across his chest. 'You'd made it pretty clear what you thought about my plans to travel before I went.'

I slipped off my stool and went to walk past him into the hall. My legs had grown strangely spongy and disconnected from my body. Maybe drinking the best part of a bottle of red wine hadn't been such a great idea after all.

'This is crazy. Why are we going over this again?' I wobbled on my heels.

Drew's hands reached out and grasped my arms, holding me steady. 'Maybe because we never finished it.'

Heat burned from his fingers into the skin of my arms through my lacy cardigan. Time seemed to pause and then he kissed me – or I kissed him, I'm not certain who started it. All I knew was that his mouth was on mine, tasting me, demanding, in a way that made desire coil in my stomach.

My arms seemed to move of their own accord, pulling him closer to me so my breasts were pressed hard against his chest. For a moment I forgot everything. I forgot Simon, my mother, that Drew and I had been fighting . . . everything was swept away by the strength of my feelings for the man in my arms.

His hands slid under the hem of my dress to cup my buttocks firmly in his grasp, manoeuvring me backwards so I was against the closed door leading into the hallway. A shiver of excitement thrilled its way along my spine as his hands slipped under the thin silky barrier of my knickers and made contact with my bare flesh. His lips moved from my mouth to blaze a trail along my neck towards my breast and it was all I could do not to cry out at his touch.

Instead, I buried my face in his shoulder while I tugged his shirt free so I could touch his body. I felt him shudder as my fingers stroked his back. He pressed against me, the hard bulge in his jeans telling me he wanted me as much as I wanted him.

'Zee . . .' His voice sounded low and ragged in my ear as I explored the skin below the waistband of his jeans.

'I want you,' I whispered and nibbled on his earlobe.

As soon as I spoke his hands stilled. 'This has to stop.' He straightened my dress and lifted his head to look into my eyes.

Embarrassment flooded through me, heating my body. I smoothed my hair and looked away. 'Guess that wine is headier than I thought.' I tried to make a joke, even though my body was still pumping out enough 'fuck me' hormones to fill a swimming pool. From the look on his face I knew that he wasn't buying my excuse of having drunk too much wine, not even for a second. My fingers trembled as I straightened the straps on my dress where they'd slipped down my arms exposing my cleavage.

'I think I'd better go.'

I stood aside and opened the door. Suddenly I felt stone-cold sober. What the hell had I been thinking?

'I'll say goodnight to Marla and Chris.' He gave me one last look and walked away, leaving me with only my humiliation for company.

I sent Simon a text once I was on board the train and on my way back to the flat. I had asked him to meet me there at lunchtime.

Drew had kept out of my way ever since he'd interrupted our kiss and walked out of the cottage. All weekend, I'd moped about, listening to mournful music on my iPod while Marla kept trying to analyse my aura. She was full of the joys of spring now that Chris was back on the scene. Even worse was her enthusiasm for the Flying Monkeys concert. She'd arranged to borrow a tent from Fran, dug out her old sleeping bags and bought a mini camping stove. We had an appointment with her consultant for the following day and I intended to raise the issue of Marla's plan to sleep under canvas.

The box containing my engagement ring formed a hard lump in the pocket of my cotton trousers. I kept fingering the rounded velveteen corners as if to reassure myself that I was finally doing the right thing. There wasn't much that belonged to me in the flat and I planned to pack it all in a suitcase and lug it back to Devon. At some point I would need to look for a room or a flat near to the school once the holidays had finished. That was something I'd have to face once I was confident that Marla would be okay.

The flat was empty when I let myself in, although I'd half expected to find Simon waiting for me. It didn't look any different from the day I'd left. I don't know why I'd thought it would. Everything was neat and orderly; Simon's PlayStation and Xbox were placed next to the big-screen TV alongside some new games. Three letters addressed to me were on the kitchen counter in the place where he liked the post to be stacked. They were all bits of junk mail.

I don't know what I had expected to see in the bedroom – some physical evidence of his unfaithfulness, perhaps. The bed was neatly made and no betraying scent of alien perfume tainted the air. I pulled my case from the storage cupboard in the hall and carried it through to the bedroom, ready to pack. Simon usually took his lunch between one and two, so I figured I had an hour and a half to get all my things together.

My clothes and shoes filled the case, while my few books and work things went into the backpack that I kept my marking and school project-work in. There wasn't anything else. My books, DVDs and music were all in the loft back at Marla's where I'd stored them when I first went to live with Simon. I'd intended storing my things to be a temporary arrangement because, of course, we were going to get married, buy a house and do all the grown-up stuff I'd always wanted to do.

Instead, I was almost thirty, single, and moving back

in with my mother. Thinking of my life in those terms felt infinitely depressing and I sat down on the end of the bed with a sigh. It was almost lunchtime, Simon should be back soon. I mentally ran through the speech I'd prepared. All the way up on the train I'd been rehearsing what I needed to say.

I was too restless to remain in the bedroom so I lugged my case into the hall and placed it next to my backpack. The taxi was booked to collect me at two o'clock; I hoped they'd send someone with muscles. As I looked around the flat, so sterile and empty, I supposed it kind of said everything about me and Simon, about our relationship.

I wandered into the kitchen, although I felt too nauseous to eat or drink anything. Not that there was anything to eat anyway. The fridge was bare and a pile of takeaway food cartons lay congealing in the bin. I checked my watch again: almost one-thirty and still no sign of Simon.

The midday sun beat against the glass and the air in the flat grew stuffy and oppressive. I wondered if he was making me wait on purpose, because for once I had been the one who had called the shots and made the arrangements. If he was running late, he could have called me. I toyed with the idea of texting him to see where he was but I desperately wanted it over with.

My legs ached from pacing up and down but I couldn't bring myself to sit down. Time ticked slowly by until it got to five minutes to two. I realised then that he wasn't coming. Anger burned in my stomach like acid as the taxi pulled up in front of the building and honked its horn. I placed the ring box on the kitchen counter. All I could find to write on was the back of one of the junk-mail envelopes. So much for my carefully rehearsed speech. Instead, I dug a pen out of my handbag and wrote: *Goodbye, Simon. I'm sorry it had to end like this. Azure.*

I left it propped up where he could see it and followed the taxi driver down the stairs with my luggage. It was over.

Marla was in the courtyard with Fran and Katya when I finally arrived back at the cottage. They were sitting around the small table with wine glasses in front of them, juice in Katya's case, and nibbling on cheese and biscuits. I abandoned my case and backpack in the lounge and got a cold drink from the fridge. The buzz of conversation ceased when I stepped through the back door and out into the yard.

'Azure, darling, how did it go?' Marla raised her hand to shade her eyes from the afternoon sunshine and squinted at me.

'Simon didn't show up. I packed my stuff and left him the ring with a note.' I gave a little shrug to show I didn't care. I'd done my crying on the train on the way back, hiding in a corner of the carriage behind a copy of the *Guardian*.

'Oh, you poor darling. Come and sit down.' Marla patted a cushion that was balanced on the low stone wall of the raised herb bed. Clearly, a fourth person had been sitting there recently and I wondered who it had been.

'We were just discussing what to do about Katya,' Fran said.

I looked at Katya for an explanation.

'Pieter is out on bail,' she said. 'Already he has been seen in the town.' She stared glumly at her feet.

'I say she should see a solicitor and get an injunction.' Fran picked up her glass and took a slurp of wine. She'd slurred the word 'injunction' slightly and I wondered how much she'd had to drink.

'It would keep him away from you, I suppose,' Marla agreed.

'He has made threats to me and also to Drew.' Katya sighed and crunched on a celery stick from the small dish in the centre of the table.

'I'll meet you each day so we can walk to work and back together,' Fran offered, waving her glass around in enthusiasm. 'Drew can take care of himself. He certainly doesn't seem worried about it and you can get an injunc— injuri— What I said before.' She gave a small hiccup and finished the rest of her drink.

'That sounds like a good idea. I'm sure he's bluffing. If he violates his bail then he'll be whisked back inside.' Marla gave Katya a reassuring smile.

I took a sip of my orange juice and helped myself to a cracker and some cheese. There didn't seem much point in getting involved in the discussion, since they appeared to have agreed on a plan of action already. I hoped Drew would be okay if Pieter started any trouble. He'd always been pretty good at taking care of himself –

the fight down by the harbour proved it – but even so, it was still worrying.

'We should go now, and let you rest. Tomorrow is your appointment, yes?' Katya looked at my mother.

'Yes, tomorrow morning. I'll be glad when I get the all-clear so I can focus on my plans.' She gave a small grimace and I wondered if she was more concerned about seeing the consultant than she'd been letting on.

'Then we go.' Katya stood and extended her hand to Fran to help her up from her seat.

Fran blinked in surprise and put down her empty glass before accepting Katya's assistance. 'Call us as soon as you get home from the hospital,' she told Marla. She swayed slightly on her heels and Katya took hold of her arm.

'I will,' Marla promised.

They collected their bags and clattered off down the hallway.

I waited until I heard the front door close behind them. 'You look shattered,' I said. The lines at the corners of her eyes had deepened and smudges of fatigue showed dark against the olive tan of her skin.

'Pish, I'm fine. I'm more concerned about you. Did Simon really not bother to meet you?' Her forehead creased with concern.

'No, I waited but he didn't come. I thought about calling or texting him but it seemed a bit pointless. Like poking the ashes of a dead fire.'

'I'm so sorry.' She gave a sigh and settled back on her lounger.

'How are you feeling about tomorrow?' I wanted to change the subject and from her reaction to Fran's question about the appointment earlier I knew she was concerned about it.

She gave a tiny shrug and picked up her glass of juice to take a sip. She hadn't joined Fran in the wine drinking. 'It's a necessary evil, darling. I've been practising my healing meditations and following all the instructions Tina gave me. There's nothing more I can do. Besides, all the readings I've done have given me positive indications.'

I was scared about her appointment and, unlike Marla, I wasn't so certain about trusting her card readings. We'd both been distracting ourselves from thinking about her illness but now it was time to go back to the hospital we couldn't ignore it any longer.

'I'm sure everything will be fine.' I tried to sound confident but I knew she'd be able to see through me.

'I should think so, the consultant was very positive after the surgery. Besides, I have far too much to do to be worrying about the hospital. I've spoken to Drew and everything is set up with Mikey from the Flying Monkeys. We've got a pitch at the campsite and Lee from the radio station is going to meet us there. He's doing interviews with the band and then we're going to go on stage. Isn't that fab?' She clasped her hands together in excitement.

'What do you mean by "we're" going to go on stage?'

'You and me, silly. Mikey thought it was a great idea. Drew is to come down with us and Chris is going to camp out too. Oh, it'll be like old times – only better.' She beamed at me.

'Marla, you really should discuss all this with the consultant tomorrow. I mean, you know you're going to be having some more treatment. He might say you shouldn't go and, incidentally, I am not dancing on any stage.' I had absolutely no intention of getting up in front of thousands of people and making a fool of myself. Why Drew would encourage my mother in this madness, I had no idea.

Her smile vanished and she shook her head. 'Azure, I've had my life on hold for too long. That's what caused all my problems in the first place. I have to put that right if I'm to rebalance my energies and recover.'

'Fine, whatever you want. Just promise me you'll discuss your plans with the doctor tomorrow.'

'If I don't, I expect you'll tell him anyway.' Her chin took on a defiant upward tilt.

Tension pain started to build above my left eye. 'I just want you to get better.'

'Then we're agreed on the main thing.' She drained her drink and swivelled her legs to the side, ready to stand. 'I need to go and change, Chris is taking me out for an hour for some supper.'

She swished past me, her bangles jingling as she walked. It would be useless to suggest she stay in and get some rest even though she looked worn out. This whole rock-concert and camping idea was ridiculous. If an hour with Fran and Katya was exhausting, she'd never be able to cope with a full-blown festival.

'Looks like it's just me and you tonight, Jethro.'

The cat regarded me for a second with unblinking green eyes before turning tail and stalking away into the house.

'Or maybe just me,' I muttered, and started to clear away the empty plates and glasses from the table.

24

I went out for a run, leaving Marla to wait for Chris. The tension pain behind my eye poked at me like a needle and I needed to get outside for some fresh air. The strain of waiting at the flat for Simon and then the worry over my mother's health were all contributing to the beginnings of a migraine.

It was still warm out and the evening sunshine felt pleasant on my skin as I jogged down the hill towards the sea. The harbourside was still busy with passengers buying tickets for the evening cruises out around the bay, and the ice-cream vendors were doing brisk business. I paused by the William of Orange statue to stretch my calf muscles before setting off past the apartments and townhouses that bordered the waterside.

I took two steps and noticed the lace on my trainer had worked loose. I bent to retie it, muttering under my breath at my own clumsiness for not having secured the bow properly in the first place. When I straightened up I saw Serena from the boat school, all dressed up in a short skirt and heels as if she was out on a date. While I watched, Drew appeared from the narrow alley near to where she stood. Instinctively, I bent down and pretended to fuss with my shoe again as I sneaked furtive peeps at them and hoped they hadn't seen me.

Serena slipped her arm through Drew's and they set off back towards the town centre together. She flicked her long blond hair and simpered up at him as they made their way out of sight. I straightened up. My stomach rolled and I felt physically sick. How could he be ready to rip my knickers off on Friday and be out dating another girl on Monday?

I set off at a steady trot down the asphalt path, skirting the water's edge. Men were all the same: impossible to trust. I ignored the pain in my heart and forced myself to focus on the steady slap, slap, slap of my trainers on the pavement as I ran. My lungs felt like they were bursting and blood roared in my ears as I upped my pace to a full-out sprint. Eventually, I ran out of path and, gasping for breath, I stopped and turned around, ready to run back the way I'd come.

A stitch nagged at my side and I placed my hand over the ache while I slowed my breathing to ease the discomfort. This far down the path was deserted. I could see people walking out on the breakwater to watch the fishermen who sat patiently dangling rods into the sea. Down by the wooden walkways and jetties other people were messing about with their boats or strolling along in the evening air.

I started to walk slowly back along the path, letting the cramp in my side ease off. Normally, jogging on my own never bothered me, but I felt a prickling sense of unease as I rounded the bulge where the sheer rocky cliff-face gave way to the start of the built-up area of town. The path was a little wider here, with a bench for weary walkers to sit and admire the view while resting their legs. At this end of the town there were no shops or stalls, nothing to lure the tourists except the opportunity to stretch their legs and admire the sea.

Tonight three youths clad in skin-tight denim jeans and black leather jackets occupied the seat. My heart rate kicked up a notch with fear when I recognised Pieter as one of the three. I kept my gaze fixed firmly ahead and prayed that they hadn't recognised me. As I drew almost level with them I thought I'd got away with it.

'Not so fast.'

Suddenly they sprang from the bench and formed a line in front of me, blocking the path. Over their shoulders I could see other walkers further along the path, but I wasn't sure I'd be able to attract their attention by shouting.

'What do you want?' My heart thumped in my chest. 'I haven't any money on me.' It was quite true – I'd left the house with just my door key; no purse, no phone, no iPod. Nothing.

Pieter took a step nearer. Being this close to him, I could see the family resemblance to Katya.

'My sister is being very annoying. I need money from her.' He scowled at me. 'You and your mother have turned her against me.'

'I don't know what you mean.' My voice wobbled.

Behind them I could see a couple with a baby in a pushchair walking closer towards us.

Pieter leaned forward, pushing his ugly little ratty features close to my face. 'Tell Katya that I need money. She will give me a thousand pounds or face the consequences.' Tiny drops of spittle landed on my face as he spat out his demand. His eyes, bloodshot and red-rimmed, glowered into mine.

'What if she hasn't got that kind of money?'

His features contorted with anger. 'Tell her to pay me, or I will make you pay too.'

One of his companions made the soft chirruping warning sound that I'd heard before at the shop. They stepped aside to allow the young family with the buggy to pass by. I seized my chance and sprinted off along the path, running for my life towards the town. I was too scared to look back to see if they had followed and the sound of my blood roaring in my ears drowned out any footsteps that might be behind me.

I didn't stop running till I was safely back inside the cottage. By then my lungs felt as if they had imploded and my legs were shaking so hard that they could barely support me. I stumbled into the hall, stubbing my toe on Marla's lucky hematite rock, and collapsed at the foot of the stairs, my head between my knees while I tried to force oxygen into my lungs.

A loud and insistent ring of the doorbell sent my heart leapfrogging into my throat. There was no way of seeing who was outside through the solid painted wood of the front door. I waited for a moment, keeping absolutely still on the stairs and hoping that whoever was out there would give up and go away.

No such luck. The bell rang again, then the flap on the letterbox lifted and I thought I was about to die of fear.

'Zee, I saw you run in, what's wrong?' Drew rapped on the door.

Relief flooded through me, liquefying my bones and relieving the black spots of fear that had been dancing in front of my eyes. Somehow I managed to pull myself together enough to open the door.

'I saw you running up the hill as if all the clappers of hell were after you.' His forehead creased with concern as he looked at me.

'I ran into Pieter down by the waterfront. He was with a gang.' My body was trembling from head to foot and my voice came out as a whisper.

Drew took hold of my arms and steered me into Marla's front room, sitting me down on the sofa.

'What happened? Did he hurt you?' He crouched down in front of me, anger sparking with concern in his eyes.

I shook my head. 'He wants money from Katya. He said that if she didn't pay, then . . .' My throat closed up and I couldn't finish the sentence.

A few choice expletives fell from Drew's lips. He stood and pulled his mobile from his pocket. 'I'd better warn Katya in case he tries her lodgings.'

I shivered as he started to text. The perspiration on my skin had started to cool and I felt grimy with dirt and sweat. I longed to get under the shower to wash off the stickiness and the horrible tainted feeling on my face where Pieter had pushed so close to me.

Drew had barely finished sending the message when his phone beeped, indicating he'd received a reply. He scanned the screen. 'She's going to stay with Fran tonight.'

'Do you think she'll be safe there?' Fran lived in a small bungalow on the outskirts of the town where she grew vegetables in her back garden and kept bees. It was a bit out of the way and I didn't know whether that would be a good or a bad thing.

Drew glanced up at me from where he was busy sending a reply back to Katya. 'I think so. I'd love to know who posted bail for him.' He finished his message and slipped the phone back inside the front pocket of his jeans.

'I'm sorry if coming up here spoiled your date.' I hadn't intended my words to sound waspish but somehow they did.

'Date?' He looked puzzled.

'With Serena. I saw you earlier as I set off for my run. You met her by the amusement arcade.' I was tempted to add a snappy 'Remember?' but stopped myself in the nick of time.

'Oh yes, Serena.' He rubbed his chin thoughtfully and the corner of his mouth twitched upwards.

'I expect you'll be in a rush to get back to her.' Jealousy mingled with annoyance and I stood up to indicate the open lounge door. 'You'd better hurry before she gets fed up and goes home.'

Drew grinned and shook his head. 'Serena is on a date tonight – but not with me. We had a quick business meeting and then she went on to meet her boyfriend in town.'

'Oh.' I folded my arms defensively across my chest. 'Well, it didn't look very businesslike from where I was standing.'

Seeing Drew with Serena and hearing his excuse had only served to remind me of all the times Simon had made a fool out of me by claiming he was held up on business, including the evening I'd gone to his office when he'd claimed he had to stay late to work and caught him attending to the receptionist's 'business' on top of his office desk.

The smile disappeared from Drew's face. 'Fine. Have it your way, Zee. We both know you're always right.'

'That's not fair.' I glared at him.

'I don't know exactly what it was that Simon did, but I'm not him.'

Heat flamed my face and I vowed I wasn't going to cry. Ever since I'd come home I'd turned into a 'regular watering pot', as Fran would say, crying over everything.

'I think you'd better leave.' It was no good. My voice gave a traitorous wobble on the last word.

Drew continued to look at me and I couldn't bear the pitying expression in his eyes. 'He really worked a number on you, didn't he? If I ever see the bastard again . . .' He tailed off as I tried to swallow a choky little sob that had somehow slipped out.

I closed my eyes in an attempt to try to squeeze away

the tears that threatened to escape down my cheeks. As I stood there, Drew's arms encircled me. Without any conscious effort on my part, I pressed my face against the soft fabric of his T-shirt.

He smelled of the sea and soap and Drew.

'I'm sorry, Zee,' he murmured in my ear as he held me tight.

'I went to see Simon today. I wanted to give him his ring back and collect my stuff.' It all came tumbling out, the whole story of my shitty day and Simon's no-show.

'And Marla has gone out with Chris and tomorrow we see the consultant and everything is just crap.' My voice was muffled by his chest but I knew from the way his muscles had tightened that he'd heard and taken in everything I'd said.

I carried on sniffing pitifully into his T-shirt while he held me. My hair had escaped from the ponytail I'd worn it in for my run; he smoothed the strands away from my hot cheek with his hand.

Something about the gentle movement and the solid feel of his body pressed so close to mine sent a quiver of longing down my spine. Almost at the same moment I knew that Drew had felt it too. The movement of his hand stilled on my hair and I raised my head to look at him.

His mouth closed on mine and I gave myself up to his kiss, wrapping my arms round his neck to draw him even closer to me. As I pressed myself against him I knew he wanted me as much as I wanted him.

'Zee, this isn't a good idea.' He lifted his head and

released me, stepping back to put space between us. His voice sounded ragged as he tried to control his breathing.

'I don't—' I started to say, but something in his expression stopped me.

'I'd better go. I'll be in touch, let me know how Marla gets on.' He was gone from the house before I could say anything else.

I sank back down on the sofa, my limbs trembling. For a while there I'd forgotten that he'd stopped me when we'd been kissing before. He might still have a few feelings for me but whatever they were, there clearly weren't enough of them. That thought hurt me far more deeply than breaking up with Simon had done.

By the time I'd finished having a good cry and taken my shower it was late. There was nothing on TV and the only thing I could find to read was one of Marla's books about astrological chart mapping. I took it upstairs and lay on my bed listening out for her return while flipping through the pages on how to determine your moon sign.

Sounds carried along the quiet street and drifted through the windows of the cottage, which I'd left wide open in the hope of moving some cooler air inside. I heard Marla's heels tapping along the pavement and the soft sound of her laughter as they halted outside the house. I waited for the front door to open but nothing happened.

I crept into Marla's bedroom at the front of the house and peeped out through the window, wondering if I'd been mistaken, but they were standing together in front of the cottage. Chris had his arms round her and they were kissing in the moonlight.

I moved away from the window and back into my own room. Minutes later I heard the front door open, followed by the sound of Marla's feet on the stairs.

'Hello, darling.' She stepped inside my room and sat on the end of my bed. Her eyes looked soft and dreamy and happiness radiated from her.

'Good night?' I pretended to be fascinated by the juxtaposition of Jupiter in the house of Aquarius. Inside I didn't know quite how I felt. I was pleased to see her so happy, but I was also scared she was going to get hurt and somewhere deep down inside, I think I was sad that I was somehow being pushed out by Chris's reappearance in our lives.

'Very.' She blushed like a teenager.

I closed my book. Not for the first time in our relationship I felt as though I was the mother and Marla the daughter. 'So, is it serious?'

She gave a tiny shrug and traced her finger around one of the cabbage roses embossed in the pattern on my duvet cover. 'I don't know, maybe. What will be, will be.'

I resisted the urge to burst into a chorus of '*Que sera, sera*'.

'Pieter is out.' I told her about the incident by the harbour. I glossed over Drew coming to the cottage.

'It would be better if Katya stayed away from the shop for a few days. I'll call Fran and see if Wendy can give her a hand.' Marla frowned. 'I'm so sorry, darling, you must have been terrified. It's a pity Drew wasn't with you down at the harbour.'

I noticed the circles under her eyes. 'You should get to bed.'

'On my way. I'll give Fran a quick call first, though.'

She glanced at the book on astrology. 'Oh, that's a good read, I'm so glad you're taking an interest.' She beamed at me approvingly and kissed my forehead before heading off to sort out the staffing arrangements for the shop.

I could hear Marla singing downstairs in the kitchen when I opened my eyes the next morning. The sun streamed in through the gap in the curtains and I realised I'd slept for longer than I'd intended. It had taken me ages to fall asleep and I'd lain awake for hours fretting about Chris and Drew. Now there was Marla's hospital appointment to get through.

She seemed to be in good spirits when I staggered downstairs.

'Morning, darling. I'm making scrambled eggs, would you like some?'

'Please.' I headed for the kettle and the stash of decent coffee that I'd hidden away in one of the cabinets behind the wholemeal flour. I could drink Marla's decaff for only so long before I needed real strong good coffee.

Marla continued to sing to herself as she cracked eggs into a skillet on top of the stove. She didn't appear to be at all troubled about her impending appointment. I waited for the kettle to boil and hoped her confidence that everything was going to be fine wasn't misplaced.

I'd booked a taxi to take us to the hospital in Torquay. Fortunately, I'd allowed plenty of time as it turned out the traffic was heavier than usual. No doubt the fine weather was drawing everyone to the coast. I'd checked on Fran and she and Wendy sounded perfectly happy at the shop. Katya was still staying at Fran's for the time being, where we all hoped Pieter wouldn't find her and Morris from the butcher's had been placed on alert in case of problems at the shop.

We checked in at reception and took our seats in the waiting area. The place was deserted and if we hadn't already been booked in, I would have thought we'd come on the wrong day. We'd only been waiting for a few minutes when a nurse called us through. Marla had a general check-up and the nurse looked at her scar before returning us to the waiting area.

A few more people arrived and were seated on the plastic chairs grouped around the room. A couple of women looked quite ill and one lady wore a head scarf which I imagined was to hide hair loss. Conversation was muted as we studied the posters on the wall until Marla's name was called and we followed a different nurse to an examination room where the consultant was waiting.

By now my heart had started to thump and my palms were damp with sweat as I braced myself for the verdict. We took our seats opposite the consultant. Marla's notes were spread on the desk before him.

'Well, Ms Millichip, I'm pleased to say everything looks good.' He smiled benignly at us. I let out the breath I'd subconsciously been holding, the relief at his words making me feel dizzy.

'So I can be discharged?' Marla asked as he stood and had a quick peek at her wound.

'Not so fast. I recommend that you have a course of

radiotherapy just to clear up anything that might be hiding away from us at the moment. It would be prudent to lower the risk of any recurrence in the future.' He sat back in his chair.

'What does it involve?' I asked.

He glanced at me. 'It means you'll need to attend every day Monday to Friday for three weeks. The procedure only takes a few minutes each time and doesn't cause any real discomfort. You may feel a little more tired and you'll need to take care of the skin around the treated area.' He scribbled away in her notes as he replied.

'And is that it, then?' Marla queried.

'Well, I'll follow you up, but that will merely be for routine appointments provided all goes well. I think we can be quite optimistic as it appears we've managed to catch you at a very early stage.' He looked up from his paperwork as she gave a little squeal of joy.

'Marla has a trip booked at the end of her treatment. It involves spending a couple of nights camping: would that be a problem?' I asked, willing him to say yes.

'Mmm, provided there's nothing very rigorous involved, I don't think it would be an issue. I take it you have good quality airbeds and things?' He directed his question at Marla, who was giving him her best doe-eyed picture-of-innocence look.

'Oh, I'm sure my daughter will make sure I get plenty of rest and we've got good equipment.'

'Then I see no reason why you shouldn't go ahead.' He beamed at us both like a jolly Santa Claus bestowing a treat.

'Thank you.' My heart sank into my shoes. He clearly didn't know what he'd just sanctioned.

We said goodbye and headed for the radiography department so Marla could be booked in and 'marked up' for treatment. We weren't a hundred per cent sure of what that meant until we got there. The nice radiographer explained about putting markings on the skin to ensure they got the same area each time they applied the treatment. By the time they'd sorted all that out and set everything up for the following week it was lunchtime.

'What shall we do now? Do you want to go home or shall we pop into town for something to eat? I think we should have a little celebration, don't you?' Marla beamed at me as we strolled towards the taxi rank.

'Lunch sounds good.' A celebration seemed in order to me. Okay, so I wouldn't be celebrating the fact that it looked as if I would be sleeping in a tent at a rock festival in three weeks' time, but Marla's excellent prognosis was definitely a cause for good cheer.

Marla called Fran on her mobile from the taxi as we headed for the seafront. She also fired off a number of texts, one of which was to Chris.

'I'll call him later, his phone is off,' she explained.

It was never a surprise if you had trouble getting anyone on their phone around Torbay as the reception could be quite patchy, depending on where you were and what the weather was like that particular day. Usually you could make calls easily in Torquay but around Brixham the reception could be awful and I'd gathered that Chris was staying in a small B&B just on the outskirts.

We got out near the harbour and made our way along the waterside, reading the boards of the various cafés that were sited there. The pavements bustled with people taking advantage of the sunshine to sit outside beneath the big parasols that shielded the tables.

A table with a view of the sea became empty so we quickly seated ourselves and picked up the menu.

'This is nice, isn't it? Spending time together like this,' Marla commented as she studied the daily specials.

'Well, I wouldn't have chosen you getting ill as a way to do it.' I looked around the tables to see if a waitress was headed our way.

'True, but all things happen for a reason, darling. I keep telling you that.' She settled back in the shiny aluminium chair and wriggled her feet free from her sandals, stretching her toes out to catch the sun.

I closed the menu and laid it down flat on the table top. 'Even Simon?' I found it pretty hard to believe that fate had any reason for hooking me up with my ex-fiancé. Unless fate had a pretty warped sense of humour, that is.

Marla gave me a pitying look. 'Especially Simon. Your aura has been very troubled lately and I don't think he's the cause.' She leaned forward to rest her elbows on the table, templing her hands together and placing them under her chin. 'I know that a lot seems to have happened quite quickly but, darling, these events have been building for a long time.'

Thankfully, I was saved from having to give an immediate answer by the arrival of the beleaguered-looking waitress. Once we'd given our order Marla tried again. 'You should tell Drew how you feel about him.'

'Marla!'

Several people at the next table turned their heads to look in our direction. Marla simply smiled and moved her hands in a fluttery, helpless gesture that made the bangles on her arms clatter and clink together.

Our waitress returned with our drinks so I satisfied myself with glowering at my mother from behind my Diet Coke. Marla took a sip of her fresh orange juice.

'If you don't talk to him, he's never going to know your true feelings and you'll never know his.'

'*Mother.*' I used the M-word in an effort to emphasise my seriousness.

'And you can't keep ignoring Chris – he is your father.'

By now I was certain that the people next to us were listening to every word. All conversation in their group had ceased and they were very carefully not looking at us, but instead feigning interest in the boats out at sea.

'I am not ignoring Chris, I *do* talk to him.' Okay, so I didn't go out of my way to do it, but I didn't cut him dead or anything.

'Not on your own. The poor man hasn't seen you for most of your life. I know there is a lot of catching up to do and I can understand your feeling cautious, but he wants to get to know you better.' She placed her hand on my arm. 'Please give him a chance.'

Her fingers, from holding her juice glass, were cool against my skin.

'Marla, I've just cancelled my wedding, you're undergoing treatment for a life-threatening illness, I'm in love with the wrong man, and now you want me to get to know a father I haven't seen since I was a baby.' I glared at her.

The people next to us were openly staring now, and even the appearance on the horizon of a larger boat couldn't pull their attention away from our conversation.

'Oh darling, you're always so melodramatic. You heard the consultant, I'm going to be fine. Simon was always a ratbag and I'm pretty sure Drew feels the same way about you as you do about him. Chris only wants the chance to become part of your life and I think you should give him the opportunity.'

'I'll think about it.' I had to say something or she would keep rabbiting on about my personal life all through lunch and I thought we'd entertained the masses with our familial dirty linen for long enough.

Our lunch arrived and I vented my feelings on the slice of lemon that came with my scampi.

'Your aura is looking very muddied,' Marla observed as I mangled the lemon with my fingers, wringing out every drop of juice over my fish as if it were Chris's neck.

I couldn't help but wonder who in Marla's cosmos I'd annoyed enough to deserve my current punishment.

26

Chris was waiting on the doorstep of the cottage when the taxi dropped us off. He bore a huge sheaf of pink roses and a white cuddly bunny in his arms. Marla's face lit up with pleasure as she slipped out of the cab and they disappeared inside the house before I'd even finished paying the driver.

Marla was out in the courtyard talking on her mobile under the parasol by the time I got inside. Chris was in the kitchen, ham-fistedly trying to arrange the flowers in a really ugly hand-decorated pottery vase that Fran had made for Marla at one of her evening classes a few years ago.

'I'll do that, if you like.' I took the flowers off him and began to trim the ends of the stems with the kitchen scissors.

'Thanks. Your mother's talking to Katya.' Chris stepped to one side so I could get nearer to the sink. He leaned back against the counter and watched as I arranged the flowers in the vase.

'These are pretty,' I ventured. With Marla's recent strictures about me talking to Chris still ringing in my ears, I tried to make some small-talk.

'Your mum always liked flowers.' He glanced through the open door to see Marla still busy on the phone. 'Azure, I hope we can get to know each other better over these next few weeks. I wish I could change what happened in the past, but I can't. You have to believe that I loved your mother very much and, now she's back in my life, I don't intend to let her go again.'

I placed the last of the long-stemmed roses into the vase and tweaked the arrangement so it looked even. 'Well, time will tell on that, I suppose.' I wished I could have believed him, but glib promises of for ever were easy to make and he'd broken them before.

His back stiffened and his expression altered. 'Yes, I suppose it will.' He walked out of the kitchen and into the courtyard to join my mother.

I carried the flowers into the lounge, guilt biting at my heels every step of the way. There was no way I intended joining my parents in the courtyard, I couldn't bring myself to sit and make polite social chit-chat when my emotions felt as if I were trapped in some giant cosmic tumble-dryer. I decided to leave Marla alone with Chris while I went out for some time on my own. A walk down by the harbour and a large ice cream would probably do a great deal to restore my mood.

I suppose I kind of hoped to see Drew while I was out, too, perhaps in the harbour teaching the children kayaking. Though what I hoped to accomplish by mooning about after a man who clearly wasn't that fussed about me, I'd no idea. It was like being a teenager all over again and I hated the slightly scary, out-of-control feeling I got whenever I saw him.

Despite my misgivings I found myself sitting on a bench near the harbourside café, slurping on a large vanilla cone topped with chocolate sprinkles and peering out to sea looking for Drew. There was no sign of the boat school, though, so I gave up and allowed myself to relax. All around me, crowds of holidaymakers ebbed and flowed while I savoured the warmth of the sun on my bare arms and the deliciously cold, milky taste of the ice cream on my tongue.

Sitting in the summer sun it was easy to forget Chris, Marla, Simon and even Pieter and his threats. I even managed to forget that I needed to find somewhere to live for the new term. One good thing was that I'd been saving some money for the wedding that I now supposed I could use for a deposit on a new rental.

I closed my eyes behind my sunglasses and focused on the sun heating my skin and warming the top of my head. For the first time in years I had no plans, no focus. It was as if my life had suddenly narrowed into one tiny bubble that floated and bobbed aimlessly in a big blue sky with me inside it.

I popped the soggy end of my cornet inside my mouth and opened my eyes to see Drew standing in front of me, a quizzical expression on his face.

'You were away with the fairies. How did Marla get on at the hospital?' He scooted up to fit himself into the narrow gap on the seat next to me.

I explained about the radiotherapy. 'I asked the consultant about the concert.'

'And?'

'He said it was okay so long as she took care and had a comfy place to sleep.' My reply came out in a sigh.

Drew glanced at me, a smile twitching the corners of his mouth. 'Marla will be fine. This is what she wants more than anything right now.'

'Yep, I know.' Although I seemed to be the only one who didn't know anything at all. I hadn't really known Simon, I'd managed to offend Chris, and I'd had so many sparring matches with Drew since I'd come back that it was a miracle he was still talking to me.

'Are you still cross about the camping and concert thing?' He leaned back on the bench and folded his arms across his chest.

'No.' I was, but there was no way I intended to admit it, especially not to Drew. Damn, why did I still have to be in love with him? It was a totally and completely bad idea. Every time we met up I was torn between arguing with him and wanting to tear his clothes off.

He raised an eyebrow. 'And what's happening with you and your dad? You know he's coming to Cornwall with us, don't you?'

'I'm trying with him, okay? It's not going great but I'm doing my best.' Wonderful. First my mother and now Drew trying to tell me to be nice to Chris.

'I'm sorry, Zee. I know it can't be easy after such a long time, but he seems an okay guy.'

'So I keep hearing.'

When would everyone get off telling me that my judgement of people was crap? I'd got the point already, thank you, it didn't need any more reinforcement.

Drew didn't answer me. Instead, he concentrated on staring out across the harbour at the huge stack of empty lobster pots beneath the harbour wall. He'd always done this when we'd argued before and I hated it. Admittedly, it was always when I was in the wrong, but he would just sit and wait for me to be the first to speak and apologise.

'Has anyone seen or heard anything from Pieter?' I tried changing the subject.

Drew shrugged. 'Dunno.'

We both continued to gaze at the stupid lobster pots. I was determined I wasn't going to say anything else. Drew and Marla could think what they liked but establishing a relationship with Chris was hard. He'd been gone for most of my life; all I'd ever seen or heard of him were a handful of grainy pictures and my mother's many reminiscences. Yet, now I was supposed to be all excited and welcome him into the bosom of my family, somehow I was the bad guy because I couldn't do it.

I took a quick peep at Drew to see if he might be ready to crack, but he still had his arms folded and his long legs stretched out lazily in front of him as if he were quite prepared to stay there for the rest of the afternoon. I was conscious of his leg pressing against my thigh as we sat squashed together side-by-side on the bench.

'This is cosy.' I couldn't help it. I hated meaningful silences and having him so close to me while we weren't friends felt like some exquisite form of torture.

'Uh-huh.'

Now he was really annoying me and my guilt chip hit overload. Sexy or not, he was pushing my buttons on my relationships with my parents.

'Look, I'll keep trying with Chris, okay? And I'll stop arguing with Marla about the concert. There, satisfied?'

Drew turned his head to look at me and he silenced the rest of the things I planned to say by kissing me on the lips and sending my half-formed words right out of my head.

'Will you stop doing that? It's not a good idea, remember?' As soon as I'd gathered what was left of my wits I placed my hand flat against the wall of his chest to keep him at bay before he could kiss me again. In truth, I would have liked him to kiss me again, but I knew it was a seriously bad plan. His kissing me and then drawing back was messing with my feelings.

I couldn't read the expression in his eyes. He dragged his hand through his hair. 'You're right. I keep forgetting.'

I wanted to ask what it was that he kept forgetting, exactly. I mean, apart from it being a bad idea for us to get together again because it hadn't worked out before, and because he was Mr No Commitment whilst, according to him, I was Bridezilla personified. Our eyes locked and my courage disappeared. Whatever his reasons were for tangling up my emotions now wasn't the time to ask. Emotionally, I didn't think I could cope with any more stress.

'I should get back. I promised Marla I'd go and check

on her allotment tonight. The old boy with the plot next door has been doing a lot of the watering but she wants me to go and tidy it up.' I got to my feet. The prospect of an evening tugging out weeds and picking beans didn't fill me with excitement but to continue sitting so close to Drew wasn't a great idea either.

'Tell Marla I'll be in touch. If you need help getting to and from the hospital, let me know.'

'Thanks.'

An elderly woman with badly dyed orange hair immediately plonked herself down in the space I'd just vacated and began to sort through her shopping bags. Drew stayed on the bench, looking out to sea as if his thoughts were already elsewhere, ignoring his new companion.

I left him to it and slogged my way back up the hill to the cottage. I listened for the sound of voices as I let myself in through the front door. Instead, I was met by the familiar strains of Marla's meditation tape wafting through the house from the courtyard.

It seemed silly to disturb her so I changed into something more suitable for tackling slugs and greenfly and set off for the allotment. Mr Poole, the man with the plot next to Marla's, had been doing a sterling job taking care of it while she was recovering. I opened up her dilapidated shed and sat down on the old lawn chair she kept inside. The heat of the day had died down but it was a long and hilly road to the plot from the cottage. I'd definitely walked off any calories from my ice cream on the way.

Marla had taken on an allotment plot long before it had become fashionable to grow your own food. I'd died a death every lunchtime at senior school when my classmates had produced neat cling-film-wrapped triangular sandwiches of chicken or ham. Marla would send me in with a pot of homemade broad bean hummus, oat cakes, carrot sticks and an apple. I would have given my right arm for a bag of cheesy Wotsits and a pre-packaged chocolate biscuit in a nice bright wrapper.

Now, of course, it would have been considered a wonderful lunchbox and if a child in my class had something like that, I would probably be delighted. But back then it had been mortifying and had made my oddness stand out even more amongst my peers. All I'd ever wanted was to fit in, and not to be the kid with the weird name and the strange mother. I'd wanted dinners made with Homepride cook-in sauces and parents who watched *Coronation Street*. Instead, I'd had organic vegetarian tofu with avocado and a mother who had refused to own a TV on the principle that it was full of government propaganda that might damage my uninformed teenage mind. She'd mellowed on that stance in recent years with the advent of satellite stations and a secret passion for *Gardeners' World*.

I gazed out over the neat rows of lettuces and runner beans, green against the rich red loam of the Devon soil, and thought again about my failed engagement. Somehow I couldn't help it – probably because I hadn't got closure from Simon's no-show at the flat. And I'd heard nothing from him since leaving the note.

Although I knew I definitely didn't want him back, it still hurt that he hadn't tried a bit harder to keep me. In a way, I wasn't surprised that I hadn't heard anything; he'd probably convinced himself that the break-up was all my fault. Just like he used to convince me that it was my fault that he'd cheated. The truth was that I'd probably already been replaced – maybe even by Elaine – the girl he'd shagged in our bed while I'd been looking after Marla.

When I'd met him he'd seemed so perfect. His parents, Jonty and Evelyn, were still together and living in a lovely detached thirties-style house in a nice middle-class suburb. Simon was good-looking and every girl in his office building had wanted to be me. He'd talked about children and houses and it had all sounded so wonderful, like every dream I'd had as a little girl was about to come true.

I'd bought into the flashy diamond ring, the white wedding and the whole 'roses around the door' dream. I realised now, though, that Simon had always been a misty, remote figure in my dreams: the fantasy baby boy and girl, Justin and Emily, that we'd intended to have and the Enid Blyton-style childhood I'd mapped out for them. I'd planned it all out, with Simon being off at work somewhere earning the money whilst I took them to the zoo and the park on my own.

Poor Simon. It seemed I'd used him as much as he'd used me. Perhaps my deception had been worse than his, because I'd never loved the real Simon at all. Only the fantasy of what he'd represented.

A tiny red and black ladybird landed on my knee as I remained seated on the battered chair, letting the jigsaw pieces fall into place.

Perhaps Drew had been right when he'd hinted that I'd tried to do the same thing with him. That he'd felt it hadn't been him I'd been in love with, but the idea of escaping from my past, with marriage as a means of creating a life I'd always craved.

Suddenly I started to see myself as he'd seen me back then, and, in my embarrassment, I wished Marla's allotment plot would open up and swallow me.

27

The next few weeks took on something of a routine. I alternated between accompanying Marla for her radiotherapy and working at the Crystal Palace while Fran or Katya went with her. Katya moved in permanently with Fran, since it turned out to be an arrangement that suited them both. Pieter would resurface from time to time, hanging around the front of the shop until Morris or the local beat officer appeared, then he and his cronies would melt away.

I received a five-page poison pen letter from Evelyn, accusing me of wrecking Simon's life. Marla snatched it out of my hand and fed it into the food blender when she realised who it was from. Chris and I remained warily polite around each other as he continued to visit the house daily and went with Marla for some of her treatments, giving Fran and me some free time.

My time wasn't really free, of course. By the time I'd got groceries, been to the allotment, taken care of the house, worked in the shop and moped around the harbour consuming my own body weight in ice cream, time slipped away.

Marla coped well with her treatment, although it made her feel sleepier than usual. Not so sleepy that she couldn't go back to doing her weekly radio spot or seeing a few of her private clients back at the cottage for readings or healing sessions, though. She also gave a series of press interviews for the local paper and apparently caused a one-woman surge in the volume of women in the area wanting to attend for mammograms.

I didn't see much of Drew. He appeared to be deliberately avoiding me. He called at the house to see Marla while I was at the shop and when I was in the shop his flat always seemed to be empty. Occasionally, I glimpsed him with the boat school out in the harbour or, rather more gallingly, with Serena, their heads close together, engrossed in deep conversation.

Plans for the camping expedition and the concert were forging ahead. At the same time, the new term was looming on the horizon and I needed to do preparatory work for my class and find myself somewhere to live. The idea of returning to school didn't depress me too much. I loved teaching, but going back to the city, possibly bumping into Simon and starting all over again in a one-room flat or bedsit, was infinitely awful. Even worse was the thought of not seeing Drew on a regular basis.

The week before the concert I arranged to go back up to town and view three small flats which had possibilities. Marla decided that since her treatment course was now complete, she would accompany me on the train.

'It's only a week till we go to Cornwall,' I said. 'Don't you think you'd be better off here, resting?'

'Oh pish, darling, the change of scenery will do me good. Besides, if it gets too much, I can always go and sit in a nice little café somewhere and you can meet me afterwards.' She waved away my objections with a careless jingle of her bracelets and I resigned myself to having company on my flat hunt.

When we arrived at the station to get the train, Katya was waiting on the platform for us.

'I thought it would do her good to get away for the day. You don't mind, do you, darling?' Marla shook out her purple cheesecloth skirt to free any wrinkles it had acquired during the cab drive to the station.

'The more the merrier.' I hoped Fran wouldn't turn up as well.

We piled on to the train and commandeered a group of seats around a table, beating off two suited business-men and a student with a laptop. Well, I say 'we', but it was Marla who commandeered the seats – for a woman who looks so fragile she can be very determined. It must have been all those years of protesting and facing off against officialdom that had given her the power.

'Katya and I will get a little shopping done while you look at your flats, if you like. I want to buy something nice to wear on stage at the concert. There are some great vintage shops in the city.' Marla smiled happily at me from her seat.

'I too need to buy new clothes,' Katya announced, digging in her bag and pulling out a foil-wrapped package. She peeled it open, releasing a pungent odour of garlic into the carriage. 'I have breakfast, would you like to share?'

Marla and I declined her offer.

'Promise me you won't overdo things. No carrying heavy bags or anything.' I gave my mother a meaningful look.

'Katya will be with me, we'll be fine. I can call in on one of my crystal suppliers and we can all meet up for lunch once you've found somewhere new to live.' Marla settled back in her seat.

I wasn't convinced that it was all going to be so simple but since I hadn't really wanted Marla trooping in and out of my potential new homes, commenting on Feng Shui principles and unnerving the estate agent, it seemed a reasonable solution. It also made me wonder what she had planned. I'd expected her to be all over my prospective new homes like a rash – after all, that was why she was supposed to be coming.

When we reached Temple Meads station Marla and Katya left to go shopping and I trotted off to the letting agents. We'd arranged to meet up later for lunch at a café where I'd taken Marla once before, shortly after I'd first met Simon. I knew the odds of bumping into him today were slim but, even so, I still felt uneasy at being back on his home ground, so to speak.

It didn't take too long to look at the flats. In my price range they were all much of a muchness even though the agent insisted on including viewings on three properties that were new to the market that she thought I might like. I'd decided to go for proximity to work and the town centre over being further out and having a larger place. My heart really wasn't in it. So long as I wasn't going to live next to an insomniac with a drum fetish or a mad axe murderer, and provided the flat looked clean and secure, that was all that mattered.

I opted for the third one on my list, a second-floor studio flat in one of the older buildings that had recently been converted. In agent speak it was 'compact and bijou'. In other words, it had a shower room because there wasn't enough space for a bath, while the kitchen didn't have room for Jethro to turn round in. It did have huge windows in the lounge that let in tons of light and it appeared to be in a nice respectable area, only twenty minutes' walk from school. More importantly, it was the opposite side of town from where I'd lived with Simon.

I handed over the deposit and filled out an inordinate amount of paperwork. All being well I could receive the keys and move in after the bank holiday before the start of term. I should have felt like rejoicing that I wasn't about to be homeless, but the thought of returning to school, facing my colleagues and picking up my life again was more than a little depressing.

Marla and Katya were seated at a corner booth when I arrived at the café. Two bright spots of colour lighted Marla's cheeks and she had a pleased-with-herself expression that didn't bode well. Katya had a pile of carrier bags from Dotty P's and New Look stashed under the table and a large hot chocolate topped with whipped cream in front of her.

'How was your morning?' Marla asked as I sat next to Katya on the vinyl-covered bench seat.

'Okay, I got a flat.' I slid a copy of the details across the table.

She skimmed through the brochure. 'It looks nice. Is it close to your school?'

'Twenty minutes' walk. Have you ordered any lunch yet?' I looked around for a menu.

'No, we have only drinks. We waited for you to come.' Katya took a slurp of her chocolate, leaving a smudge of cream on her upper lip.

'The menu is on the wall. What would you like? I'll go and order, your feet must be aching after all that traipsing about looking at flats,' Marla offered.

Actually, my feet did ache. A surprising number of the places I could afford had been either in cellars or up several flights of stairs. Although I'd tried to keep the agent to only viewing the three flats on my shortlist, we'd also seen several others that she'd insisted might be suitable.

'Jacket potato with tuna, please,' I said, having perused the menu on a blackboard behind the till.

Katya wanted the same thing so Marla drifted off to order.

'How was your morning?' I asked Katya as soon as my mother was safely out of earshot.

'It was good. I have got lots of new clothes and some shoes.' Katya licked the cream from around her mouth.

'It's usually quite an experience shopping with my mother. I'm amazed she didn't drag you into the vintage shops.'

To my surprise Katya's cheeks pinked. 'I am going to them alone while Marla saw to some business.'

I waited until my mother returned with two mugs of tea before tackling her on what she'd been up to while I'd been viewing apartments.

'Azure, darling, I was going to tell you later, after the concert.' She looked at Katya, who gave a tiny, almost imperceptible shrug.

'Tell me what?' My heart fluttered in panic. I never knew what my mother might have decided to do. Whatever it was, the chances were I wasn't going to like it or else she wouldn't have sneaked off to arrange this 'surprise' behind my back.

'Well, you know my list?' She wriggled forward a little on her seat, her face glowing with excitement. 'I booked it.'

'Booked what?' I tried to remember exactly what she'd put down apart from interfering in my life and dancing on stage at a rock concert.

'My trip, darling, to go and see the Serengeti and the vistas of Africa!' She waved her hand for emphasis, as if a vision of safari parks was about to materialise in front of my face.

'What, you mean like a package tour?' My hands trembled as I reached for my mug of tea, praying that was what she'd booked.

'Well, not exactly . . . It's more free-form than one of those holidays where they simply bus you around looking for giraffes and wildebeest like a kind of glorified zoo. This is a real African experience, camping under the stars.' Her eyes shone and her bangles clinked as she tried to make me see the magic of being stuck in the bush and separated from man-eating lions by only a thin sheet of canvas.

'But you'll be part of a group, surely?' I'd watched *Wild at Heart*; usually they sent men with guns and a qualified cook with groups into the bush, didn't they?

Marla hesitated, nibbling on her bottom lip.

'Oh God, what have you done?' Of course my mother wouldn't have booked anything sane or sensible like a guided tour or an escorted group . . .

'It'll be perfectly fine. Chris has been there a few times and he knows the area quite well. Obviously, we'll have a guide for the Serengeti. We want to see that together, exactly like we planned when we were expecting you.' She breathed a dreamy sigh and I could almost see little red love hearts forming in her eyes.

'You planned this trip with Chris?'

A quick glance at Katya and the guilty flush on my mother's face told its own tale.

'I bet Fran knew as well, and Drew? Did anyone apart from me not know?' I couldn't believe she'd been planning to head off for the wilds of Africa on a DIY tour with my estranged father and hadn't bothered to mention it.

'I knew you might be a bit upset. Chris and I were going to tell you together, at the party.' Marla shifted uncomfortably in her seat.

'What party? The going away to Africa party?' I bet everyone but me knew about this party too, although Katya looked a little startled also.

A waitress arrived and slid our lunches in front of us while Marla and I glared at one another silently across the table.

'I knew we should have said something, but really, darling, it's all happened quite quickly. Your father and I, that is . . . we, well . . . we're going to get married.' She rushed the last part out and the words lay on the table in front of us, looming over the jacket potatoes.

Katya appeared as surprised as me by this latest turn of events. 'Congratulations,' she said.

I pushed my plate away and slid out of the booth. 'I hope you'll both be very happy.'

I caught the first train back to Torquay. Marla had always been impulsive, so her decision to marry a man she hadn't seen for almost thirty years and disappear off to Africa with him shouldn't have come as a shock. After all, she'd sprung other stuff on me when I'd been younger that would have sent most people screaming to a psychoanalyst. Let's face it, most people's mothers don't see auras or believe that meditating with rocks helps them make good life decisions.

I suppose I was hurt more than anything else. I was worried about her health too, and the Serengeti would be far more hazardous than a camping weekend at the Eden Project. I was also worried that Chris might be taking advantage of her. It wasn't until the train pulled into Torquay station that I realised I still didn't know anything about the party she'd mentioned.

There was no way I wanted to go straight back to the cottage, so I decided to spend some time in Torquay. A pootle around the shops and a Devon cream tea with a mountain of clotted cream felt like the best cure for a squashed ego and worries about a mad mother.

I wandered along, aimlessly browsing in the shop windows and trying to think of what I'd say to Marla when I returned home. I'd reached the bottom of the main street ready to cross the road to see what was on at the French Market, which was spread out along the seafront, when I noticed a familiar figure.

At first I wasn't sure if my eyes were playing tricks on me. It was definitely Drew, but not as I'd ever seen him before. Instead of his usual jeans or cargo shorts and faded T-shirts, he was dressed in a navy formal suit, with a crisp white shirt and sober tie. He'd emerged from the bank and was walking towards the multi-storey car park. I almost called out to him but something about his clothes and the set of his shoulders held me back.

I gave the French Market a miss and took the bus back to Brixham; I figured once you'd seen one croissant you'd seen them all. Marla was in the courtyard, sitting on her favourite chair with Jethro on her lap when I arrived home.

'Darling, I've been so worried.' She jumped up, tipping the cat on to the floor.

'I'm sorry. You took me by surprise, that's all.' I dropped my bag down on to the worktop and stepped out into the courtyard.

She reached to take my hand. 'I wanted to tell you sooner – we both did – about the trip to Africa, but I didn't know how you'd react. Chris only proposed to me last night; I hadn't told anyone about that. You must have seen Katya's face, she didn't know either.'

'And the party?'

'Is a celebration party for the end of my radiotherapy, crossing one of my items off my list, and now, I suppose, the engagement. I hadn't set a date or anything. You are pleased for me about the engagement?' A worried frown puckered her forehead.

'Sure.' I gave her a gentle hug. I'm sure she knew that I wasn't fine, but I had decided on my amblings around Torquay that I would try to be happy for her if Chris was what she truly wanted. I figured she'd tried to do the same for me when I'd been engaged to Simon, so it only seemed fair.

She eased herself away from me and held my arms so she could study my face. 'Darling, I know that to you this seems to have happened quickly, but I've been in love with Chris all my life. Fate has sent him back to me just when I needed him most, but you're still my daughter – you know?'

I managed a nod of my head. I couldn't speak as emotion had clogged up my throat. Despite my mother's craziness I loved her and, deep down, all I really wanted was for her to be happy, especially when only a few short weeks ago I'd thought I might lose her.

Jethro interrupted our mushy moment by entwining himself around our ankles and mewing piteously to remind us that he was still there and not at all happy at having been dumped on the floor.

The doorbell rang. Katya, Fran and Wendy were on the step. Katya had wasted no time alerting the coven to Marla's good news and they were armed with organic champagne, Fairtrade chocolate truffles and fresh flowers. They were quickly followed by the guys from the radio station and a flurry of phone calls from the local press. Chris appeared in the midst of the chaos and got swept off by the horde before I could say anything to him or he to me.

At first he appeared rather flustered by all the attention, but he was soon installed in the courtyard next to Marla, talking to the reporter from the radio station. I went back into the kitchen to hunt out more glasses for our unexpected guests when a hush fell over the group outside. Chris was on his knees in front of Marla and I watched from the door as he carefully slid a ring on to her finger amidst applause from the onlookers.

A big lump came into my throat as I remembered Simon producing my ring from the inside of a specially made Christmas bauble and slipping it on to my finger on Christmas morning.

Fran came into the kitchen, wiping her eyes on the sleeve of her cardigan. 'Oh, that was so romantic. He's had a special Celtic ring made with lapis lazuli, so symbolic.' She snatched a tissue from the box next to the kettle and blew her nose.

I wracked my brain, trying to remember the significance of lapis lazuli. I knew it bonded love and relationships but there was something else too. My thoughts were interrupted by the doorbell again; this time the reporter and the photographer from the local paper were on the step bearing more champagne. I led them into the cottage. At this rate I would need to dig around at the back of the pantry to unearth Marla's Christmas and New Year glassware.

The kitchen was filling up with people so I rummaged around and poured crisps from my hidden stash of naughty, unhealthy food into dishes for people to nibble. Luckily there was a ton of freshly made hummus and avocado dip in the fridge so I chopped up carrots and cucumber and put those out as well. Someone, I think it was Katya, turned on some music and the party really got going.

Before I knew it, the doorbell had gone at least another half-dozen times. Morris from the butcher's had arrived, along with a couple of Marla's clients. Fortunately, Morris had brought a couple of quiches with him and the clients added more wine to the festivities. As darkness fell, Marla lit the citronella torches and tealights out in the courtyard and Fran switched on the fairy lights that were strung along the whitewashed walls. The place took on an enchanted fairy-like atmosphere and people spilled into the lounge, the hall and the rest of the house.

Someone else answered the doorbell when it rang again. I was busy cutting chunks of cheese to go with olives and crackers in the kitchen.

'I bought some extra supplies,' a masculine voice murmured in my ear. My body snapped to attention as Drew materialised at my side, clutching a carrier bag full of French sticks.

'I guess you heard the news about the engagement too.' I accepted the bag of bread from him, eager to keep my hands busy so he wouldn't be able to guess my real feelings about my parents' engagement. The French sticks felt too fresh to have come from the local eight-till-late and I wondered if he'd bought them at the French Market in Torquay.

'Katya called me from the train and told me about it.' He picked up a knife and started to spread butter on the chunks of bread as fast as I could cut them.

'Oh.' I paused in my cutting, wondering what else Katya might have said.

'Chris and Marla do seem to be potty about each other,' Drew murmured as Fran collected one of our plates of buttered bread and carried it off to feed the crowds.

'I know, but they've been apart for almost thirty years and now, after only a month, they're engaged.' I turned my attention to a block of cheddar and started to hack slices off it ready to put on the bread.

'You don't think that if you loved someone – really loved them – you would still feel the same when that person came back, even if you've been apart?'

Something in his tone compelled me to look at him. His face was serious. I wasn't sure if he was talking about Marla and Chris or me and him. Except that he hadn't loved me – at least, not in the way I'd loved him. Like Chris, he'd gone away and left me.

'I was thinking practically.' I returned my attention to the cheese, not least because his query had stirred up all kinds of feelings deep inside that I'd been trying to suppress. I'd wanted to say that yes, I still loved Drew as much now as I had then, but it was hopeless. He might want to go to bed with me but he still wasn't offering me what I really wanted: what Chris had promised Marla; not so much the wedding, but the for ever love, the knowledge that he would stay. Perhaps that was my problem. I was a little bit jealous of Marla for having what I'd always wanted – permanence.

'Of course, practicality, nothing to do with romance or how someone might actually feel.' Drew's tone was neutral.

'Chris vanished, leaving Marla and me alone in a manky, dirty squat with no money. Now my mother is settled and financially secure, he shows up just when she's vulnerable and, all in the space of five minutes, they're engaged.' I jabbed the point of my knife deep into the block of cheese.

'You think he's after her money?' Drew asked.

'No. Yes. I don't know. I don't know anything any more. No one tells me anything, I'm always the last to know what's going on. Do you know, when I was little, Chris was always talked about as if he were a cross between Robin Hood and Thor, as if he was the leader of the eco-warriors. My father, the big hero who would come back and rescue us from living in Godforsaken squalor. Then he finally turns up almost thirty years too late and he's a bus driver from bloody Basingstoke.' I hadn't noticed I was crying till a big tear splatted on to the cheese board, narrowly missing the cheddar.

Drew slipped his arm round my back and steered me out of the kitchen and along the hall. Before I knew it we were standing in the street outside the cottage.

The night air was cool against my bare arms after the bustle and warmth of the kitchen. Music and laughter drifted out to us from the open windows.

'Let's walk.' Drew wrapped his arm round my waist, solid and comfortable, and we strolled down the hill a short way until we came to a quiet spot overlooking the bay and all its twinkling lights. It felt like a lifetime ago since I'd stood there with Simon the night we'd arrived back in Brixham.

'Marla planned to give a party for after the concert. I think she intended to tell everyone then about her and Chris.' I dabbed under my eyes carefully with a tissue. My mascara had probably run all down my face, so it was a good job it was night-time.

'Katya's big mouth put paid to that,' Drew said. He moved his arm from round my waist and leaned his elbows on the top of the stone wall in front of us, looking out at the built-up sprawl of the town spilling towards the sea in the darkness.

'Did she tell you they're going to Africa together? It's one of the things from Marla's list, to see the dawn over the Serengeti.' My voice gave a little wobble as I joined him in leaning my elbows on the wall.

'What are you going to do? Katya said you'd got another flat back in Bristol.' I heard his feet shuffle on the asphalt.

'I signed a short-term let today. I move back next week ready to start the new term.'

He didn't say anything for a moment. We both

continued to stare out over the bay. On the horizon I could see the pale orange lights of a slow-moving ship. I wondered where she was headed and who was on board, while inside my heart broke into a million tiny pieces.

'Have you heard from Simon?'

His question took me by surprise. I'd been hoping Drew might have asked me to stay here with him. Stupid really, but I wasn't feeling my usual practical self. All I knew was that my heart would be with Drew even while my body was eighty miles away.

'Nothing. I've had a poison pen letter from his mother but nothing from him. I don't expect I shall hear from him again.'

'I'm sorry it didn't work out for you.'

'It was all an illusion. I didn't love him.'

Silence weighed heavy between us once more.

'I'll walk you back, it's late.' He turned away from the bay and we started back up the slope.

The last little bit of hope that he might have asked me to stay or told me that he loved me faded and died.

Chris had hired a small minibus to drive us and all our camping equipment to the campsite, while Drew was to make his own way on his motorbike. Our party included Katya as Marla felt that a few days away would do her good. I think it was also a ploy to get her out of Torbay and hopefully away from Pieter's harassment; also, she and Lee, the guy from the radio station, seemed to have had a bit of a thing going on since the engagement party. The radio people were going to meet us down there too as they were arranging press passes, backstage access and all that jazz.

We were booked into a small campsite about a mile's walk from the Eden Project. Apparently strings had been pulled to secure us a spot as everything within a ten-mile radius had been snapped up the minute the concert had been announced. Plus it was a bank holiday weekend, so we would have been struggling anyway.

The last couple of days since the party had been a frantic whirl of washing and packing. Marla had been sorting out cover for the shop with Wendy and Fran. The press had been ringing up, and even some of the national papers wanting to get in on Marla's story of love reunited. I hadn't seen Drew since he'd left me at the door of the cottage the night of the party. He'd simply kissed me on the cheek and walked away.

At least the weather forecast was good – for once. Usually a bank holiday was the signal for the heavens to open and monsoon-like deluges to swamp everything. Today, though, we hummed along the road with the sun shining on our bus and the sound of the Flying Monkeys' last album blasting from the speakers.

I chomped my way through a packet of fruit pastilles and tried to be optimistic about the upcoming torture. Chris, Drew and Lee, the radio guy, were sharing one tent whilst Marla, Katya and I would be in the other. I'd been assured by Marla that the site had proper toilets and showers and even, allegedly, a small clubhouse with a bar. I had a feeling I would need alcoholic support or a lot more fruit pastilles to get me through the next couple of days.

Ever since the night of the party Chris had kept trying to take me to one side for a chat. I must admit, I'd been wriggling out of talking to him. I didn't feel ready, my emotions were still all over the place. I had, however, duly admired my mother's engagement ring; it was so completely her. A narrow band of white gold carved with Celtic runes clasping a bright blue lapis lazuli. I'd looked up the significance of the crystal in one of Marla's books. I had been right about it having another meaning besides the bonding of love relationships – the book had said it could also reverse difficulties caused by not speaking out in the past.

I didn't have to be a genius to figure out the significance of Simon's choice of ring for me. It had been all about possession and show, a demonstration to the world that I belonged to him with the size of the stone emphasising his status. The stone had been as cold and empty as his heart. Unlike Simon, Chris had obviously done his homework.

We reached the site at lunchtime. Chris helped my mother down from the minibus while Katya and I stretched our legs in the car park. The promised clubhouse turned out to be a pleasant-looking whitewashed converted Cornish farmhouse and we piled inside for a drink and some lunch from the bar before tackling our tents.

After half a pint of cider and a Cornish pasty the sun was still shining and I discovered that the campsite looked better than I'd expected. We were guided to our pitch by the site owner, and left to put up the tents. Our pitch appeared to be the only one still vacant on the site, slightly apart from the other campers and bounded on one side by long grass and a tall tree. Lee arrived and he and Chris set upon the task, with Marla giving instructions and Katya passing over tent pegs and hammers. I felt rather redundant amongst the lovebirds so I set off to fill the water carrier.

I was tugging the water butt back along the gravel-topped road on its little wheeled trolley when I heard the putter of Drew's motorbike behind me. He halted next to me and throttled the bike down.

He pushed up his visor. 'How's it going?'

'Chris and Lee are putting up the tents with Katya and Marla.'

'Okay, meet you up there.' He knocked his visor back down and drove off towards the tents.

It took me a good five minutes to finish slogging my way past my fellow campers to reach our pitch. By then the bike was parked up and Drew was seated on a folding chair drinking a can of Coke. Sunlight lit up the scene. The tents were both up, standing side by side, and a small camping table and folding chairs were out front next to a metal barbecue. Katya and Marla were seated next to Drew while Chris and Lee were still pulling sleeping bags and coolboxes from the back of the bus.

Drew saw me coming and put down his drink to come and relieve me of the water carrier. His strong muscles made short work of tugging the heavy butt over the bumpy grass to set it up next to the tents.

'What do you think, darling?' Marla called. 'Looks good, doesn't it?'

'Lovely.' I smiled politely and tried to banish memories of staying in a 'Stop the Bypass' protest camp when I'd been six or seven years old during a cold, wet spring.

'I was just saying to Marla that we need to go over to Eden to sort out things for tomorrow. Mikey from the band gave me a call this morning to say we were all invited for dinner tonight. Rick, the lead singer, has a house not far from here, where they're all staying. The guys are keen to meet your mum,' Drew said.

Lee and Katya looked impressed, while Marla immediately got to her feet to embrace Drew.

'Oh, thank you so much for arranging this! Azure, darling, do you think you could go with Drew to collect the passes and talk to the stage people? I'm still feeling a little tired and if we're going out tonight I think I'd better conserve my energy.' She beamed hopefully at me but despite her cheerful expression I could tell she was feeling the strain of the journey.

I didn't want to go on Drew's bike again – feeling his body so close to mine and knowing he didn't care would be an exquisite form of torture. Then, again, I didn't want Marla overdoing things; she really did look as if a rest would do her good. So, against my better judgement, I accepted his spare helmet and wriggled on to the bike behind him for the short ride to the Eden Project.

I'd visited Eden before about three years ago, when I'd brought my Year Five class to look at the plants and the giant domes there as part of their curriculum work. I'd forgotten how spectacular the site was, with the giant biospheres set in the old chalk pits, now landscaped and filled with all kinds of sculptures and plants. The concert stage was huge, set right in front of the biomes with their giant honeycomb structures.

I was relieved to see that there were no big screens so at least if you were a distance away you wouldn't get to see my mother looking too foolish on the stage. We met with the team who were looking after the concert and collected all our passes once they'd verified who we were.

'Go down and take a look at the preparations, but don't get in anybody's way,' we were instructed.

Dutifully, we put on our official passes and walked down the path to the venue. The area was full of visitors all being kept at bay from the backstage and electrical area by a small security team. We flashed our passes and were allowed through.

'Wow!' I stood on the stage near a man who was carrying out some sort of sound check and looked at the huge bowl of the arena. All around the top of the seating areas I could see poles bearing pennants of multi-coloured cloth. Overhead, a huge steel gantry carried lights with men working on them while the back of the stage was protected from the weather by a massive canvas half-shell.

'Proper job, this, isn't it?' Drew joined me, the familiar West Country phrase bringing a smile to my lips.

'I think I'd be terrified if I had to go out here.'

A local member of the crew overheard my comment. 'Wait till you see it tomorrow night, my lover, with all the lights and smoke and everything. Bloody marvellous, it is.'

'They light up the biomes too.' Drew smiled at me.

A shiver ran up my spine like someone walking over my grave. 'Marla *will* be okay, won't she? I mean, the band will look after her?'

Drew gave another small smile. 'You're meeting them tonight and she'll be fine. She's going on for three songs, that's all. This is her dream, remember?'

I followed him off the stage, ready to walk back up the hill to the main entrance. By the end of tomorrow night, it would all be over. Marla would have achieved her ambition and the day after that we'd be back in Devon and I'd be getting my things ready to move back to Bristol. Somehow those thoughts made me feel lonelier and more desolate than I'd ever been in my life.

Halfway along the path I stopped to look back at the arena and tried to picture it all lit up with thousands of people listening to the Flying Monkeys. It was hard to believe it was going to be a reality.

'Come on, we'd better get back to the campsite,' Drew said.

As we drove back, weaving in and out of the traffic, I tried to savour every last minute of being so close to Drew. The heat from his body, the smell of his skin and the soft cotton of his T-shirt . . . I stored it all away in my mind knowing this might be the last time I would be this close to him.

It would be hell having him so near to me for the next couple of days. It was as if my body had tuned in to his so that I knew where he was without even having to look. It would make it harder with Marla and Chris billing and cooing about the place and even Katya had found a smile now Lee was around.

We arrived back at the tents to find that Lee and Katya had gone for a walk while Chris and Marla were lying out in the sunshine on a couple of tartan travel rugs. Gentle snores came from Chris's direction.

'I'm going to pop out for a while, there's someone I need to see. I'll be back later. We'll need to leave here about seven to get to Rick's house tonight.' Drew turned his bike around, the noise making Chris startle and alter his position on the rug.

'Oh, okay.'

I watched Drew ride off with a weird, deflated feeling in my stomach. I wondered if he really did have someone he planned to see, or if it was simply that he didn't want to spend too much time with me. I filled the kettle with water from the butt and put it on the little camping stove to boil. Marla eased herself up from Chris's side and came over to join me.

'Darling, when are you going to tell him how you really feel?' She took a seat on the folding chair next to mine.

'Marla, please, I don't want to talk about it.'

She laid her hand over mine. 'He loves you, Azure. His aura changes whenever you're near him. I've seen how he looks at you.'

'No.' I shook my head. 'You're wrong. It's simply the remnants of our old physical attraction, that's all. It didn't work out for us before and it won't work out this time either. I have a life in Bristol. I need stability and certainty. Drew is a free spirit. He's here now, but for how long?' I freed my hand from hers to pull the mugs and teabags from the coolbox.

'You're the one who's wrong, darling. I'm sorry, but you are. At least tell him how you feel. What have you got to lose?'

I plopped the teabags in the mugs, adding an extra one as Chris began to wake. 'Please, Marla, just leave it. It isn't going to work and that's that.'

Chris sat up, rubbing his eyes and effectively ending Marla's attempt to convince me to talk to Drew. What would I say to him anyway? I could hardly go up to him and tell him I was madly in love with him. Last time I'd tried something similar all those years ago, he'd turned tail and I hadn't seen him for nine years. I decided I'd try and enjoy what I could of the weekend and keep those memories for when I was alone in my new flat in Bristol.

Since neither Katya, Marla nor I knew what the appropriate dress code would be for dinner with a rock band, Katya and I opted for jeans while Marla stuck with her usual bohemian look of gipsy skirts and bangles. Drew returned just before seven and we all piled into the minibus with Chris driving and Drew directing us.

Rick was the lead singer and keyboard man for the Flying Monkeys. Mikey was the drummer, Kev was bass guitar and Zumo played lead guitar. We travelled along what seemed like miles of twisting country lanes bordered at the sides by dry stone walls and green mossy banks studded with tall, purple foxgloves and yellow-hearted white daisies until we finally arrived outside a huge set of black wrought-iron gates embellished with a stylised metal guitar.

'Very Graceland,' Lee quipped.

Drew spoke into the intercom and the gates swung open to allow us inside on to a gravel driveway. A quarter of a mile further down, we finally arrived at the house: another whitewashed converted farm building. To one side stood two huge stone barns which Drew informed us were for Rick's car collection and a music studio. We clambered nervously out of the bus as the front door of the farmhouse opened and a slim, pretty young woman came out to greet us carrying a small curly-haired toddler in her arms. She had the kind of open friendly smile you couldn't help but like.

'Come on in, I'm Chloe, Rick's wife. Everyone's out back by the pool.'

We all introduced ourselves and she led us through the hallway and into a vast modern farmhouse kitchen then out again on to a stone-flagged patio next to a swimming pool. Before I could blink I found myself installed on a teak garden seat with a glass of white wine in my hands, looking out at a stunning view of the Cornish countryside with distant glimpses of the sea.

Chloe and Rick proved to be the perfect hosts. I don't know quite what we'd been expecting from a rock band, but this wasn't it. Everybody seemed so normal and laid-back. Marla was busy chatting to Zumo and from the slightly confused look on his face I guessed she was reading his aura. Katya and Lee were talking to Kev while Chris had been drafted in to help Rick with the barbecue. Chloe took her toddler, Willow, off to bed. Drew introduced me to Mikey, the drummer, who had arranged the whole thing.

'How did you and Drew meet?' I'd been wondering about this ever since Drew had said he knew Mikey.

They exchanged glances. 'It's okay, Zee can be trusted,' Drew said.

'Thailand. Usual kind of story, I guess. The band

wasn't very well known then. We'd just started to make it. I met Drew in a bar and we got talking. I was into taking stuff then.' Mikey paused and glanced around as if to check that no one else was listening to the conversation. 'I took some bad shit, you know? I was out of it, man . . . could have died. But Drew got me to the medics in time.' He shook his mane of artfully cut jet-black hair and slapped Drew on the back. 'That was it for me. My parents flew out, thinking they would be bringing me back in a box. I got clean after that.'

'Wow!' I didn't know what to say. Drew looked faintly embarrassed.

The evening turned out to be a lot of fun. Rick didn't cremate too many burgers and sausages and I lost track of how many glasses of wine I'd consumed. Eventually it grew properly dark and we decided we'd better head back before the campsite closed and locked its gates for the night.

My legs felt strangely unsteady as I staggered to my feet and I stumbled on a flagstone. Drew caught me round the waist, preventing me from falling.

'Whoops, clumsy me . . .'

The wine had obviously lowered my defences and I enjoyed the sensation of Drew's arm round me, keeping me upright with the lean hardness of his body pressed close against mine for support.

Chloe and Rick led us around the outside of the house back to where we'd parked the bus, Chloe pausing en route to show Marla her vegetable garden in the moonlight. Katya was snuggled up to Lee and Marla was on Chris's arm. The evening air had cooled considerably from the heat earlier in the day so I nestled closer to Drew as the fresh air sent my senses spinning.

I couldn't resist sneaking my arm round his waist and sliding my hand under his T-shirt to caress the firm, warm skin of his back while Chloe showed Marla her courgettes. He stiffened at my touch, which made me giggle.

'How much have you had to drink?' he whispered.

'Only a little glass of wine,' I whispered back, and this time I slid my hand down under the waistband of his jeans so I could admire the curve of his bum. Meanwhile, our small group moved forward again towards the front of the house.

'You're drunk,' Drew murmured as I stumbled once again on the path.

'And I want to sleep with you,' I murmured back, placing my mouth up close to his ear and taking a nibble of his earlobe.

I don't remember much else. I woke up the next morning to the sounds of Katya snoring next to me like a giant orange caterpillar inside her sleeping bag. It all came back to me as I lay there with my mouth feeling like the bottom of a birdcage and wondering if I would wake Katya if I tried to get out to go to the loo. I wracked my brain, trying to recall what had happened once we'd got inside the bus for the drive back, but all I got were a few snippets of me trying to sit on Drew's lap.

By now my bladder was bursting, so I slid the zip down on my sleeping bag to try and get past Katya. I was still dressed in my jeans and top from the previous night, so whoever had put me to bed and however I'd got in my sleeping bag, I had no idea.

'You are awake. Last night you drank much wine.' Katya opened one eye as I attempted to clumsily commando-roll out of my bag.

'Was I that bad?' Ouch . . . even the sound of my own voice hurt my ears. I needed to find some aspirin from my handbag, and fast.

'You were very funny.'

I tried sitting up. I've never been very funny. Well, at least when I'm sober I don't think I'm funny. God knows what I'd said last night.

'You and Drew were very friendly,' Katya continued.

What did that mean? What kind of friendly? Blurry unfocused snatches of memory returned of my kissing Drew and trying to unzip his jeans. Oh God, what had I done?

'I think I'm going for a shower.' I grabbed my toiletry bag and towel along with a change of clothes and stumbled out of the tent. The bright morning sunlight hurt my eyes as I stood blinking by the camping stove.

'Oh, darling, you look rough. I'll make you some tea.' Marla was sitting at the table eating a bowl of muesli. The zipper on the men's tent was still firmly shut.

'Thanks, I'm going for a shower.'

I wobbled off across the field towards the toilet block, thanking heaven for small mercies – at least Drew hadn't been outside my tent when I'd emerged. God knows how I was going to face him when he did get up – or the others, for that matter. I must have made a real fool of myself.

I swallowed some painkillers for my thumping head-ache and took a quick shower. Every stroke of the hair-brush through my damp hair hurt my scalp and I decided I couldn't face the noise of the hair dryer. I did my best with under-eye concealer, mascara and lipgloss and hoped for the best as I headed back to camp to face the music.

Marla had disappeared and Chris was in her place. 'There's some tea with your name on it.' He slid a steaming mug across the table towards me as I flopped down on one of the folding seats.

'Thanks.' Embarrassment caught at my throat and I found myself tongue-tied. Glancing at the men's tent, I realised it was empty.

Chris noticed my expression. 'Lee and Drew are over at the shower block. You must have missed them on the path.'

'I'm so sorry about last night. Was I really awful?' I took a sip of scalding hot tea and my stomach instantly protested.

Chris grinned. 'No, not really. You sang a few unlady-like songs and you wanted to sit on Drew's lap, but other than that you were fine.'

'Oh hell . . .' I buried my face in my hands.

'It's okay, I think everyone here has done a lot worse things when we've had a few. At least you weren't sick over anyone's feet.'

I peeped at him through my fingers. 'I feel so terrible.'

Chris grinned at me. 'I quite liked it. I had begun to wonder if you ever let your hair down or if you were even really my daughter.'

I blinked at him in surprise. Was that how he'd seen me, a miserable, prissy woman?

'I hoped this trip might help us get to know one another better, Zee. I know I can't make up for what went wrong in the past. If I could, believe me, I would. All I can say in my defence is that Marla and I weren't much older than Katya when we had you. We were young and idealistic. We thought we could save the world and that it was our duty to do so. I love your mum very much – I'm a lucky man that she is who she is and that she's prepared to give me another go. I'd really like it if you could bring yourself to do the same – give me a go?'

I looked deep into his eyes and, for the first time since he'd re-entered my life, I got a sense of a connection. He held out his hand for me to shake. Instead, I stood up and hugged him hard. When we finally let go of each other we both had tears in our eyes and Marla and Katya were standing a few feet away, sniffing with emotion.

Marla immediately hurried to embrace both of us. 'I knew this trip would be wonderful. I can feel the karma and synergy between you,' she announced.

In the distance I noticed Drew and Lee strolling back towards us and I wondered how much synergy and karma Drew felt towards me after last night.

Lee's face split into a big grin as soon as he saw me. 'How's the head?' he called cheerfully.

'Not good. I apologise here and now for anything I said or did while under the influence of Rick and Chloe's white wine.' I figured it would be better to take the initiative early and just blame everything I might have done on the alcohol.

Drew stowed his towel inside the open flap of the tent and came to stand next to me while the others busied themselves with making tea and finding breakfast.

'So you didn't mean any of the things you said to me last night?' His breath, fresh and minty from toothpaste, tickled my ear.

'I guess I'm not too good when I've had a drink.' Since I couldn't remember everything I'd said last night, I hoped I hadn't said anything too terrible. Apart from asking him to sleep with me, it was difficult to think how much worse it could be.

Drew's dark green eyes narrowed as he looked at me and my face heated up.

'Pity,' he said, and walked off to claim a mug of tea.

31

Chris and Marla decided we should all spend the morning down by the sea. Marla thought the air might help clear my hangover and it would give us a nice break before we headed to Eden for that evening's concert. Apparently, while I'd been getting nicely plastered last night, she'd been with Zumo and Rick, working out exactly what she'd be doing on stage with them. I vaguely remembered her dancing with Zumo by the side of the pool at one point while Mikey drummed out a beat on the patio table with a fork.

We piled into the bus with our swimwear and towels and a cooler bag full of soft drinks, sandwiches and cider. We ended up at Fistral Beach so that Chris, Lee and Drew could hire boards and go surfing. Katya went with them, as Lee had promised to teach her the basics, while Marla and I sat on the sand and watched.

Chris proved to be surprisingly good on a board, and I have to admit that it wasn't exactly a hardship to hide behind my sunglasses, drooling over a half-naked Drew.

After a picnic lunch on the beach we set off back to the campsite for a few hours of rest before the big night.

The guys and Katya left to hit the showers as soon as they got off the bus, leaving Marla and me to tidy up around the camp. I unzipped the tent flap and went to hunt out more aspirin from my toiletry bag. Although my headache was much better, I decided to take one as a pre-emptive strike before spending the evening listening to a rock band.

A torn piece of paper lay on top of one of the sleeping bags. I didn't remember anything being there when we'd set off that morning, so I picked it up to see what it said.

Don't think you can get away. Have money ready for me. P.

My heart fluttered in panic. I carried the note outside and handed it to Marla. She scanned it quickly and then handed it back to me, pursing her lips as she did so.

'Pieter must have followed us down here,' she said.

'What do we do? Should we tell Katya?' The relaxed mood of the morning leached away. Poor Katya – every time she thought she was free of her horrible ratbag of a brother he reappeared, and she had been so happy lately since she'd been staying with Fran and now that she'd met Lee.

'I don't think we have much choice. She needs to know so that we can protect her.'

I dropped the note down on the table. 'Perhaps Drew will know what to do.' Personally, I would have gone to the police, but I knew that suggestion wouldn't go down well with any of the other members of our group. Thinking about it rationally, I wasn't sure what they could do anyway. The note didn't contain a direct threat and since we had no idea where Pieter might be, the chances of them picking him up somewhere were slim to say the least.

When everyone was back from the showers we showed them the note. Not unnaturally, Katya was distraught.

'He will do something bad, I know it.' She clutched Lee's arm.

'I can't see that he's going to be able to do anything at Eden,' Drew said. 'The security is too tight. Providing one of us stays with Kat all the time, then she'll be fine. We just need to stick together and keep an eye out.' Drew screwed the note up and burned it to a crisp on the flame from the camping stove.

We all murmured in agreement. There were plenty of us and only one of Pieter. At least I hoped Pieter was on his own and not accompanied by his cronies. I tried not to think about the threats he'd made when he'd cornered me on my run a few weeks before.

'You don't know. When he has the need for drugs, he is crazy,' Katya muttered, clearly not convinced by Drew's assurances.

Finding the note had cast a cloud over us and we were a sober little group as we prepared to leave for the concert.

We arrived at the Eden Project during the brief lull between the day visitors leaving and the concert-goers arriving. We flashed our passes and, once inside, made our way towards the stage. Marla's face was alight with excitement and in that moment I could see what she must have been like as a young girl.

She had chosen to wear a crinkly cheesecloth dress in shades of bright blue and green which merged and swirled into one another. The bodice was cross-banded in gold in a kind of Grecian style and it should have looked awful, but on her it didn't. As usual she had a dozen bracelets on each wrist, while round her left ankle, next to her tattoo of some shooting stars, she wore a silver anklet that jingled as she walked. Her long dark hair was loose and she looked beautiful.

The band was already backstage. Zumo was checking something out with a guitar technician and Mikey and Rick were playing cards while Kev appeared to be 'brain training' on a Nintendo DS.

'Hey, guys!' Mikey looked up from his hand of cards. 'Wow, you look great, babe.' He stood and took my mother's hand while she performed a twirl for him.

'Thanks.'

Outside we could hear the rumble of voices as the vast open space inside the bowl began to fill with people. All around us sound and lighting men scurried about, finishing off last-minute jobs as the sun began to slide lower in the sky and the air thickened with expectation.

Lee recorded an interview with the band, his face flushed with excitement. Rick read a bedtime story to Willow down his mobile phone and Chris attempted to help Kev with a maths challenge on his DS. Out on stage a local blues group had started their warm-up act and the crowd were showing loud appreciation of their efforts.

Marla's eyes were bright with excitement as the first

act finished and they trooped backstage to go and chat to Lee about their experience.

'Wish me luck!' Marla kissed me and went to stand in the wings as the Flying Monkeys took to the stage.

I joined Chris, Katya and Drew at our VIP viewing spot as the music kicked off. Time flew by as we joined in with singing our favourite tracks. Marla was amazing; she danced with Rick and Zumo to two tracks and sang part of the chorus on another song. Rick introduced her to the crowd as Mystic Marla, their special guest. In the background, the biomes glowed pink and blue in the night sky like special effects from a sci-fi movie.

'Your mother is very incredible!' Katya yelled over the noise of the crowd.

'Yeah,' Chris and I both answered, grinning at one another.

Finally it was over: the light show ended, the smoke machine was switched off and silence, apart from the hum of the crowd laughing and gathering their things, returned. We made our way backstage, our ears still ringing from the music. The band were towelling down and gulping back great draughts of bottled water while roadies scurried around like ants packing up the equipment. Marla was waiting for us, her slim frame quivering with excitement.

Mikey shook hands with Drew in a macho, fists pressed together, boys-in-the-hood kind of way.

'That was cool, man,' Rick said.

'The best,' Marla breathed, embracing Chris and kissing him tenderly.

We said goodbye to the band and made our way back through the almost deserted grounds to the car park. Everyone was still buzzing with excitement from the concert. Chris pushed the Flying Monkeys CD into the car stereo and we decided to collect an Indian takeaway to eat back at camp.

Drew had been rather quiet all evening. I'd seen him using his mobile a couple of times and had wondered who he'd been calling. Now, as we clambered off the bus laden down with carriers of aromatic tin-foil containers, it dawned on me that after tomorrow I wouldn't see much of him. Once we were back in Brixham, I had to start packing and I would leave the next day to move into my flat ready for the new term.

Solar lanterns illuminated our pitch along with the glow from a small electric lamp that marked each camping spot. There were still plenty of people around, sitting outside their tents drinking beer and wine and talking in the warm night air. A few hapless moths flapped against the light as Lee uncorked a bottle of wine while Katya and I dished up the takeaway.

Chris and Marla took their food to go and sit together on one of the blankets while Lee and Katya opted for a blanket on the other side of the tents. That left me to sit with Drew at the table.

'I'm sorry about last night. I made a real idiot of myself.' I took a sip from my can of Coke. I'd decided it would be wise to give alcohol a miss after yesterday's antics.

Drew's face was in shadow and I couldn't read his

expression. 'I didn't mind you trying to seduce me too much, although it would have been nicer if your parents hadn't been there.'

I grew hot at the reminder. 'I suppose that'll teach me not to underestimate the powers of Chardonnay.'

'I asked you earlier if you'd meant any of the things you said to me last night.' His voice was low so our companions couldn't hear our discussion.

I wished I could remember exactly what I *had* said to him. There had been something about wanting to have sex with him, I remembered that part. 'I meant the bit about sleeping with you. But I think we both know it wouldn't be a good idea.' Even as I spoke I felt desire start to heat, low and primeval, deep in my abdomen.

'What about the other things?' he asked.

I stared at him blankly. All sorts of possibilities ran through my head, surely, I hadn't told him the truth, that I loved him? Oh God, how embarrassing would it be if he were trying to let me down gently?

'I don't know, I say a lot of things when I've had a drink.' I shuffled uncomfortably on my seat at the face-saving fib.

He opened his mouth to reply but I don't know what he intended to say, because the ugly wailing sound of a car alarm suddenly split the night air.

'Damn, that's the minibus.' Chris grabbed the keys from the table and ran past us, quickly followed by Lee and Drew.

No sooner were they out of sight than Katya gave a

small shriek. Marla and I turned to see what had happened, half expecting to find that one of the large Bob-howler moths had flown into her face and startled her.

Instead, Pieter stood close by her side, a cruel smile tugging at the corners of his mouth. He had one of Katya's arms twisted up behind her back and the sharp glittering blade of a knife pressed against her throat.

'Give me all your money, quickly!' he hissed at us. Katya's face contorted with pain and terror as he wrenched her arm higher behind her back.

Marla let fly with a torrent of swear words as she shook the contents of her bag out on to the table.

'Cash, hurry!' he spat, then muttered something in his own language to Katya as Marla pulled notes from her purse. My fingers felt clumsy and uncooperative as I did my best to follow her example. I added my notes to hers together with the meagre pile from Katya's own purse.

He backed Katya away into the shadow of a tall tree so that they were less visible to anyone approaching our camping spot. 'Bring me the money!'

Katya let out another terrified squeak as he gave her arm another twist.

'Just take it and leave Katya alone.' I held the money out to him.

He moved the blade a few centimetres away from Katya's throat to snatch at the money. With his attention momentarily diverted, Marla struck. Before I could stop her she had whirled and karate-kicked at his outstretched hand, sending the knife spiralling off into the long grass on the edge of the field.

He didn't get a chance to react. She followed it up with a swift kick to his groin while Katya took advantage of the attack to wriggle free from his grasp. Pieter fell forward, bent double on the ground groaning, as Marla whacked him on the back of the head with her purse for good measure.

In the distance I heard the rapid dull thunder of running feet as Drew and the others raced across the grass towards us.

'Phone the police!' I called out, as I joined Marla in sitting on Pieter's legs to prevent him from escaping.

Drew and Lee arrived slightly ahead of Chris, who jogged to a halt next to us, panting, about half a minute later. Drew already had his mobile out and was punching in the nines.

'What the hell . . . ?' Lee asked.

'Marla is so very brave.' Katya collapsed, sobbing, into Lee's arms. He steered her away and sat her down inside one of the tents at a safe distance from her brother.

'I knew those self-defence classes from when we lived in Peckham would come in handy,' Marla announced as she was helped up by Chris so Drew could take her place.

Despite her breezy assurance and her adrenaline buzz from rescuing Katya, I noticed her favouring the side where she'd had her treatment and I hoped she hadn't hurt herself. If she had, then Pieter would be getting another kick in the balls, this time from me.

The kerfuffle attracted the attention of some of the nearest campers and a small crowd gathered to see what the commotion was all about. The police arrived on the scene remarkably quickly. Once Katya explained about the injunction and they discovered that Pieter was already out on bail, they soon had him in handcuffs in the back of the police car.

By the time we finished giving brief statements and they had driven Pieter off to cool his heels in a cell, it was the early hours of the morning. Too late, I realised as I crawled inside my sleeping bag, to find out whatever it was Drew had been about to say to me when the minibus alarm had gone off.

32

The next day found all of us at the cop shop, filing detailed statements about last night's incident at the campsite. Katya was still upset by the whole thing but Lee seemed to be looking after her very carefully. Pieter had been kept in custody and the desk sergeant told us it was very unlikely he'd be let out again in a hurry.

Drew had already set off back to Brixham when we broke camp. Serena had called and asked him to take a class late that afternoon so he had to go on ahead of us. I watched him ride off with his kitbag on his back, knowing I might not see him again before I left for Bristol.

There had been no opportunity to talk to him on his own, not that I would have known what to say anyway. He'd given me no indications that he planned to come and see me before I left Brixham or that I was ever going to find out what he'd intended to say when the alarm had interrupted us. My heart weighed heavy and sore in my chest all the way home and it was a struggle to concentrate and make conversation with the others.

Chris dropped Katya and Lee at Fran's house before taking me and Marla back to the cottage. Once we'd unloaded our bags he left to return the bus to the hire place. I stuffed our dirty clothes into the washing machine and looked in the fridge for something to eat while Marla sat down and called Fran at the shop to fill her in on all the juicy details of our adventurous weekend.

I toyed with the idea of walking down to the harbour to see if I could see Drew once he'd finished his class, but dismissed the idea almost as soon as it came into my head. I'd already made an idiot of myself when I got drunk and since we seemed to have agreed that it would be a bad idea to sleep together, then what was left?

Drew was one of those people who liked to drift from place to place. The only permanent thing in his life was his motorbike. I needed stability; I had a job I loved and I still had plans to buy a home of my own one day. Somewhere that would be mine, where I'd never have to worry about the vagaries of a landlord again. Perhaps it was better not to see Drew again before I returned to Bristol. I had to start moving on at some point.

I'd learned a lot about myself over the last few weeks. I wasn't the same girl who'd arrived back in Brixham engaged to Simon, blithely planning a fictional future straight from *Homes and Gardens* magazine. Something had altered deep inside me, even my name didn't bother me any more. I knew I still wasn't the kind of person who could abandon everything and set off into the unknown, but I could take a chance and be a little bit wilder and more adventurous.

Most of the things I'd collected from Simon's were still packed, but I would have to buy kitchenware when I moved in to my new flat. Before I'd lived with Simon I'd had a room in a house-share which had been pretty laid-back, and where all the things we used had been communal. It would feel strange to live alone in my tiny shoebox flat. I'd never properly lived by myself before unless you counted my room in halls when I'd been at uni. Maybe I'd finally grown up.

'You know you can take whatever you like from here,' Marla said as we finished our omelettes at suppertime. It was almost as if she'd been reading my mind.

'Thanks.'

'I'm sure you'll find your feet in no time.' She patted my arm. It was typical of my mother to be keen to reassure me.

I'd been worried about her after the karate-chopping incident. After everything she'd been through over the last few months I was concerned she might have hurt herself. Dancing on the stage had taken more out of her than she'd anticipated and I knew she was still sore from the radiotherapy.

'Everything'll be fine. It's a nice little flat and handy for work.' If Chris hadn't been around, then I couldn't have gone and left her so soon.

'You could stay here, darling. There are always jobs in the town and you could get some agency work as a supply teacher until a good post comes up.'

I shook my head. 'I've got a perfectly good job waiting for me back in Bristol.' I knew she was concerned about me being alone, or running into Simon. That seemed unlikely – knowing Simon, I suspected he would probably have some other girl installed in his life by now. We had always moved in different circles. If it hadn't been for one fateful night when my housemate had decided to fix me up with this old friend of her brother's – who turned out to be Simon – our paths would never have crossed.

'And what about Drew?' As usual, Marla knew exactly how to put her finger firmly on the sore spot.

'What about him?' There was nothing to say. However much my heart might ache, we were going nowhere and always had been. He'd walked away like he had before.

Marla sighed and picked up her glass of water. 'You love him and, unless I'm going blind, he loves you too.'

'It's never going to work. It didn't work last time and it isn't going to work now.' Tears prickled the backs of my eyes. I guessed that somewhere deep inside I'd hoped we could make it work, and that even now a part of me wished he would come and knock on the door of the cottage to ask me to stay.

Marla frowned. 'Give me your left hand.'

'Marla!' I knew what was coming. Although my mother's first loves were her crystals and her tarot cards, she was also pretty good at reading runes and palms. It had been a long time since she'd studied my hand.

'Come on, darling, let me see.'

Reluctantly I uncurled my fingers and laid my hand, palm up, on the table.

'Hmm . . .' She studied my heartline and then my headline. I knew she wouldn't make a prediction from my palm, and that she was checking to see if the events happening in my life were as they should be. 'Why don't you let me do the cards again for you?'

'It won't make any difference.' I moved my hand away from her scrutiny. 'You're always telling me that "what will be, will be".'

She gave another sigh. 'I know, but I don't want you to be unhappy. If Drew is the one for you, then don't make the mistake that Chris and I made. Don't lose each other again.'

My heart tore a little more as I said: 'We never really had each other in the first place.'

Chris and Marla came with me to the station to see me off.

'We'll come to see you at the weekend.' Chris helped me tug my case on to the platform to wait for the train.

'Oh darling, I'm going to miss you so much.' Marla locked me in one of her full-on embraces, albeit a little carefully because of her treatments.

'You too.'

I was surprised to find that I meant it. A few weeks ago, I'd dreaded coming home to spend time with my mother but, like a twist of a kaleidoscope, the pattern had shifted. Absence is supposed to make the heart grow fonder but for me and Marla it was being together that had brought us close; the way my mother had always wanted us to be when I was younger.

The station tannoy boomed out an arrival announcement as the train pulled to a halt at the platform. Chris helped me haul my case on to the train.

'Look after her for me,' I murmured to Chris as he gave me a goodbye hug.

'I will. We'll be up to see you soon.'

I settled into my seat and scanned the thin row of people on the platform, hoping against hope that Drew might arrive like a scene from the movies to beg me to stay. But a few minutes later the train pulled out with just Chris and Marla arm-in-arm waving to me from the platform.

The flat came furnished with a double bed, a cheap sofa upholstered in a floral pink fabric and a square imitation-teak coffee table. I was relieved to find the mattress on the bed appeared to be new and still wrapped in plastic. I unpacked my clothes into the tiny fitted cupboard and uncovered a selection of gifts from my mother carefully wrapped in the legs of my jeans.

There were a tiny handmade dreamcatcher and a wind chime for my bedroom window, a small jade Buddha statue to bring me good luck, a lump of amethyst to clarify my dreams, rose quartz to bring me love and another chunk of hematite to give me good fortune. A few months ago, the gifts would have exasperated me, now they brought a lump to my throat and made me want to go home to Brixham.

I arranged them around the flat and then I went out shopping for basics. Two hours later I had bedding, cutlery, plates, glasses, crockery and a kettle, along with an assortment of other odds and ends. By the time I'd been to the local grocery store I'd got enough food to last me for the next couple of days and some magazines to keep me occupied until Marla and Chris could bring me my books and some of my other things at the weekend.

The flat looked altogether more cheerful once the bed was made up and there were a few things in the kitchen. I even bought a bunch of carnations that had been reduced for a quick sale and stood them in one of my new glasses in the centre of the coffee table.

Getting the flat ready and preparing my clothes for work the next day helped to keep my hands occupied, but still my thoughts drifted back to Drew. I wondered what he was doing, if he knew I'd gone and, more importantly, whether he cared.

I'd been dreading returning to school but my colleagues were sympathetic about Simon and as they knew about Marla's illness thanks to Joyce, the school secretary, there weren't too many awkward questions when I returned to work the next day. My friend Megan, who'd been my confidante when Simon had let me down, had joined the staff in a permanent post. I told her everything that had happened over the summer. All about Drew and how it wasn't going to work out.

'Talk to him when you next go home,' she urged.

I knew it would be a long time before I could face going home.

The rest of the working week dragged by despite Megan's support. My new class was sweet, with the usual small bunch of challenging students who felt they were duty-bound to test my limits. Unsurprisingly, some of the older children noticed my missing ring.

'In't you getting married no more, Miss?' Zoe, one of the braver souls, asked while I was on playground duty.

'No, I decided not to.' I gave her the kind of smile that should have deterred any further questions.

'Din't you love him, Miss? My mum, she don't love my dad no more and he's gone to live down the road with Josie Higgins's mum instead, but I still see him on Saturdays and he takes me to McDonalds,' Zoe informed me, hopping from one leg to the other like a plump kangaroo.

'Really . . .' I wasn't sure what else to say in reply to that piece of information.

'I'd marry you, Miss Millichip,' Daniel Sugden, one of my favourite miscreants, piped up.

A deep familiar male voice added, 'I'd marry you too, Miss Millichip.'

I spun round to see Drew standing in the midst of a curious circle of nine-year-olds.

'If you'll have me, that is,' he added.

Behind him I could see Megan and a couple of my colleagues looking on with anxious faces, clearly worried that they may have done the wrong thing by letting him in to the school grounds. I smiled to reassure them that everything was okay.

'How did you get here?' I asked quietly.

'I spoke to your head teacher. She checked me out to make sure I wasn't a loony. Good job I'm CRB-checked and everything.'

My pulse raced. I couldn't quite believe he was really there in my playground.

'You haven't given me an answer.'

I suddenly realised he was holding something out towards me; his eyes were bright and anxious.

The children sidled over to see what he had in his hand and my heart skipped a beat when I saw that it was a ring.

'I thought you was supposed to kneel down,' Zoe whispered loudly to a friend. Then she turned to me and urged: 'Say yes, Miss!'

'You want me to marry you?' I asked.

'Do you want me to kneel?' Drew said in reply.

My throat had closed up with emotion and all I could manage for a second was a tiny shake of my head.

'Drew, we . . .' Words failed me for a second time and the children groaned. 'Class Five, can you excuse us for a moment?' I said in my most authoritative voice. The children backed away, grumbling at being denied the chance to watch me get engaged.

'This was a bad idea.' Drew tucked the ring back in the pocket of his jeans. 'I'm sorry, I should have thought this through. It's just –' he raked his hand through his hair – 'I love you, damn it. I've been going crazy knowing you'd come back here and I hadn't told you how I felt. I wasn't sure if it was too soon for you – after Simon, but when you were at the Eden Project and you told me you'd never loved him I thought maybe I had a chance.'

I stepped forward to take his hands, my heart beating so quickly I thought it would fly out of my chest. 'I love you too. I've been so miserable because we didn't talk before I left. I wanted to tell you that over the last couple of months I've changed. I still need some certainties, I probably always will, but I'm willing to take a chance now, to try things that aren't sensible and practical. I want to take my chances with you. I couldn't love Simon, not when I was still in love with you.'

His mouth quirked, 'I'd been waiting till everything was finalised. I didn't know you would be coming back to work so soon. I've been buying Serena out of the boat school with the money I saved while I was travelling. It's easier to save money when you're living on other people's property and they're providing your board. One of the beauties of boat sitting and yacht hauling. The business is all mine now.' A dull trace of red stained his cheeks. 'I wanted to prove to you that I could be practical. That I could . . . plant roots somewhere, take care of you. Then when Marla and Chris said you'd already gone, I thought I'd left it too late and I'd lost you again.'

He pulled the ring from his pocket once again. My fingers shook as I held out my hand for him to slide it into place. No flashy, meaningless diamond this time; Drew had chosen a delicate pink topaz, the hope stone.

My future had become crystal clear. Maybe it wasn't the one I'd clung to all those years when I'd been a displaced little girl. Instead, it was better and brighter than I could ever have imagined. Drew's heart shone in his eyes as the ring settled snugly into place and I knew that it wasn't having a house or a job that could give me the stability I'd craved, it was Drew. Being with the man I loved and who loved me was everything I would ever really need.

He clasped me in his arms and as he kissed me, somewhere in the background, I heard Class Five cheering.

little black dress

brings you fantastic new books like these
every month - find out more at
www.littleblackdressbooks.com

Why not link up with other devoted Little Black
Dress fans on our Facebook group? Simply type
Little Black Dress Books into Facebook to join up.

And if you want to be the first
to hear the latest news on all things
Little Black Dress, just send the details below to
littleblackdressmarketing@headline.co.uk
and we'll sign you up to our lovely email
newsletter (and we promise that we won't share
your information with anybody else!).*

Name: _____

Email Address: _____

Date of Birth: _____

Region/Country: _____

What's your favourite Little Black Dress book?

_____

How many Little Black Dress books have you read?_____

*You can be removed from the mailing list at any time

Pick up a *little black dress* – it's a girl thing.

ITALIAN FOR BEGINNERS
Kristin Harmel
PBO £5.99

Despairing of finding love, Cat Connelly takes up an invitation to go to Italy, where an unexpected friendship, a whirlwind tour of the Eternal City and a surprise encounter show her that the best things in life (and love) are always unexpected ...

978 0 7553 4743 8

Say 'arrivederci, lonely hearts' with another fabulous page-turner from Kristin Harmel.

THE GIRL MOST LIKELY TO ...
Susan Donovan
PBO £5.99

Years after walking out of her small town in West Virginia, Kat Cavanaugh's back and looking for apologies – especially from Riley Bohland, the man who broke her heart. But soon Kat's questioning everything she thought she knew about her past ... and about her future.

978 0 7553 5144 2

A red-hot tale of getting mad, getting even – and getting everything you want!

You can buy any of these other
Little Black Dress titles from your
bookshop or *direct from the publisher*.

FREE P&P AND UK DELIVERY
(Overseas and Ireland £3.50 per book)

TO ORDER SIMPLY CALL THIS NUMBER

01235 400 414

or visit our website: www.headline.co.uk

Prices and availability subject to change without notice.